The
Commandments

Óskar Guðmundsson

Translated by Quentin Bates

CORYLUS
BOOKS

Published by Corylus Books Ltd

The Commandments is first published in English the United Kingdom in 2021 by Corylus Books Ltd, and was originally published in Icelandic as *Boðorðin* in 2019 by Bjartur.

Copyright © Óskar Guðmundsson, 2019
Translation copyright © Quentin Bates, 2021

Layout and cover by Barry McKay

Cover image: Yuliia Chyzhevska/Dreamstime

This book has been translated with a financial support from

 ICELANDIC LITERATURE CENTER

Corylus Books Ltd

corylusbooks.com

ISBN: 978-1-9163797-7-0

'It's a remarkable thought. This is the person I made every effort to erase from my memory, to wipe it totally clean. I started to focus on this around ten years ago. But thinking it over now, then this is the one I think of the most, practically every single day.'

A victim

1995

Saturday 25th March, 1995

'Congratulations,' the director said to the company as he stormed into their smoke-filled dressing room, reaching for a wine glass. Anton looked at him, surprised that Helgi hadn't been seen since the performance had ended. There had been four curtain calls, which had to be *pretty damned good*, as one of the bit-part players had said as they clinked glasses.

'It's all the cast's families and friends out there. What did you expect?' Anton said as he sank into a chair and poured beer from a can into his glass. He watched the cast as they laughed, high-fived, slapped each other's shoulders and hugged.

'You worked like Trojans,' Helgi said, pushing his hair, which had come loose from its ponytail, back from his forehead and behind his ears. He wiped his face with the towel he had draped over his shoulders, and which Anton realised had to be damp with sweat. The middle-aged director had himself played a modest part in the production, but that hadn't been so physically demanding that it could account for all that perspiration.

'And not just the cast. Every one of those who put a shoulder to the wheel, day and night, to make this all come true,' he said, looking down at the company. 'The lighting was immaculate, the sets have been impeccable, and you, Anton... The costumes are just magnificent. I mean, stand up and see for yourself,' Helgi said, coming uncomfortably close, taking him by the hand and hauling him to his feet.

Anton didn't meet his eye, instead concentrating his gaze on his coarse skin, which still carried the unmistakeable scars of a tough battle against youthful acne.

'It's fantastic. Here's to you. And here's to everyone!' Helgi called out, turning around, glass in hand.

Anton took in the scene, looking at the angels and disciples, Jesus in person and Lucifer. The cast clapped and called out – *Bravo! Hurrah! Whoo-hoo!* Someone ruffled his hair and someone else slapped him on the back far too hard so that beer spilled from his glass.

He sat down again. In his eyes, all this was exaggerated and overplayed.

Anton had never managed to get a handle properly on this director person. More than likely there were others who felt the same, but nothing was said out loud. He was admired in the local community for his selfless youth work, and for *playing a significant role in ensuring a bright future for the upcoming generation*, as someone had written. *One of those with a sharp eye for the underdog, and who has, with hard work and dedication, worked steadfastly to provide support for the younger generation which will undoubtedly pay dividends for the community in the future*, according to the YMCA blurb.

On top of all that, he was active in Dynheimar's theatrical circle, served as a deacon, preached the occasional sermon and was a relief religious education teacher at the Síða school. Anton wasn't the only one who found it unsettlingly tactless that Helgi should take such an active part in the first night celebrations, and that he should so enthusiastically clink glasses with them, *the upcoming generation*.

Anton had first encountered Helgi three years previously at the Síða school. He took religious education and confirmation classes through most of that winter as the local priest had been taken ill. During one lesson he had expounded upon creation with great conviction. Anton and his pal Rafn had rebelled, citing the theory of evolution.

That's a load of crap, they had said.

They talked about the fish that had crawled onto dry

land, and pointed to the well-known picture of the ape straightening its back, step by step, finally standing bolt upright in image of the human being that we know today. Anton recalled that one of the girls had made a sarcastic point, asking if the ape had evolved only into a man, and the class was still laughing and chuckling over this for days afterwards.

Once they had made plain their heathen tendencies, Helgi had asked the pair of them to stay behind after the lesson.

That was when it had all started.

First sweets. Then money. Finally, there had been booze.

Everything changed.

Anton felt the anger swell inside him. He was about to stand up and walk away from the party, but changed his mind as the door opened and Rafn silently walked in. Anton watched as he went to the table, fetched himself a beer and folded himself into the chair next to him. He jerked his head sideways to toss his long, dark fringe away from his forehead.

Someone had turned up the music, GusGus's 'Chocolate', and some of them took notice and began to sway to the beat.

'Did anything happen?' Anton asked. He had been waiting for the right moment. He glanced over at his friend a couple of times, noticing how he stared fixedly ahead through the fringe that had again flopped forward. His thoughts appeared to be far away. There was nothing to indicate that he had sensed the music, not even a knee moving to its rhythm. Anton wondered if this had been the wrong moment – or if he hadn't been heard.

'Rafn. Did the bastard...?'

'Hey, shut your mouth,' Rafn said as he got to his feet. Anton was about to do the same, but Rafn put out a hand, his palm in Anton's face, pushing him back into the chair. Anton sat frozen in shock as he stared. He watched as Rafn disappeared into the crowd.

Anton was shaken from his daze when the show's lighting

3

manager suddenly appeared in front of him, a grin spreading across his face. He dropped to his haunches and held out his hands.

'On the house,' he said, offering him a shot glass of clear liquid.

Anton looked at the glass uncertainly, and then knocked back the contents. He could feel the heat in his throat as the spirit burned its way down his gullet.

Kneeling, Anton opened his mouth. With kindness in his smile, the priest laid the wafer on his tongue and held the chalice to his lips. For a moment, Anton looked into it. There was none of Christ's blood to be seen. The chalice was brimful of black sand. He hesitated and caught the priest's eye. His smile widened a little, and there was an encouraging twinkle in his eye, telling him there was nothing to fear. Anton leaned his head back, opened his mouth wide, and felt the fine sand slip down his throat, easily, as if running through an hourglass. He stood up, walked across the church and opened the doors. Outside it was pitch black, without a breath of wind. The weak yellow glow from the light in the doorway showed him an open grave just beyond the church steps. Anton walked towards the grave, and without stopping at the edge, stepped forward and fell in. Instead of hitting the bottom, he felt himself float in a vacuum, as if he were in space. Then gravity suddenly took hold of him and he hurtled at a terrifying speed to land hard on the ground at the bottom of the grave.

Anton opened his eyes and put his hands to his head. Once his eyes were able to focus, he saw the wooden legs of a coffee table and realised that he had toppled from the sofa. He supported himself against the table, hauled himself up and looked around. He could feel the stale stench of beer and tobacco overwhelming his senses.

He saw Rafn asleep, mouth open and eyes half-closed, on the red sofa. Each breath he took echoed as if through a drain. His dark hair, long and tangled, obscured part of his face.

Anton stood up slowly so as not to aggravate his headache

even more and looked over the coffee table, crowded with wine glasses and overflowing ashtrays. He shifted a few of the stubs around with the tip of a finger, found one that was half-smoked, and lit up. As he went over to the gable window, the floorboards creaked beneath him and his socks stuck where beer had been spilled. It was bright outside, but there were few people about. He tried to get his bearings.

He crossed the living room floor and came to a side room. After peering through the half-open door to see three naked people motionless inside, he finally found the toilet. He looked around in a daze. A shower cubicle with no curtain occupied one corner and in the other was a curry-powder-yellow basin where someone had vomited. A neat circular mirror hung over the basin. Anton almost fell as he slipped on the damp white floor tiles.

He threw the cigarette stub into the toilet and looked in the mirror. His body probably didn't have the energy to summon a reaction to a shock.

Anton went right up to the mirror and looked long and hard at the face that had been painted white, apart from the black rings around each eye, with lines above and below.

He could hardly recognise the face that looked back at him that put him in mind of a spirit of the dead, or was it some rocker? *What the hell is the guy's name? One of those from Kiss?* No... Yes, now the name came to mind. Alice Cooper, a singer his father had adored; he had once hung a poster of him on the living room wall back when Anton had been a boy. His indistinct memory was that his mother had torn it down that same day. His memory of the ensuing row was clearer – not that it could exactly be described as a row. It was more of a fight, with insults hurled, along with plates, glasses and ornaments. There were never half-measures. Afterwards they always came to him to talk, separately, once he had gone to bed. Year after year after year. Choose a team. Mum's side, or Dad's side. He managed to be on both sides without either of them knowing. They were the kind of people who were far too honest with their opinions and said plenty of inappropriate things, way too many of them and way too loud, whenever they disliked some aspect of his behaviour. They always believed that they had been able to keep the fury inside the walls of their own home. Maybe some people were taken in by all that, as he sometimes heard distant relatives telling him what kind and gentle people his parents were, and that he was the luckiest lad alive to get to grow up in a home full of such love and warmth. But most of the people around them were aware of what went on. Those people knew the truth, not that anyone said a word out loud, they all acted as if nothing was amiss.

He could see it in these people's eyes. He had never once had the strength to tell anyone of the depth of hatred he felt for his parents; and how much he loathed the people who turned a blind eye.

Fuck, he said, deep inside his own thoughts.

He tried to recall the previous evening's events. He could remember a few indistinct, mundane fragments. The gaps seemed to be huge, and the last thing he could be sure of was leaving the theatre with a couple of other people. Ah, that brought back another fragment of memory, the taxi. He had jumped in a taxi with someone or other outside Dynheimar, on Hafnarstræti where the amateur dramatics society was based. From then on his mind's black eraser had wiped any further memory.

He glanced down to turn on the tap, and that was when he noticed what he was wearing – a grubby white shirt that reached half-way down his legs. Someone had used a felt-tip to sketch a cock and balls over his crotch. He turned sideways in front of the mirror and could make out the tattered angel's wings at his shoulders. He could remember nothing of putting on any these things, all of which had been his own work in his efforts to prepare for the performance.

He turned on the tap, filled his cupped hands with water and splashed it on his face. He fumbled for soap in the dirty sink, but found none. He picked up a towel and, despite the smell of vomit clinging to it, dried his face. He looked in the mirror. There were shadows of his actual skin colour to be seen beneath the white face paint, and the black had dribbled its way down his cheeks. It was as if Alice Cooper was melting before his eyes. He didn't have the energy to wash any more, and dropped the towel on the floor.

You've no idea how much I hate you, he said with quiet vehemence to the figure in the mirror. *Just think how many people will be delighted when you're gone. You're a useless arsehole.*

His toe connected with something that rolled across the floor. He felt under the sink, unsure what it could be, and picked it up. Red lipstick. He snapped off the cap and screwed the waxy red cylinder up.

He stared in the mirror for a moment. He remembered the lipstick.

As Anton opened the front door and stepped out of the flat, the chill immediately began to nip at his cheeks. There was deep snow on the ground and he carefully made his way along the slippery path to the pavement. Although he didn't remember much of the evening or the night, he was fairly sure it hadn't been snowing. For a moment he wondered if he had been there for a few days. *Not necessarily,* was his conclusion. A few hours of heavy snowfall could change everything.

Once he had enjoyed taking deep breaths of cold, fresh winter air, he took a gulp of Southern Comfort from the bottle picked up in the kitchen and lit a half-smoked cigarette. He stubbed it out after a few puffs. Ice-cold rays of sunshine pierced his eyes.

The Glerá church was there in front of him as he reached the next crossroads. The sight of a group of children having a snowball fight by the church doors brought a smile to his face. They tried to dodge each other's snowballs, and sometimes even managed it – although not every time. They were some way from him, but their chatter and laughter echoed inside

Óskar Guðmundsson

his head.

A man in a black suit stepped outside just as the church doors swung open. The sight was followed by the shock deep inside that follows an unpleasant surprise, stabbing right through him. It felt as if all his powers of concentration and self-awareness had been cranked up to the maximum when he heard the man laugh. He could almost feel the touch of the man's hand, as he patted the heads of some of the children, with a gentle stroke of the hand down to the neck. The bottle clattered from Anton's hand without his noticing it.

With slow steps he approached the church, and it wasn't until he was close that the children all stood still, frozen like statues in the middle of a game. They stared at this lipsticked, filthy angel, complete with his scrawled cock and balls. The priest took a while to examine the appearance and face of this tattered angel, then told the children to be on their way home. *Right now!* he snapped as some of them failed to respond.

'Good morning, my friend. Won't you come inside?' the priest said, opening the church door and extending a hand.

Anton's thoughts flashed back to when he had sat with Rafn the previous evening after the performance, when Rafn had placed a hand on his face and forced him back into the chair. That was when Anton realised what had troubled him. He could *feel* it. It was a smell he knew; the smell of genitals, the smell of dick, the smell of spunk.

And as he looked down at the priest's hand, his mind was filled with the same smell.

Rafn surfaced from sleep on the couch. He looked up, wiped the drool from his chin and touched his tongue gingerly, certain that it had morphed into the coarsest kind of sandpaper.

He struggled to keep his balance when he stood up. After a long pause, he looked around. He stepped over a sleeping body on the floor, went into the hallway and peered into the bedroom where someone was asleep. He spoke Anton's name twice in a low voice, but nobody answered.

In the bathroom he was fairly satisfied at how smoothly he managed to get his dick out through his flies, and even more satisfied when he managed to aim most of the stream where it was meant to go.

He didn't bother to flush, and leaned against the sink. He looked in the mirror. It took a few seconds to realise what obscured the reflection of himself. He took a step back and squinted. Then he saw her, the image in red. She was magnificent, or so he thought. A face, drawn in red lipstick, stared back at him. The artist had given the image lips by kissing the mirror. The face was one of concentration and threat, but there was also something erotic about it. Maybe it was the lips, Rafn thought, and then he read the three sentences written on the mirror in the same red lipstick.

2014

Friday 22nd August 2014

Hróbjartur held the plate under the flow of hot water until it had washed away the worst of the remnants of curry sauce. He wiped the rest away with the tip of one finger and placed the plate in the drying rack. He took a cloth and dried splashes of water around the sink. He glanced thoughtfully out of the window that looked to the west, wiping the condensation from the pane. The sun hid behind Sauðaneshnjúkur and he gazed at a sky that seemed to be on fire.

As he switched on the kitchen light, a mirror image of himself appeared in the glass and he examined himself for a moment. Had he really aged that much in a day and a night? he wondered, running one heavy hand over his cheek. His fair hair had turned paler during that unusually sunny summer. The grey at his temples had become more prominent and he considered whether or not to go to the bathroom and apply some dye to his hair. Although he felt the colour suited him, he sometimes wondered whether people even noticed. He thought back to a conversation with a friend in the same position.

The worst bit's buying the fucking dye. They look at you like you're buying rubber johnnies, he had said with a laugh.

Hróbjartur had occasionally smiled to himself at the recollection. But not this time. He examined his own face carefully. He switched off the light and his reflection vanished.

Tears rolled down his cheeks. He wiped them away with

the dishcloth and tossed it onto the table. Next to it was yesterday's paper. This was the paper that had kept him awake all night and ruined the following day, most of which he had spent pacing the floor. He had meant to pay a visit to a neighbour he hadn't seen for ages, but decided against it. Instead, he had lurked indoors, his mood swinging from misery to anger and back again.

How could someone do this to him? He hadn't done anything. He repeated it to himself in his mind. Every now and again he'd say it out loud. 'I've done nothing!'

But every time the thought came to him, a voice deep inside his head whispered to him, *that's not quite true, is it, Hróbjartur?* Or sometimes, *what about the boys?*

Try as he might to find where these thoughts came from, they had dug themselves so deep that he couldn't reach them, as if these were the final remnants of conscience that did their damnedest to make themselves at home in the depths of his mind. There was no way to wash them away.

No way to drown them out.

He snatched up the newspaper, took it with him into the bedroom and lay on the bed. He looked over the front page and read the headline.

Yesterday he had been to the shop. He'd said hello to everyone as he pushed a trolley in front of him, greeting people as he went on his way. *Hello, mate, morning, love. Nice to see you. Good to see you the other day.* Usually there had been nothing but platitudes about nothing special. But this time people seemed to be going out of their way to avoid him. Once he had encountered the third person who had no wish to say hello, let alone stop and chat, he began to suspect that something wasn't quite right. Every time he made eye contact, it was as if his gaze burned deep. People avoided catching his eye.

It wasn't until he steered the shopping trolley up to the cash desk and was already placing his things on the conveyor

13

belt that he glanced at the rack of newspapers. For a second it was as if he had been swept up and carried to a dark room where he stood alone. On the cover was a photograph of seven priests and he knew every one of them.

Including himself.

He put a hand on his heart. He could feel the pounding inside, as if someone had clambered up next to his heart, giving it a hammering.

The headline screamed out at him.

Church covers up child abuse
Victims tell all

That was all he could recall. He didn't remember buying the newspaper, or leaving the shop. He didn't even have any recollection of driving home.

As Hróbjartur lay in bed, he thumbed through the paper to scan the article for the fifth time. He muttered to himself under his breath as he read.

'It has been shown repeatedly that the victims are not known to each other. Therefore, there is no conspiracy at play here, as some people have suggested. Although some of them have come forward anonymously, it is simply not possible to overlook the fact that here is a group of individuals who have spoken up, all with much the same story to tell, and the same accusations to make. This speaks for itself. The church ethics committee will examine these new accusations, as well as investigating older cases. As a society we have a duty to get to the bottom of this. We must bring everything out into the open, and there are people who must accept responsibility and take their punishment. We will leave no stone unturned as this matter will be treated with the utmost seriousness,' said the reverend...

'This is just bullshit... The case was thrown out,' he said out loud, throwing the newspaper to the floor. He folded his arms and stared at the ceiling, sighed heavily and closed his eyes.

Hróbjartur was unsure when he opened his eyes whether or not he had briefly fallen asleep. He sat up. Had he heard something, or was it something he had dreamed? He listened and watched out through the open bedroom door into the living room.

He started as he heard it, a rattling sound.

Then silence.

He sat upright, listened and heard the rattle again.

Cautiously, he got off the bed and went to the door. He looked around and went slowly into the living room and from there to the kitchen. He could smell something, a smell that was out of place, because...

... the rattle was there again, louder than before. Now he realised what the smell was. The coffee machine was spitting the last few drops of hot water into the filter.

He saw his reflection in the window once more. Hadn't he switched off the light?

Hróbjartur stared at the percolator and tried to think back, to recall if he had made coffee and then simply forgotten about it? It went without saying that he hadn't been his usual self after the shock of reading that article.

I've done nothing! he thought angrily.

That's not quite true, is it, Hróbjartur? he heard his deep inner voice say, and he put his hands to his head. He stared at the coffee machine and the steam that dribbled upwards from it. He watched a tar-black drop as it dripped from the filter. He felt the world around him slow down to a crawl. The drop fell with immeasurable slowness and formed a circle as it hit the smooth black surface of the coffee in the jug.

'Hello, Hróbjartur,' a voice said behind him.

Hróbjartur yelped and spun around. He stared at the figure in black standing in a corner of the kitchen.

'Who are you?' Hróbjartur's voice grated, once he had his breath back. 'What are you doing here?'

'We don't know each other,' the stranger said in a voice so calm it was disconcerting. 'But we're going to get to know each other better. Not that much better, though. There isn't time for that. We need to talk.'

'Talk?' Hróbjartur said in surprise. 'Talk about what?'

'Sit yourself down,' the man said, stepping forward and drawing a chair from under the table. 'I made coffee.'

Hróbjartur stood motionless, as if rooted to the spot. He glanced around and saw his phone lying on the worktop, plugged into the socket to charge the battery.

'Ah,' the man said, following Hróbjartur's eyes. 'I took out the SIM card,' he continued, fishing it from his pocket and holding it up. 'Sit down. Coffee.'

Hróbjartur took slow steps towards the man. He weighed the difference in size between then. He himself was brawny and in pretty good shape, apart from a slight paunch; one metre ninety, and a hundred and five kilos. But he was also sixty-six years old, with a bad back and suffering from osteoporosis. He quickly abandoned the notion of attacking the stranger. The man looked to be a good few years younger, beefy and fit.

'What... What do you want?' Hróbjartur asked as he sat down. He placed his hands on the kitchen table, and took in the sight of the black leather gloves the man had placed on it.

'Don't look like that, Hróbjartur. You seem sulky,' the man replied after he had filled two mugs and taken a seat on the other side of the table. 'Shall we begin with this? Is there something you want to tell me?' he said as he turned the newspaper to face him.

For a long time Hróbjartur stared at the newspaper. He had failed to notice that it no longer lay on the bedroom floor where he had thrown it. He looked hard, but in fact he could see nothing more than some jumbled, unreal thoughts that flashed past his eyes.

'What do you want me to say?' he asked at last.

'Up to you,' the man said, almost cheerfully and took an apple from the fruit bowl on the table. He looked at it for a while, turning it in his hands, and put it back. 'But what happens in the next stage of this unexpected visit depends entirely on your answers.'

'I don't understand. What am I supposed to say?' Hróbjartur said in sudden terror as he stared back at the stranger.

'Take that look off your face. I already told you once,' the man rasped and Hróbjartur winced. 'But I'll give you a clue: the truth.' He pulled on one glove. 'You tell me the truth, and everything will be fine.'

'Yes... But. It's... I don't know how I... I haven't done anything that...'

That was as far as Hróbjartur got. The man moved fast and a leather-clad fist crashed into his nose.

Hróbjartur howled and snapped back in his chair, but not so far that he was thrown to the floor. He put his hands to his face as blood spurted from his nose.

'There, there,' the man said gently, reaching for a dishcloth that lay by the kitchen sink. 'Here you go. It wasn't that much of a punch. The next one is going to hurt a lot more and you won't even feel the third one. The fourth one will be lethal. All the same, there'll be some pain between the third and fourth. That'll be something you don't want to experience. So, the truth, Hróbjartur. If you tell the truth, then none of this will need to happen. There, wipe your nose and we'll start again.'

The Commandments

The man waited patiently while Hróbjartur wiped blood from his face.

'No doubt you've read more than a few times the article about the pervert priests and the cover-up perpetrated by the Church. All those accusations. And, after all that, most of those cases were dropped through lack of evidence or because the statute of limitations kicked in. But there are things that can still come to light if people tell the truth, Hróbjartur. That's precisely the reason I'm here right now. I want to hear the truth, and you can start right away.'

Hróbjartur still had the dishcloth held to his face as his eyes flickered from the man to the newspaper and back.

'There's... There's... a lot that could have been so much better,' Hróbjartur said, almost choking on his own words. 'But please believe me when I tell you that I've done nothing wrong ... and there's not a shred of evidence to say I have. Nothing has come up that says I've done anything. At any rate, the case was thrown out and...'

A heavy blow struck Hróbjartur's hands that were still covering his nose, and something could be heard cracking.

He howled, louder than before, falling to one side and landing on the floor. The man stood up and went to his side. He took hold of him under the arms, lifted and placed him on the chair.

The stranger took a roll of kitchen paper from beside the sink and placed it on the table in front of Hróbjartur before again taking a seat facing him.

Hróbjartur's face was flushed red and tears of pain coursed down his cheeks. He tore a few sheets of kitchen roll and held them to his nose, where they were immediately saturated with blood.

'Remember? You won't even feel the third one. Now then,' he said brightly, and opened the small knapsack he had brought with him. He extracted a bundle of papers, put them on the table and pushed them towards Hróbjartur.

'What's that?'

'These are diary extracts. You can go to where I put the markers and read from there.'

Hróbjartur looked at the stack of paper in terror, as if it were a contagious disease there in front of him.

The man banged the table with a fist and Hróbjartur looked up in alarm.

'Read!'

Hróbjartur thumbed through the bundle to the first of the five marker notes the man had placed between the pages.

He read in silence.

As he read, he shook his head or groaned. He couldn't be sure if the words that came to mind, *this is dreadful*, or *good Lord*, were in his thoughts or spoken out loud.

In the meantime, the man had stood up and filled their coffee cups.

Hróbjartur finished reading and looked down at his hands.

'I can understand that telling the truth is likely to be a painful ordeal for you,' the man said in a low voice. 'But that's what I'm here for. So let's try again, Hróbjartur.'

5

A falcon with wings outstretched rode the wind over the Lax River in the Mývatn district. The river flows from the lake at Mývatn and along the Laxá valley, above the Brúár falls and the Laxá hydro-electric plant. No doubt the falcon was scanning the ground below for prey. It probably wouldn't have to search for long, since the bird population along the banks of the river is among the most varied to be found anywhere in Iceland, with many species on the menu that are found nowhere else.

The river slipped gently around Salka as she stood in the middle of the stream. She had never before experienced such a strong connection to the natural world, bursting with life all around her along the banks of the river – considered by those in the know to be the best in the country for trout.

Salka tried to cast her mind back to the last time she had been to the Lax River. Yes, fifteen years ago. She had been twenty-three and it was as clear in her memory as if it had been yesterday. Her boyfriend – or rather, aspiring boyfriend – had pursued her and invited her to go with him. Eysteinn had taught her the art of fly fishing, and she had fallen for the whole package, the river and him. She wasn't exactly sure, but she had long ago convinced herself that their daughter María had been conceived during that very first fishing trip, down there among the tussocks in the most beautiful spot by the river. Born prematurely, she had been such a tiny piece of life, with her thick mop of hair as red as fire. Salka laughed as she recalled lying for the first time with her in her arms after she had been taken from the incubator, and had made a tiny plait of her hair.

Three years later they had walked up the aisle together.

It hadn't been just the fishing trips that had tipped the balance while he was pursuing her. Eysteinn was quite simply one of the good guys. He was reliable, and he could be as funny as hell. And he'd been dynamite in the sack. As time passed, it hadn't done any harm that he did well in business and they never had to worry about money. She had never been acquisitive, had never been one for piling up earthly possessions or splashing out. Maybe they had been different in that respect.

Four years ago they had moved to Britain. Eysteinn had landed a position leading the design department of a fairly new and adventurous tech company, partly owned by people in Iceland who had set up a branch in London. She had found a civilian niche with the Metropolitan Police as a crime analyst working with a CID team. The sun shone on the little family. The thought made her smile. But the smile wilted as she recalled what had changed everything: the arguing, the yelling. The time she walked out, slamming the door behind her, driving away from the house. Then she...

She was startled out of her thoughts as a fish jumped downstream. Salka lifted the rod and flicked it back and forth. She gradually let out the line as it swirled above her head like a ballerina stretching her limbs back and forth. The dry fly landed gently on the surface exactly where she wanted it. She had planted the fly for a fish in exactly this spot before now. The fly was carried by the soft current, leaving fine lines of a wake behind it. She dipped a hand in the water to wet her fingers and ran them through her hair.

Salka leaned slightly forward and peered, not sure if she could make out something watching the fly in the sunshine. She finally caught sight of it glittering on the surface as it approached the catch point, just below an outcrop of rock to one side. She could feel a rush of adrenaline and prepared to pull the line in as the fly reached the rock. It passed the outcrop – and nothing happened.

She straightened up and was about to reel the line back in

when her phone rang in one of her waistcoat's many pockets. She sighed. She was sure that she had left the phone back at the chalet. She patted her pockets and found the phone.

'Hello.'

'Hello, my dear. It's Mum,' a gentle voice announced. 'Am I disturbing anything?'

'Well... hey. You don't have to introduce yourself, Mum. You and your voice are very familiar,' she said with a laugh.

'What are you up to?'

'I'm actually a bit busy right now. Is it all right if I...'

'How are you feeling?'

'Feeling?' she asked, and fell silent.

'Are you still there?' her mother asked after the silence had hung for too long in the air.

'I feel fine. Was there anything in particular? Is everything all right?'

'Sure. Your dad's better. He'll start treatment after the weekend, I hope.'

'You hope?'

'Oh, you know what the health service is like these days. But we're hopeful.'

'Well, that's good,' Salka said, and could hear that she'd had a drink. She was about to ask her mother how she was, when it all happened. It was as if someone had pulled at her hand with all their strength. The rod bowed and the line whined as it was hauled off the reel. Drops of water were cast from it as it spun, landing on her freckled face.'

'I'm sorry, Mum, I'm a bit busy right now. I'll have to call you back. Is that all right?'

'No problem,' her mother assured her.

The hook in its mouth, the big fish had twice danced on its tail across the river's surface before she managed to put the phone away and get a grip on the rod.

The feeling of wading against the flow to follow the fish was similar to when she put her exercise bike on its hardest setting.

The fish shot upstream and down again, and after ten minutes it seemed to have taken the decision to dive to the deepest point in the middle of the river, and to stay there, motionless.

Salka breathed fast and stood stock still with as much tension as she dared on the rod. She could feel the rush of adrenaline. She noticed a duckling by an islet in the river. It must have been separated from its family and Salka knew it wouldn't survive long. It would quickly become prey for the falcon, or else for a trout that was nothing but an underwater predator. Several times she had gutted fish that had gulped down whole ducklings or field mice.

The duckling twittered ceaselessly and she watched it dart again and again from under the high grassy bank of the island, as if in confusion.

She thought of her mother, who probably felt much as the duckling did. Salka's father had recently been diagnosed with cancer, and he simply vanished, as if at the wave of a wand. He retreated inside himself, taking with him most of the characteristics that marked him out as a person, his opinions, determination, initiative, his smile and his sense of fun. And her mother was left alone and at a loss.

Salka glanced at the curve of the rod and watched the line, leading away under tension into the depths where the trout had sought refuge.

She jerked the rod with all her strength. The line whistled as she saw it zip past her face, minus the fly. She waded ashore, sat on the grass and felt for her phone.

'Hi, Mum, I'm free now. How are you?'

'Sorry. Did I interrupt you while you were fishing?'

'No, it's all right,' Salka fibbed. She took the thermos from her fishing bag and poured coffee into the lid.

'I worry about you, Salka.'

'There's no need to. I feel absolutely fine here and I'm going to make the most of being here for a couple of days.'

She managed to untwist the cap of the half-bottle of

cognac she had bought especially for this trip and poured a slug into her coffee.

'You used to go so often to Lax River...'

'Well, we did,' Salka said, cutting her off. 'But I've seen plenty of fish about, and the food at the house is much better,' she said, realising that she had just delivered a couple of non sequiturs as a way of changing the subject. It was all to no effect, as her mother simply continued.

'Heard anything from Eysteinn?'

'No.'

'He hasn't called?'

'No. He hasn't called,' she said sharply, and immediately regretted it. She could almost feel his breath on her neck. She could hear his words, indistinctly.

... I give up ... It's all your fault. I'm out of here...

'How's Dad?' she asked, banishing unwelcome thoughts from her mind.

'He's so quiet, as you know. You'd hardly know he was there, so to tell the truth I couldn't say how he's feeling inside. He says he's fine. I just have to believe what he tells me,' she said with a low laugh.

Salka was very familiar with the shades of her mother's laughter and couldn't miss how forced it sounded this time.

She reached for the fishing bag, which strictly speaking belonged to Eysteinn, and pulled it closer. She opened a side pocket, taking out a lighter and a box of Café Crème cigars. She couldn't stop herself from smiling. Smoking was something that neither of them ever had ever done, except when they went fishing.

'Give him a kiss from me,' Salka said, as she lay back in the grass and gazed up at the sky above. She drew the smoke deep and grimaced. She felt the harshness of the bone dry tobacco fill her mouth. All the same, she liked the sensation. 'I'll come and see you soon,' she said, blowing a stream of smoke hard at the black cloud of midges that had gathered over her head.

She recalled when María had caught her with a cigarette in her hand. María had been ten years old and wept tears of fury. It had taken Salka such a long time to convince her daughter that she was just dabbling, that she hadn't started smoking. Which was in fact the truth of the matter. She allowed herself the occasional smoke with a drink. It had also taken her ages to convince María that she wasn't about to die.

'Are you smoking?' her mother asked.

Salka was taken by surprise, and sat up.

'No. What makes you think that?' she said, as she noticed a fisherman wade into the stream from the other side of the river, looking as if he was about to cast a fly by her rocky outcrop. She watched as he looped his rod until he released the line, so that it lay like a feather on the water upstream from the rock.

'What did you say?'

'I asked if you had heard anything from Pétur?' her mother said.

'Pétur? Why would I hear from him?'

She watched the dry fly float downstream towards the rock.

'I ran into him yesterday. He promised... Said he'd get in touch with you. The police here in Akureyri are so short-staffed.'

'Mum, don't. Please,' Salka implored her.

'What?'

'I'll apply for jobs when I'm ready. There are things you don't need to worry about.'

She knew her mother well enough to know that this would make no difference. Her mother had always been the one to take the initiative, call the right people, go to the right place, sort things out. Salka felt that this was the best way to be; all the same, her mother tended to go into things at full tilt.

'You know that my happiness is your happiness, Salka. I

just thought it would do you good to be back at work. Take your mind off things and work with what you do best. There are plenty of good people ready to give you a job.'

Salka watched the man cautiously reel in his line, then cast again. She heard the whirr of the line and saw the fly land nearer the outcrop than before and drift towards it.

'Mum, please stop all these calls and inquiries on my behalf. I'm an adult. It's not like it was when you were applying for summer jobs for me,' she said, and sighed. She knew that she was coming across more sharply than she had intended. 'I know you only want the best for me, and I love you for it. But I'm fine and I can sort myself out. Now that's pretty good...' she said as the man's fly vanished from the surface just below the outcrop. A large trout broke the surface, jumping clear of the water.

Salka grinned and got to her feet.

'What's pretty good?' she heard her mother say.

'Nothing. I'll give you a call later,' she said, ending the call. She went down to the riverbank.

'Need any help?' she called out to the fisherman. He had been struggling with the fish, which had fought hard and then gone to ground under a rock by the islet, refusing to move.

'That would be much appreciated,' he called back.

Salka picked up a fist-sized stone and waded out some way downstream, towards the islet where the current flowed faster. She was up to her waist in water and knew that one more step and the fast-flowing stream would snatch her off her feet. She saw where the line lay, close to the islet, and threw the stone so that it landed as close as she dared to the line. The trout immediately set off upstream, judging by the line's position, heading straight for her. Salka leaned over and almost lost her footing as the line swept past, just missing her head, even though the man had lifted his rod as high as he could.

Salka waded over to the man and as she reached him, he

handed her a landing net.

'You use one of those?' she said, after having glanced at him in surprise.

'What do you mean? Other than what?'

'Hands,' she said, grinning.

They sat on the bank after the man had brought the fish into the shallows, where Salka had caught hold of it and brought it ashore.

The man didn't hesitate. He took out a wooden club and gave the trout three sharp blows to the head.

'Magnús,' he said abruptly, offering his hand.

'Salka,' she replied, taking it.

His grasp was firm, like hers, and lasted for a while, as if there was no hurry to let go.

'Yes, I know.'

'Really?' she said, ready to withdraw her hand.

'Aren't you Didda and Steini's daughter?'

'Well, yeah. You know them?' she said, gazing down at the water.

'No, not exactly. I'm in the police myself and... Yes,' he said and coughed. He seemed to have realised that his words were falling on stony ground. 'That was quite a fight back there,' he said, trying to lift the tone. 'With the fish, I mean,' he added after she stared at him with blank eyes.

She knew exactly why he had changed the subject. Her father had retired after a career in the law, during which he had defended many of Iceland's worst criminals. After his success in getting Akureyri's most notorious criminal off the hook, he had in turn been convicted by society, especially in Akureyri. She had never been able to fathom why this continued to be such an emotive issue, even though that had been more than fifteen years ago.

'Just a bit,' she agreed, shaking off dark thoughts. 'I see you know how to cast a fly. Been fishing long?'

'You could say that,' he said, wiping his knife clean on the grass after gutting the fish. 'Since I was a kid. There haven't been many opportunities in the last couple of years, but I go when I get a chance,' he said, and she discerned a touch of a northern accent in his words.

'Where are you from?' she asked, passing him the brimming cap of the cognac bottle.

'Hrafnagil. Very peaceful, and good to live away from the noise in Akureyri,' he said, knocking back the contents of the lid, and passing it back to her.

He took off his cap and flapped it from side to side. The midges had been making a concerted assault on him. He smoothed back his dark hair and smiled, a delicate smile. His greenish eyes were mild and bright. Salka guessed he had to be around forty. There were creases in his forehead, and clear lines ran from his nose to the corners of his mouth. There was a striking cleft in his chin.

'And you?'

'Here and there, I suppose,' Salka said. 'I suppose you're in the Akureyri police?'

'Yes. Drugs squad.'

'It's not always peaceful at Hrafnagil. Isn't that where there was a fire last year? I'm sure I read something about it online.'

'Yes, that's right,' he said, a serious edge to his voice. He paused for a moment before continuing. 'That was a real tragedy. The house burned to the ground in no time at all. The couple who lived there had no chance.'

'Were you there?'

'No, I wasn't,' Magnús said. Salka noticed that he was deep in thought. 'I was up on the heath hunting for ptarmigan.'

'Did you know them?'

'No. I didn't know them, exactly. They were people who had moved there from somewhere out of town. But I knew the place, and not in a good way. They were people with troubles of their own. They'd been seen earlier that evening in a bad way. The house burned down that night.'

'The Special Unit was called out, wasn't it?'

'Yes. Shots had been heard inside the house. But by the time the Special Unit was on the scene, the house was already in flames. Tragic,' he said, and lay on his back. Salka did the same.

'Have you been here before? To Lax River?' she asked after they had watched the sky in silence.

'No. First time. Wonderful river. And the area's a real paradise... It's ruined,' he said and smiled.

'What's ruined?' she asked in surprise, and they both sat up.

'The fly. It's had it,' he said and showed her the dry fly. In the struggle with the trout, the bindings had given way. 'Are you still in the police? CID?' he asked.

'You seem to know quite a bit about me,' she laughed.

'Ach. I'm sorry. I know Pétur very well. You know, the senior officer in Akureyri.'

'Yes. I know him.'

'I had a word with him the other day and he mentioned that you'd be fishing up here. All the same, I reckoned I'd be more likely to run into you at the chalet than down here by the river,' he said, sounding apologetic.

Salka rolled her eyes, and thought of her mother.

'Well, I understand. But no.'

'No, what?'

'I'm not a serving officer. Not at the moment. I'm on leave.'

'Weren't you working with CID in London? Pétur said something about that.'

Salka said nothing.

'Well,' she said, and forced a smile as the silence became awkward.

'You wouldn't consider joining us in Akureyri? Pétur mentioned that we're short-staffed.'

'I don't believe in coincidences ... Magnús,' she said after a pause. For a second she had forgotten his name. 'I was talking to my mother just now, and she said exactly the same.'

'I'm sorry. It looks like I've been stalking you. That wasn't the intention at all...'

'It doesn't matter,' she said, inspecting a daisy held between her fingertips. She had to laugh. 'It's funny, I suppose,' she said, catching his eye.

'Hey, look,' Magnús said in surprise. He had been about to put the fish in a bag when he noticed something in its mouth. He took a pair of pliers from his bag, eased them into the trout's mouth and showed Salka what he had retrieved. 'He had another fly in his mouth,' he said, laughing out loud.

'That's my fly,' she said quietly.

'What do you mean?' he asked doubtfully.

'That's my fly. This fish took it earlier.'

'You're joking! What sort of a coincidence is that? The same fish took both our flies?'

'I told you I don't believe in coincidence. This fish is so big that he wouldn't let anything else onto this stretch of river. Like any other predator, it has its own territory. So there's no coincidence. You caught my fish,' she said, and it was her turn to laugh.

'Remarkable,' he said, and fell silent. He looked a little abashed, and a smirk appeared on his face. 'Actually, I had been watching you.'

'What do you mean? Watching me?'

'When you were fishing earlier. I could see you knew what you were doing when you cast down towards the rock there. You knew there was a fish down there, didn't you?'

She stared at him.

Damn, you look good, she thought.

She had already noticed the absence of a ring on his finger.

'Yes. I knew. Are you alone?' she asked and felt herself flush. She was surprised at the emotion that surfaced inside her, which felt a lot like a twinge of conscience. 'I mean, did you come here with a group?'

'No, I'm on my own. Arrived this morning and I'll be spending a few days here,' he said, and looked into her eyes, for a long time.

6

Hróbjartur opened his eyes as wide as he could. He couldn't figure out what was restricting his vision. He closed them again, and gradually recalled the events in the kitchen. At the same time, he felt the pain in his face intensifying. He had a hazy recollection of what had happened, but he was sure that there had been a bunched black fist in there somewhere. Now he remembered, and opened his eyes. He could feel the pain in them. That man had been quite right. He hadn't even felt the blow. To begin with, he wasn't sure where he was. He looked to one side, where a familiar lamp cast its glow from the bedside table. He saw the Bible that lay next to the lamp. He was in his bedroom. *Thank God*, he thought, and tried to sit up. But he couldn't. He could make no movement at all. He felt that his arms and legs were tied to the bed. Something squeaked every time he moved. He swung his head to one side, and discovered that a sheet of plastic had been laid under him, covering the whole bed.

'Awake, are you?' asked the man, who now stood in the doorway.

'What happened?' Hróbjartur asked, his voice hoarse and trembling.

The man went over to him and whipped away the blanket from Hróbjartur's naked body. Lifting his head as far as he could, he realised that he wasn't tied only hand and foot. Three yellow bands held down his legs, waist and chest.

The man took a seat on the edge of the bed. He looked at Hróbjartur for a long time. Then he leaned close and whispered.

'The truth, Hróbjartur. If only you had told the truth, then you wouldn't be in this unfortunate position. It was in the text you read just now. But you won't accept the truth,' the man said and looked at him again.

'Yes, I'll tell you everything...'

Hróbjartur's words were cut off as the man placed a strip of silver coloured tape over his mouth. He leaned over him again, and whispered.

'Shhh. It's too late now,' he said with a smile. 'You're a man of the Church, Hróbjartur. Do you know how many of you there are, priests, I mean? Well?'

He raised himself up and looked into Hróbjartur's eyes. He leaned down again and whispered.

'There are around a hundred and fifty of you. One hundred and fifty good men who carry out your duties to God and men. Ach, I'm sorry. There aren't a hundred and fifty of you. I forgot the bad apples. Those bad apples spoil so much. And they're all over. In fact, bad apples don't get to go to market. They get thrown in the bin. But among people we can't throw away the bad apples. These rotten individuals find their way into every corner of society, banks, politics, sports clubs, youth clubs. The Church. The house of God. Are you the rotten apple in God's house, Hróbjartur? How come you, the spoiled fruit, were able to hide yourself away there so well, and for so long?'

The man again straightened his back and looked down with a smile at Hróbjartur, who stared back at him. The smile vanished, and he again leaned forward to whisper.

'You know how it is with the house of God, the church. All those symbols. Don't you? Yeah, you know them all. All right, I'll see what I can remember of it,' he said and stood up. He paced the floor. 'The church itself symbolises heaven. It's also often likened to the ark Noah built to save men and animals from the great flood. There are churches that leak like sieves and anyone whose path lies that way doesn't come back unscathed. Apologies, Hróbjartur. That stuff about Noah's just a distraction,' he said and laughed. 'The doors of the church are the symbol of Christ. Jesus said, "I am the door".

The church spire represents the good news and the bells are the bringers of the word. The space between the door of the church and the altar is the holy road. Beautiful, isn't it?' the man said, and fell silent.

He stared for a long time at a heavy wooden cross that hung on one wall, and the gilded figure of Christ crucified on it.

'Talk to him now and again, do you?' he asked in a low voice and went over to the cross.

Hróbjartur mumbled and fought back a stifled cough.

The man turned and ripped the tape from Hróbjartur's face; he gasped for air.

'Jesus. Do you talk to him? Do you get any answers? Maybe the right answers that echo inside your head when you beg for forgiveness?'

There was no reply.

'It doesn't matter. There's more interesting stuff to come. All this symbolism. It's all very beautiful, and don't misunderstand me. I mean what I say. Very beautiful. Let's go on,' he said and sat again on the edge of the bed. He leaned close to Hróbjartur and whispered again.

'The height of the church symbolises hope. The walls of the church represent the three apostles. Well, what about that?'

'Four,' Hróbjartur said, his voice a hoarse rasp.

'Good man. It's all there at your fingertips. Of course there were four of them. You know all this stuff,' he said, getting to his feet. 'And all this is your guiding light when you are inside God's house. Noah's Ark and...' He got no further, and exploded into laughter. 'My God. All this stuff is fantastic. I'm sorry, I just pictured you in front of me, dressed up in all the ceremonial trappings and preaching to God-fearing people,' the man said, and wiped tears from his eyes.

He stood up, went to the end of the bed and picked up a black leather bag that he placed on the bed, before taking out a knife, scissors, pliers and a balled pair of socks.

The Commandments

Hróbjartur struggled and called out, hoarse cries for help. The man went quickly to him, and stuffed the bundle of socks into his mouth, taping his mouth shut. He squatted between Hróbjartur's legs, picked up the pliers and examined them. He seemed to be about to make use of them, then paused, as if he had remembered something.

'Ah. There are still a few more items we need to cover. I almost forgot,' he said with a laugh. He got up, and again sat on the edge of the bed next to Hróbjartur to whisper.

'It goes without saying that you have the ethical rules of the church at your fingertips, don't you?'

Hróbjartur's breathing came in quick gasps and he squeezed his eyes shut.

'Right at the start, they tell you that the rules are there to provide support and guidance in serving God and men. It even states that the fundamental rule of personal relationships is that *everything you would want others to do for you, you should do for them*. There are twenty of these rules altogether. I'm not going to quote the whole lot right now, but here are a few interesting ones. The seventh, as an example, states that one should never misuse one's position or jeopardise an individual's welfare, such as with inappropriate behaviour, with verbal, attitudinal, sexual or any other kind of abuse. The eighth rule is interesting as it reminds us that each individual is unique, so that a touch could be easily misunderstood or could cause discomfort. Do you reckon the boys misunderstood when you touched them? Do you think they misunderstood when you rammed your dick into their arseholes?'

He was silent for a long time before continuing.

'I have an idea that you'd like the ninth rule, the one that forbids forming inappropriate relationships with members of the flock. Hey! Hróbjartur, did you break that rule? Or maybe this one, number fifteen: being aware that you have a stronger position than the child you are working with, you should under no circumstances misuse your position? Well, you've certainly made a mess of things, as granny would have put it.'

He laughed and looked down at his hands.

'I get it, Hróbjartur. When men go hunting, they use the right equipment, or weapons. And you? You used your garments. You wear the hemp. Remember the Commandments? The tenth tells us that we shouldn't covet our neighbour's wife, his servant or maidservant, his ox or his ass, or anything that is thy neighbour's. Hmm,' the man said, straightening his back after allowing himself a moment's thought. 'What's missing, of course, is the word *child*. Although that could be counted among the neighbour's things that one should not covet. But the word itself is missing. *Child*. Don't you think? Thou shalt not covet thy neighbour's child. Then maybe you'd never have done what you did,' he said, sighing after a pause. 'No. You'd have found a way around the rules, all the expectations, to sneak past God's watchful eye. Past this guy,' he said, pointing at the cross on the wall.

The man stood up, went to the end of the bed and sat down.

He picked up the pliers, then the knife.

'There's a fruit bowl in your kitchen. It contains twelve apples. That's it, just think. The same number as the apostles. I noticed that one is spoiled, with a dark brown patch. What would you have done with that apple? Thrown it away? No. You'd have fetched a sharp knife and cut away the bad part. And that's exactly what I'm going to do.'

7

Saturday 23rd August 2014

Salka stepped out of the shower, reached for a towel and dried her hair. She ran her fingers through it and could feel the grease left by the silica in the water. It wasn't just in her hair, her whole skin had taken on this fine layer. She examined herself in the mirror. She couldn't help noticing that the freckles had spread across her face during her stay by the river.

She pulled on blue pants and a white tank top, opened the bathroom door and glanced along the accommodation block's corridor, which was deserted. That was understandable at twenty past five in the morning.

An hour earlier her phone had begun to vibrate on the bedside table. It wasn't a number she recognised and when she quickly looked it up in the online directory and she found that it belonged to Pétur, she could hardly believe her eyes.

She decided not to answer, and closed her eyes. All the same, there was no chance of getting back to sleep. She knew he was keen to add her to the police team, but there was something very weird about calling long before the first cock crow.

So she had got up, and decided that she would take a shower before calling him back. She had just closed the bathroom door behind her when the phone buzzed again.

'Hello?' she said in a low voice.

'Hello, Salka. Pétur here. You remember me?'

'Yes. I know. I imagine you're aware what time it is?' she said, with just the right note of sharpness in her voice.

'I know. I'm sorry to wake you so early. Kolla... Kolbrún, I mean, you know her?'

'Yes, your superintendent.'

'She asked me to get in touch with you. She's out of the country herself at the moment and in any case, I had meant to get in touch with you at a more reasonable time of day to see if there's a chance of you coming to work with us.'

Salka said nothing, just waited for him to continue.

'Well, Kolla suggested I call you right away. We're in crisis here right now. We're short-staffed and overworked... I can tell you we're drowning in workload in every single department and our people are bogged down.'

Salka still said nothing.

'You're still there?'

'Yes.'

'We've just had a report of a man murdered in a church.'

'Church?' Salka asked, astonished.

'That's right. The victim is the local priest and I was going to ask you if you could go out there and take a look?'

'Out where?'

'Ach. I'm sorry. I've only just been woken up. It's at Grenivík, not far from where you are. Ideally as soon as possible.'

Silence.

'That's... Assuming you're ready to start work with zero notice.'

'Pétur, I don't quite get this. To start with, Grenivík is closer to Akureyri than here. I'm on a break and hadn't expected to go back to work right away, and certainly hadn't decided what to do, whether with the police or something else completely.'

'Yeah, I understand perfectly,' he said, and there was another long pause. 'Kolbrún has been pressuring me to tempt you back, and in all honesty, I'm supposed to pull out all the stops to make it happen.'

'Then you've a long way to go still,' she said and smiled. 'I understand about being short of manpower and endless cases needing attention. But I can't believe that it's not possible to pull in a team for a case that should get top priority.'

'Well, yes. That's true,' Pétur said, and Salka sensed the tension in his voice. 'The thing is, you've investigated this man before. This priest.'

'Really? What do you mean?'

'2010. It was a case you worked on before you went to London. The abuse case that involved several priests. He was investigated, along with a few others, when charges were brought against them. You must remember it?'

'Of course. There were three... no, four women and two men who made accusations against these priests, and all of the cases were dismissed.'

'That sounds about right. After you went abroad there were a few more linked cases that cropped up, but it was never possible to prove anything, what with statutes of limitations, one man's word against another's, and... well, you know all that. According to the records I've been looking through, you questioned this man, the one found murdered.'

'Who is it?'

'Hróbjartur.'

There was a long silence. Salka remembered the man clearly: devious and difficult to pin down. She recalled the man's pomposity and the smile that seemed to be a permanent feature of his face. She even remembered his huge hands.

'And why do you want me working on this?'

'You know him. You've investigated him before. According to the report from the officer on the scene, it's brutal. And Kolla knew him pretty well.'

'Understood.'

She could feel her resistance ebbing away. That would make Kolla happy.

'I've been in touch with forensics down south and they're ready to go, but there's a thick fog over Akureyri right now

so there are no flights. Hopefully, it'll burn off before long.'
'What?'
'The fog. Hoping it'll lift when the sun's higher in the sky.'
'All right, Pétur. I understand. I'll leave right away.'

Salka quietly shut the bedroom door behind her. The
morning brightness made its way into the room around
the edges of the blinds that were supposed to darken it.
The chalet was showing its age. It was in fact a six hundred
square metre prefab block that had previously been used
as accommodation at the Blandá hydro-electric plant. The
walls were paper-thin and full-throated snores came from
both of the neighbouring rooms. It would have been easy to
let herself be irritated by this, but she couldn't help smiling
as she wondered if Magnús was one of the snorers.

After their encounter by the river, they had each gone
their own way. After a day's fishing and dinner in the
evening, she had gone to her room. She had been about to go
to sleep when Magnús had knocked, asking if she would care
to share the bottle of red wine he had been given. They sat in
the common room where other fishermen had gathered, and
talked over the day's events. One of those present seemed
to have at his command some kind of supernatural wisdom
and deep knowledge of fishing that left his companions
speechless. Salka wondered if this was down to sincere
admiration, or good manners and a reluctance to call out the
other man's tall stories.

Salka and Magnús sat and talked, and at two in the
morning they left the common room and went together along
the accommodation block's corridor. The words formed on
her lips. She even opened her mouth, ready to invite him into
her room, when he said good night and disappeared into his
own room.

Salka dressed and left the room, having packed her
things and fishing gear. In the dining room she scowled as

she pressed the button on the coffee pot and found that it was empty.

It was bright daylight outside and she took a deep breath of the fresh morning air. She glanced up at the flagpole next to the chalet, where the fishing club's flag hung limp.

A field mouse scurried over the grey gravel and disappeared under the wooden steps to the fly-tying room.

Salka sat behind the wheel of the white Volvo XC90, set off and took a right turn at the junction with the main road to head for Akureyri. An hour later she was driving past Víkurskarð's pitted cliff face, from where she could see the fog cloaking Eyjafjörður below. The fog bank stretched out along the fjord, denser towards the town. They would have to wait a while for forensics to turn up, she thought.

On the flat ground by the coast, she took the sharp right turn for the road to Grenivík.

8

Her first sight of the fishing village of Grenivík, the most northerly settlement on the eastern side of Eyjafjörður, reminded Salka of the approach to Blönduós, with green pastures speckled with bales of hay and grazing livestock. She drove past grassy fields and meadows on both sides until the village appeared as if from nowhere, nestling at the side of the fjord between Thengilshöfði and Kaldbakur.

During the hour's drive, Salka had seen only two other cars. It was just seven in the morning when the car's wheels crunched over the gravel drive leading to the yard outside Grenivík's church. An empty police car stood in the car park in front of the church.

The smell of seaweed carried on the breeze as she got out of the car. She slipped a band from her wrist to tie back her hair, and took in the sight of the white-walled church with its roof of red steel sheets. Within the walls of the churchyard there were graves that ranged from recent to ancient. She used her phone to snap a couple of pictures of the church and its surroundings.

There wasn't a cloud in the sky from where she stood with a view over the village, part of which was clustered below the church, straggling towards the sea. The place looked to be made up of mainly conventionally bland detached and semi-detached houses. The silence was practically tangible – there was nobody to be seen anywhere. The only sound that broke the tranquillity was when a snipe dived from a height like a wartime Spitfire, its tail feathers humming as the air flowed over them.

Salka went to the lychgate in the churchyard wall. She swung it open and paused, standing still as the gate marked where consecrated ground began. She wasn't sure who had told her... Yes, it was her father who had said it, on the way to church when she had been a girl, that when you stop at the centre of a lychgate, you're neither in the world of the living, nor of the dead. She had asked him if you became immortal in such a place.

'Good morning,' called a young man who was standing in front of the open church doors. 'Good to see you. I'm Gísli. Akureyri police force,' he said as Salka made her way towards him. 'I've been expecting you,' he said with a smile. 'But not quite this early.'

She climbed a couple of steps up to the church doors. He was of average height, with short fair hair, combed to one side. Some people would have described it as golden, courtesy of the unusually long spell of summer sunshine Iceland had been enjoying. It looked as though he hadn't had time – or allowed himself time – to take a shower or comb his hair properly before his shift, as the hair at the back of his head was tousled. It seemed that he noticed Salka's look, as he quickly patted down his hair with his left hand.

'Have you checked the scene?' Salka asked.

'Yes, a quick look. It doesn't look good. But I've not been here long. It was one of the council staff who found him,' he said, one foot sweeping fresh glass clippings from the path.

'Council staff?'

'That's right. Skúli. He works for the council and keeps things maintained around the village. He's something of a lost soul.'

'And what do you mean by that?'

'Well, you know... ' he said and glanced at Salka, who smiled back. 'You'll see when you meet him.'

'What time was it when he got here?'

'It was...' he checked his notebook. 'Around half past two in the morning. Maybe a little earlier. He called in to raise the alarm. He'll be here shortly.'

'Why isn't he here now?'

'He has a bitch at home that's about to pup.'

'Isn't there anyone else who can look after the dog? By rights he should have waited here.'

'He'll be here before long. I know him pretty well.'

'What was he doing here in the middle of the night?' she asked, looking at the walls of the church, which could have done with a coat of paint.

'He was walking the dog, said she'd been restless. Shall we take a look inside?' he said, opening the church door.

Salka followed Gísli into the narrow, bare lobby that was furnished with nothing more than a couple of coat hooks on each wall. Gísli opened the door to the nave where flecks of dust danced in the shafts of sunlight creeping through the windows. Banks of pews, upholstered in red, flanked a dull carpet.

'There he is,' Gísli said in a low voice, pointing towards the altar.

Salka's gaze travelled along the church floor and she didn't appear to hear Gísli's voice behind her. She didn't feel comfortable in the church, or in churches in general. It wasn't that the church had taken anything from her, but more what it stood for: the House of the Lord. He was precisely the one she felt had failed her.

'Are you all right?'

'Why are you whispering?' Salka whispered, glancing at Gísli.

'I don't know,' he said, looking back at her in surprise.

She knew perfectly well why. You never speak loudly in church. Unless you're singing, you whisper. But churchgoers don't always lower their voices. She recalled clearly attending a service as a girl with her parents. She joined enthusiastically in with 'Jesus is my friend', singing with such gusto that she distracted both the congregation and the priest, and her father had tapped her on the back of the head. *Shhh*, he had said, and she saw the shadow of a smile on his face. The recollection always brought a smile to her face as she knew what her intention had been – to drown out the priest's dreadfully out-of-tune singing voice.

Salka took slow steps towards the altar, looking up at the light blue dome of the roof above, speckled with golden stars, before she stopped at the altar rail. The gate in the rail stood open. Above the altar was an image of the risen Christ with outstretched arms. The altar measured no more than a few square feet and there – inside the altar rail – slumped the priest. She took a long look at him. His back was against the altar itself, while his legs, straight and slightly apart, extended beyond the gate. His arms lay at his sides, clenched fists with the knuckles uppermost. His head lolled slightly forwards. His face was swollen and badly beaten, but there was no blood to be seen, as if it had been carefully washed.

'Are you the only one here?'

'Yes. I was on a routine patrol through Vaðlaskógur when the report was called in. They were going to send a team, and then there was an update to say that you were on the way.'

'And that's Hróbjartur?' she said, as if to herself, after squatting to peer more closely at the bruised face.

She heard Gísli flipping through his notes.

'That's right. He's been the parish priest for... some time. Not quite sure how long, but I understand he had a good reputation.'

'Who told you that?'

'Unnar. He lives around here.'

'Unnar who lives around here,' Salka repeated, standing up. 'Are you telling me that you've told someone here in the village what's happened?'

Gísli stared at her. He opened his mouth and was about to reply, but closed it again, as if he had swallowed what he had been about to say.

'I know him,' he said at last. 'He was rolling home from a party somewhere, and came past the church, and went inside. So he saw Hróbjartur. He was drunk, so I escorted him out again.'

'It's going to be great to read about this in the morning papers.'

'No, it's all right. He won't say anything. It's confidential.'

'Sure,' Salka sighed. She closed her eyes for a moment. 'How do you know this...?'

'Unnar? I'm from around here, I mean from Grenivík, and know pretty much everyone. Spent my college years more or less in Akureyri. But Unnar's one of those who likes a drink. He's a colourful character.'

'Precisely. And I suppose that's why you're certain he won't breathe a word of this?' she said and smiled.

'Well, no... Or, he's...'

'Let's not waste time on this, Gísli,' she said, holding his eye for a long time. 'News is going to get out soon enough anyway,' she said, placing a hand on his shoulder. 'How many people live here?'

'I'd guess two hundred to two hundred and fifty here in the village, and another hundred in the countryside around it,' he said, gesturing with his open palms, the relief evident in his voice.

Salka took out her phone and called up a map of Grenivík.

'The forensics team will be on the way as soon as the fog over Akureyri lifts and hopefully they'll be here as soon as possible. Are any of your guys on the way?'

'Two cars on the way. They should be here soon.'

'You can meet them outside. You need to fence off the crime scene and the approach to the church. You also need to knock on the doors of all the houses that are within sight of the church,' she said, holding the phone so that Gísli could see the screen. 'It looks like ten or twelve houses below the pasture. So it's a question of whether anyone saw anything,' she said, turning back to Hróbjartur.

'Sure,' Gísli said and she could hear his uncertainty.

'So maybe you could make a start on that, Gísli,' she said when she saw that he hadn't moved.

She heard him mumble and the creak of the floorboards

as he went towards the church doors. Salka sighed. She felt uncomfortable at how sharp she had been with him. He seemed a decent enough lad, but young and green, and somehow damned simple. No, he wasn't simple, she thought, she was being unfair. He was simply insecure, and that was entirely understandable.

'Where did Hróbjartur live?'

'In Akureyri. I don't have the address but I can find it...' he said and was about to set off when there was a knock on the door. 'Reinforcements are here,' he reported once he had opened the door. 'They say Skúli's here.'

'Give them instructions, and then you can sit with Skúli in your car. I'll be right with you,' she called after him.

Gísli opened the door and looked over at Salka with unasked questions in his eyes. He seemed about to say something. She caught his eye. He swallowed, looked down at the floor for a second and was about to shut the door when Salka called him over.

'Gísli, now we need to get a handle on things. If you're going to work on this with me, you need to pull yourself together. How many guys have come from Akureyri?'

'Four.'

'Two of them to close off the road to the church and two to do the door-to-door stuff. You sit with Skúli in the car, but don't talk to him until I get there. OK?'

'Got it. No problem,' he said and left the church.

She stepped over the altar rail, checked the table beneath the altar and examined the gilded candelabra in the centre, the Bible and the book of Psalms. Everything appeared to be untouched and carefully arranged. Looking down at the altar floor, there was no blood to be seen. She bent down to lean closer to Hróbjartur. He wore black vestments with a white ruff. Salka was not wholly familiar with the customs and practices of the church, but she was aware that black was worn only on Good Friday and for funerals.

A tiny patch on the chest of his cassock glittered, at the

centre of a tear she guessed to be around twenty centimetres long and the work of a knife. She made out black trouser legs beneath the cassock, and black shoes polished to shine like mirrors. Salka found the sight of him disturbing. Fair hair had been neatly combed back from a high forehead, greying at the sides. His mouth hung slightly open. The puffed eyelids were shades of blue, red and yellow. A tracery of purple veins lay along a big nose that had been pushed to one side, more than likely by a blow. He had a broad jawline and thin lips. His fists were almost frighteningly large. Almost everything about this man was too big, just as she recalled from the last time they had met. Salka decided that whoever had attacked him had to be powerfully built. It would take determination to pick a fight with someone this size, she thought. Or would it? It wasn't always size that mattered. It was courage. You can be small in size but still think big. She knew that when your life is threatened, the body's instinctive brakes unconsciously stop working, providing access to huge reserves of strength in the struggle for survival.

Salka felt cautiously around his hips and chest, hoping to find something that would indicate that he had a mobile phone or anything else in his jacket or trouser pockets, but they appeared to be empty.

She peered closer at his left fist and saw the light catch something. As long as her eyesight hadn't failed her in the dim light, she was sure she could make out the glint of a dark, twisting hair caught between his finger and thumb. She took a deep breath.

She stepped over Hróbjartur to check his clenched right fist. The light caught the same sort of hair there as well.

Salka looked closely at Hróbjartur's face. She switched on her phone's torch and played the beam of light over his mouth, and adjusted his chin so that his mouth opened further. She covered her mouth and nose with a hand as the powerful stench came at her like an ambush.

'What did you do that was so bad you deserved this?' she muttered and stood up.

The Commandments

She stepped back to crouch at his feet, picked up the hem of the cassock and lifted it. She clicked on the phone's torch. She dropped the cassock, rushed through the nave and out. By the time she reached the lychgate, she was retching.

9

'Are you all right?' Gísli asked, half out of the patrol car, as she walked over to him and sat in the passenger seat.

'Yes, fine,' she said, and turned to look at Skúli who was sitting behind the driver's seat. 'Hello, my name's Salka.'

'Hello. Do you know who murdered him?'

'Murdered?' she asked in surprise. 'Who said anything about murder?'

'Well. I thought he had been killed.'

'We haven't got that far yet. Do you know what happened to him?'

'Me? No,' he said firmly, and sounded offended. 'You're off your head if you think I know anything about this.'

'Skúli,' Gísli said, looking in the rear view mirror. 'Mind your manners.'

'What happened to you?' she asked, nodding at Skúli.

At first he didn't seem to be sure what she meant, then he lifted a hand to the bruise and the swelling across his right temple. The skin must have been broken, as he had fixed a circular plaster over the centre of the swelling.

'That? I just walked into something with a bit of a bang.'

'It looks recent. How did this happen?'

'The sink at home was leaking,' he said after a second's hesitation. 'I was bent double down there inside the cupboard and banged my head.'

Salka turned to face forward. She glanced at Gísli, who appeared apologetic on Skúli's behalf.

It was immediately clear to her that Skúli was different to most people. He came across as childishly direct. She guessed he must be somewhere around twenty-five to twenty-seven. He was chubby, with fair hair down to his shoulders and it wasn't easy to work out whether it was unwashed and uncared for, or styled to look that way. He had an outdoor complexion, his eyes were sharp and he appeared to be physically powerful. The grubby grey military-style jacket he wore over a black tee shirt could have done with being a size larger as it stretched over his bulky torso. Maybe it was the jacket that emphasised the colour of his eyes, making them look greyer than they really were.

'Tell me about what happened when you went to the church,' Salka said gently.

'It was three in the morning and I saw Hróbjartur. It was a horrible sight.'

'I can well believe it. What did you do when you saw him?'

'Well, I called the cops right away. And Gísli turned up pretty quickly.'

'Did you know Hróbjartur?'

'I want a lawyer,' Skúli said in a low voice.

'What?' Salka said, twisting around to face him. 'Why do you want a lawyer?'

'I don't want to say anything until I have a lawyer present.'

'Did you have anything to do with what happened?'

'No.'

'Skúli, you don't need a lawyer,' Gísli said. 'You haven't been arrested and we just want to talk to you.'

'Then at least I want to talk to Valgeir.'

'Who's Valgeir?' Salka asked, turning to Gísli.

'He's a police officer and he's running things while Kolbrún is away. Valgeir's Skúli's uncle,' Gísli said quietly and glanced at Skúli. 'You don't need Valgeir here. We just want to talk and find out what happened.'

'I don't want to talk. I don't want to say something I shouldn't,' he said and folded his arms over his chest, as if he were cold. He looked out of the window at his side.

'Don't be daft, Skúli,' Gísli said sharply. 'We just want to go through the events of last night, that's all.'

There was silence from the back seat.

Óskar Guðmundsson

'Well,' Salka said, as if speaking to herself. 'We'd better take a look at your home.'

'Why?'

'That's routine in a case like this,' Salka said, after a pause.

'Then you need a search warrant for that.'

'Yes, sure. But do you have anything to hide?'

'No, of course not. But you still need a warrant.'

'Skúli, what's got into you?' Gísli said, clearly irritated, after twisting around in his seat to look at him.

Salka looked over her shoulder and saw Skúli's expressionless face.

'Those are the rules,' he said finally. 'Apart from that, Mother doesn't like having people with no business there rooting around her house.'

Salka turned back to face the windscreen and smiled to herself.

'You live with her?' she asked.

'Yeah. Or she lives with me. We live in the same house.'

'So shall we go and have a chat with your mum?'

'No,' he snapped. 'She's not home.'

'Where is she?'

'She had to go over to Dalvík. She'll be back today.'

This isn't going our way, Salka wanted to say, but instead she just sighed.

'Then I suppose you'd best come with us to the station, Skúli,' she said gently.

'What for?' he demanded, edging forward in his seat and catching hold of the headrest in front of him.

'Routine in this kind of case, and it's not as if you're being co-operative.'

'I'll have to go and check on the dog, she's about to have pups.'

'How far gone is she?' Gísli asked.

'Four weeks or so.'

'Then you don't need to worry. She's got at least the same again before she drops them.'

'What do you know about that?'

'I know a thing or two.'

'You have a dog, do you?'

'Skúli, I know something about dogs,' Gísli said, his irritation showing more clearly. Salka smiled, but took care to look to one side, out of the passenger window.

'By all means check on the dog, as long as we come inside with you,' she said.

'Absolutely not.'

'Fine. Then we'll go to the station in Akureyri,' she said, and turned to catch Skúli's eye. The man put her in mind of a recalcitrant, overgrown child.

10

Salka drove to Akureyri, with Gísli following behind her with Skúli in the back of the patrol car. They parked behind the police station on Thórunnarstræti, looking down on the town below. A female officer was at reception and Salka asked for Skúli to be taken to an interview room, as she didn't have the heart to have him put in a cell.

All of a sudden they were aware of a man standing among them, asking if there was anything they could say at this moment. They stared at him in surprise.

'You've no business here,' Gísli said with determination, striding towards the journalist.

'Who's the dead person in the church? Is this a murder case?'

Salka shook her head and thought of Gísli's discreet friend who had shown up at the church during the night. She watched Gísli and another officer march the journalist out, past the gate he had ducked under, which barred access to the station from Thórunnarstræti.

Gísli returned and Salka asked him to track down Skúli's mother.

'You must be this Salka I've been hearing so much about,' said a slim man in an official white shirt and black tie, who appeared from a doorway at the end of the corridor when she reached the second floor of the building. 'We need to talk.'

Salka caught the man's eye and went over to him. The tone jarred. *This Salka*. She was surprised to see the spiderweb veins on his face, at this time of year.

'Of course,' she said, and went into his office. She could sense he wasn't delighted, as she hadn't been invited in. 'And you are...?' she asked, as if his name had been plucked from her memory – even though she knew perfectly well who this man was.

'Valgeir,' he said, pushing glasses with golden frames higher up his nose. 'You've come direct from Grenivík?'

'That's right,' Salka said, making an effort to stifle a yawn. She almost managed it, taking a long breath through her nose. The stuffy air of the office had made her aware of how tired she was. She glanced at the clock on the wall, and saw that it was twenty past eight.

'How are your parents?' he asked, planting himself in his office chair so that it quivered beneath him.

Salka sighed involuntarily.

'They're fine.'

'And your dad? Still working?'

'No.'

'Really? How come?'

Salka wondered whether to take the chair facing his deck, or the sofa that stood against one wall of the spacious office. The chair option would leave her uncomfortably below Valgeir's eye line. She chose the sofa and noticed that he shot a look of annoyance her way, past the computer screen on his desk.

'What did you want to talk to me about?' she asked, as she picked up a crumpled crocheted cushion that was on the sofa and put it to one side.

'I've heard from my guys in Grenivík. I've instructed them to go door-to-door at every house within sight of the church to see if there's anyone who noticed anything unusual.'

'That's good,' Salka said and smiled. She could let him have the glory of having taken that decision.

'I understand you have some legal documentation for me,' he said.

'Then you understand wrong,' she said quietly.

Valgeir glared. She knew what he was thinking. He didn't like her tone.

'I don't have anything to confirm your presence,' he said.

'I'm here at Kolbrún's request. She must have sent some paperwork?'

'Understood. She's on holiday and I'm in charge in her absence,' he said in a dry voice, without taking his eyes from the screen in front of him. For a moment Salka though he was looking at the ceiling, and then realised that he was using the reading point of his multifocal glasses.

A printer spat out two sheets of paper.

'Let's see,' he said, reaching for them. He hummed a few times as he read, a little too often for her liking, obviously taking his time.

'I see that you handed in your warrant card in June 2010 when you moved to London and were with CID there. Then you came back to Iceland in October 2013 and... haven't been involved in police work for around a year. Why's that?'

'Why's what?'

'Why haven't you worked during this time?'

'There's nothing about that in your file?' Salka asked.

'No,' he said, drawing out the word as he appeared to search through the document in his hands.

'I've no idea what you're looking at. If there's nothing stated, then that's probably because there's nothing that should be stated there,' she said and gave him a smile, a narrow little smile.

'Hmm?' he grunted. 'Why on earth shouldn't this be mentioned?'

'Probably because it's a personal matter. Apart from that, I'm pretty sure that I wasn't supposed to be coming to you for a job interview today.' Valgeir opened his mouth to speak, but Salka continued in her measured tone. 'I'm here entirely at Kolbrún's request. Probably on a temporary basis. She wanted me to investigate the case concerning Hróbjartur,' she said, feeling herself getting hot under the collar. 'And is Pétur here somewhere?'

'No, he's not here,' Valgeir said, taking off his glasses and rubbing his nose. If anything, his face was even more flushed than before. He put his glasses on again, and seemed to be about to speak, but Salka again beat him to it.

'I'm going to get myself a cup of coffee, so maybe you could let me know when he turns up?' she said, ready to get to her feet.

'What about Skúli? He's waiting to be interviewed.'

'It'll do him no harm to wait a little while.'

'Couldn't you have talked to him at the scene?' he asked, his voice sharper than before, as he took off his glasses again, which this time came across as a theatrical gesture. He blinked rapidly and Salka wondered if he could see anything at all.

'I spoke to him when I met him outside the church, and he wasn't as co-operative as he could have been. I want a longer chat with him.'

'He's a lovely lad and has...'

'I know he's your nephew, Valgeir. But we have to follow procedure. I'll talk to him later and if it all goes well then he can go home to Grenivík. It's not that far.'

'You can't just waltz in here...'

'Valgeir, I don't understand where you're going with this,' Salka said firmly, standing up and forcing a smile. 'A murder has been committed. I've been asked to investigate it and I don't honestly care one way or the other whether you like it or not. The same goes for whatever opinion you might have of me. I'm simply here to do my job. I'll run the investigation and we can work together in peace and harmony, or it can be a pain in the arse for both of us. It's up to you.'

The computer in front of him pinged.

Valgeir snatched up his glasses. Not the golden ones this time, but a pair of red-framed reading glasses that fitted badly, probably the kind of emergency glasses sold at filling stations. He pored over the screen and puffed through his nose, before looking up at Salka.

The printer hummed.

'Fine,' he said and took the sheet of paper it spat out. 'Fine,' he said again, shifting in his chair. 'Your temporary accreditation. Kolbrún sent it just now.'

He opened a desk drawer and took out an old-style stamp. After he'd pressed it against the ink pad, Salka expected he would bang it down hard on the paper in front of him. But the opposite happened. He placed the stamp with great care on the paper and pressed down, then picked up a pen and signed his name across it.

'Here you are. Welcome back,' he said and smiled – a cold smile that was a long way off from reaching his eyes.

11

It was half past nine when Salka took a seat in the Blue Jug on Hafnarstræti with a mug of coffee and a baguette sandwich. She had called or checked online every hotel, guest house and Airbnb in the area. No vacancies. When the last one she tried turned her away, she was about to ask if she could just curl up in a corner somewhere.

She had considered staying with her parents, even though that would mean sleeping on the sofa. But she quickly dropped the idea. The sofa was as hard as rock and too short for her to stretch out her full one metre seventy. The cash-strapped police authority would have to cough up for a place where she could lay her head, although that would inevitably take time.

Salka was startled by a knock on the window. She looked up to see a man grinning from ear to ear on the pavement outside.

'Hello, Pétur,' she said and was about to get to her feet as he came across to her table, but he told her to stay where she was.

Salka dropped her eyes to the table when she realised that she had been staring at his face, and felt a stab of shame. It was six or seven years since she had last seen him, and she recalled a man with a mass of dark brown hair and a red beard framing a strong face. Now neither were to be seen. His hair was cropped short, clipped close at the side and the beard was gone. But it wasn't this change that was painful to see. The burns had healed into scar tissue that covered the left side of his face and distorted his ear. The skin that covered the scorched half of his face reminded her of marzipan.

'Good to see you, Salka. And thanks for coming,' he said as

he took a seat opposite her. 'I can see from the look on your face that you hadn't heard about this,' he said with a smile, pointing at his own face.

'No. I had no idea. Can I ask what happened?'

'We had a report of gunshots being heard at a house in Hrafnagil, so the Special Unit was called out. Then there was a report that the place was on fire. We were there ahead of the fire service and when we got there, the upper storey was burning merrily. We knew there were people inside, so, like an idiot, I went in. Should have realised there was nothing I could do. I was on my way out again just as the house started to collapse on top of me, and that's how this happened. The place just went up in smoke. My wife says she likes the sexy new look,' he said and laughed.

'That's the fire last year?' Salka asked, astonished at how positive his outlook was.

'That's the one.'

'Magnús didn't mention what happened to you when he talked about the fire,' Salka said, hesitating for a second as she mentioned him.

'You met him fishing?'

'Yes.'

'I don't think anyone talks about it any longer. He probably thought you knew. But enough of all that,' Pétur said, glancing at his watch. 'I hear you've met Valgeir. He didn't upset you, did he?' He laughed. 'He can be a real pain in the arse.'

'It was a bizarre encounter, but I reckon it would take a lot more than that to upset me.'

'And you've been to Grenivík. I hear it wasn't a pretty sight.'

'That's about the size of it,' she said and gave him a brief description of what she had seen. 'And I'm stopped in my tracks now that the forensic team can't fly because of the fog.'

'I have to say, I really appreciate you coming. I know I said Kolla had been pushing me to bring you in, but it's important to me as well. I don't know if you were aware, but your dad and I get on well these days,' he said with a smile.

'Really?'

'We're both in the Odd Fellows. I've developed a lot of respect for him since we got to know each other. He's taught me a lot.' Pétur fell silent for a moment. 'I know he's been on the receiving end of some harsh words, as well as ... what shall we say...? Criticism for some of the cases he took on, especially that last one. But as they say, someone has to look after the bad guys as well.'

'It's all right, Pétur. It doesn't bother me. I know Dad and what's behind what you see. That'll do for me.'

'Can I get you anything?' asked a young waiter, approaching the table.

'Not for me, thanks. I have a meeting to get to,' he said.

'But you could bring a cappuccino for me,' said Gísli, who appeared by the table, a smile on his face. 'Hello, Pétur. Good to see you.'

'I imagine you know each other?' Pétur said.

'Gísli was at the church when I got there,' Salka said. 'He's going to be working with me on this case.'

'Really?' Pétur asked, glancing from one to the other.

Salka noticed Gísli's look of astonishment.

'Well, that's fine as far as I'm concerned,' Pétur said as he stood up to leave.

Salka could hear the doubt in his voice. This was a decision he would probably have preferred to discuss privately. Gísli had never been involved in a CID investigation. But an inner voice was telling her that he deserved a chance. She had faith in him, and she liked him.

'I imagine you must have met Valgeir,' Gísli said as he took the cup brought by the waiter. 'Was he as cheerful as he usually is?' he asked, with a spark of amusement in his eye.

'Yep, happy as Larry.'

'I've known him for a long time. He can come across as being a crusty old grump, but he's all right,' Gísli said when he had stopped laughing. 'Anyway, here's an aerial picture

I found of Grenivík. I've marked all fifteen houses that are within sight of the church. We've spoken to residents in all of them, and nobody saw a thing,' he said as he placed the sheet of paper on the table. 'Have you spoken to him?'

Salka looked at him and frowned.

'Skúli, I mean.'

'I know who you mean. I'll have a chat with him later. Are you worrying about him as well?'

'No, not at all. I know he was a pain this morning... but he's a decent lad.'

'How does this work? Does everyone here know everyone else?'

'No, it's nothing like that. Well, sort of. This is a smaller community than you see in the city.'

'So how do you know Skúli?'

'Since primary school. Then secondary school, which he never actually finished. I've had to respond a couple of times to call-outs that have been to do with him. A bit of noise and bother, but never anything serious. Skúli wouldn't... he's never hurt a fly.'

'I don't know anyone who hasn't hurt a fly,' Salka said with a smile.

'No, I suppose not,' he said thoughtfully.

'What's he like? I mean, personality-wise? It was like talking to a child in your car.'

'Yes, I know. He's always been like that.'

'Like what?'

Gísli sat for a moment in thought.

'I remember him from way back. Back then he was pretty immature. As a kid he was often still playing with the toys that the rest of us had outgrown. Yet at other times he was like an old farmer. That's to say, he talked like ... the vocabulary he used was grown-up. Maybe that's because he mostly grew up with his grandparents. I've noticed this whenever I've had to deal with him in the last few years. One minute he's like a child and the next he's as sharp as a knife and speaks

61

completely differently.'

'Sounds like, what's it called? A personality disorder, or something like that,' Salka said, dabbing with a serviette to remove a drop of sauce that had strayed from her sandwich to the sleeve of her sweater.

'Exactly. Poor chap,' he said and Salka frowned, already tired of what seemed to be Gísli's sympathy that bordered on enablement. 'At any rate, he's devastated after what he saw when he found Hróbjartur. He told me just now...'

'Just now? You've spoken to him?'

'Yes, up at the station.'

'Gísli, I thought I'd given clear instructions that nobody was to speak to him. There are reasons why I'm letting him wait, alone. There's a process going on here. You said you spoke to him?' she asked, and felt the heat rising in her face.

'Yes. I did.'

Salka sighed and looked out of the window. She watched the tourists who walked past, open-mouthed and smiling with delight at things that locals had long stopped noticing.

'Did you get hold of Skúli's mother?'

'That's why I went to speak to him, to get her phone number and ask when she would be likely to be coming back from Dalvík. He didn't know when she would be going home. He also said that she hardly ever hears her phone ring. In any case, I wasn't able to get hold of her.'

'Keep trying. What about...?'

Salka was interrupted by her phone ringing. After a short 'yes, no, all right, speak to you later' conversation, she ended the call.

'The forensic team still hasn't left, but they should be able to take off shortly,' she said. 'What was I saying? What about the search warrant for Skúli's place? Any progress?'

'Yes. The house is actually in his mother's name, so maybe she'll allow access.'

'Let's get the warrant anyway, just in case. And what's the score with this place? Is there any chance of finding somewhere to stay in this town?'

'That could be a problem. But there are a few empty cells,' he said with a grin. 'Have you tried many places?'

'Every single one I could find.'

'I should be able to sort something out. Like you said, everyone here knows everyone else.'

12

Gísli worked some magic over the phone and Salka found herself with a place to stay above a tourist shop on Hafnarstræti. It was a warm, neat hotel apartment with a living room that doubled as a kitchen. Salka put her bags down and let herself collapse onto the sofa. She was immediately disappointed, finding that it wasn't as soft as it looked.

As she lay on her back, she thought of Magnús, after which, contrary to what she would have preferred, her thoughts went to Eysteinn. She sat up and took out the paperwork Eysteinn had sent her. She flipped through it. Six months ago he had sought a divorce, and now she had the decree nisi in her hands. She hurled the documents across the room, buried her face in her hands, and wept.

It went without saying that this had been the only possible outcome after everything that had happened. There was the shame, her own self-reproach, plus what someone had told her, that self-destructiveness was not the way to put anything right. She had implored Eysteinn for them to seek counselling. But by then it had already been too late. That had been what he asked for when their world had been turned on its head, but at that time she hadn't listened and allowed herself to be drawn deep into a darkness of her own to which nobody else had access. She had been there, or so it had felt, for an eternity and could no longer see any point in this life. When she finally emerged from the blackness, Eysteinn was as good as gone.

Salka reached for her wallet in the pocket of her moss-green denim jacket and took out her wallet. In it was an old, creased photo of their daughter María, grinning at the camera and tugging her red hair to one side. She recalled what María had once said.

Mum, I have twenty-three freckles. I just need one more and we'll be just the same.

She picked up her phone and called. It rang a few times until a happy voice answered.

Hi, this is María. I'm soooo busy right now. Don't call back, I'll call you… If I remember.

The message ended with a peal of laughter.

Salka unlocked the door to the room where Skúli had been taken on the police station's second floor. She had hardly stepped beyond the threshold before Skúli was on his feet.

'About time,' he barked, hands waving. 'What's going on here? Why have I been locked away in this cubbyhole?'

'Looks more like a suite to me,' she said, looking around. 'You've clearly never been inside a cell.'

He did as she asked and followed her, taking a seat at a desk beneath the window in one of the interview rooms. She sat opposite him, took off her jacket and hung it over the back of the chair. She took out a notepad and her phone, and placed them in front of her.

Salka unhurriedly checked her notes and switched on the recorder.

'What are you recording for? I've already told you everything I know.'

Salka didn't reply.

'Can I get you something to drink, Skúli? Coffee, water? Soft drink?'

'Have I been arrested?'

'No, but your status is that of a suspect, and you didn't tell me anything at all.'

'That means what?'

'What means what?'

'Being a suspect?'

'That means I can keep you here for twenty-four hours.'

Skúli slapped both palms down hard on the table and stood up. He puffed out his chest and glared down at Salka.

She flipped through the notepad's pages, as if searching for something. Skúli's reaction had taken her by surprise. She managed not to show it, and Skúli's chest deflated as if it had been punctured.

'Sit down, Skúli,' she said quietly, without looking at him. 'If you do that again I'll have no option but to have you cuffed.'

After staring at her for a moment, Skúli dropped back into his seat. She was sure she heard him curse under his breath, but couldn't be certain. He continued to grunt as he sat opposite her.

'Shall I get you a fresh plaster for that?' she asked as she glanced at him, indicating the plaster that was half hanging from the injury to his temple.

'What? No, it's all right,' he said, pulling it off, and feeling the place with his fingertips. 'It's stopped bleeding.'

She could see a small cut there in the swelling and the skin had flaked away from it.

'That's a hell of a shiner you have there. How did you say you got it?'

'I was fixing a leak under the sink at home and managed to bang my head.'

'Where, exactly?'

He thought for a moment.

'I'm not completely sure.'

'I mean, did you catch yourself against the outflow pipe, or against the cupboard itself?'

'What difference does it make?' he blustered.

'Just between ourselves, Skúli, I'll give you a piece of advice,' Salka said gently, putting the notepad aside. 'How you reply to questions can have a negative effect on how all this plays out. I'm here to ask you simple questions. Your job is to answer them. I'm a police detective and I have a great deal of experience in figuring out whether or not people are telling the truth. My advice to you is to tell the truth. Speak from the heart. Can you see where I'm going with this?'

'Yeah,' he said after pausing for thought.

'This interview is purely so that I can piece together what went on. Understand?'

She leaned forward a little and raised an eyebrow.

Skúli said nothing.

'Fine. At any rate, I can tell you that you saying you don't remember where you banged your head sounds very unconvincing. When people knock into something and hurt themselves, the instinct is to put a hand to the sore place and look at whatever it was that got in their way. Often people get angry and swear,' she said. 'I stubbed my big toe against at home, and it hurt like hell. I looked down at the doorstop and swore like a bargee,' she said and smiled, maybe because she was lying about something personal. 'So I'm asking you, Skúli. Where did you hit your head?'

'The drain pipe,' he said, without catching her eye. 'I banged my head against the drain.'

Salka watched him. He still wasn't convincing, and she allowed the seconds to tick past before continuing.

'Tell me about when you went out with the dog. Or, first explain to me what took you out?'

Skúli looked at her and settled a little into the chair.

'Húbert's pregnant...'

'Hang on... Húbert is a she?'

'Yeah. Húbert is a *she*,' he said with emphasis on the *she*. 'She's carrying pups.'

Salka let it pass with a nod, and as the silence became awkwardly long, Skúli seemed to sense that she was waiting for him to continue.

'Well, I couldn't sleep, and Húbert wasn't happy, so we went for a walk.'

'What time was this?'

'Around two-thirty, I reckon.'

'Why do you reckon that?'

The Commandments

'I looked at the clock when I went into the kitchen and then it was a quarter past. So sometime soon-ish after that.'

'And you took the dog for a walk in the middle of the night. Is that normal?'

'No. It's unusual. But she was bit needy.'

'Does Húbert usually get needy? And at night?'

'That's two questions. Does she get needy? Yes. That started after she got pregnant. But in the middle of the night? No. Or if she does, I sleep through it. But I think she must have been aware of some movement outside because she barked by the living room window.'

'And did you notice anyone about?'

'No.'

Salka placed the map of Grenivík on the desk in front of Skúli.

'You live here, don't you?' she asked, sliding it across to him and pointing to the house at the edge of the open space below the church.

'Yeah,' he agreed, leaning back in the chair after peering at the map and pushing it back to her.

'So you have a good view of the church,' Salka said, examining the map.

'I can see it clearly from the living room window.'

'What made you take Húbert out?'

'Because she was whining and wanted to go out. She was scratching at the door. Do you have a dog?'

'No.'

'There you go. If you had a dog then you'd understand when they need to go outside.'

Salka sighed, almost silently. She slid the map back across to him.

'Show me where you went with Húbert.'

He leaned forward and pored for a long time over the map.

'I just went out here onto the grass,' he said, tapping the spot with a finger.

'You went out the back door? You usually do that?'

'Yes. I told you Húbert was scratching at the back door. I opened it and she ran up to the church. She stopped by the steps.'

'And then?'

'When I came closer to the church, I saw that the doors were open a little way.'

'And at what point did you see that?'

'I would have been about here,' he said, his finger on a point in front of the church.

Salka picked up a pen and marked the spot with an X.

'Then what happened?'

'I went into the church. And that's where I saw ... I saw ... Hróbjartur.'

'Did you go up to him?'

'No... I don't remember. I don't think so. I ran out of the door and home. Called the cops.'

'You can't have seen much if you didn't go into the church?'

'Well, I might have gone closer. It's all hazy.'

'Did you have your phone with you?'

'No,' he said firmly. 'I forgot to take it with me.'

'Do you have it with you now?'

'No. It's at home.'

'What's the pass code for your phone?'

'What do you mean?'

'The number to get into your phone.'

'That's none of your business.'

Idiot, Salka thought. She wasn't going to bother telling him that it didn't matter, that the forensic team would easily find a way into his phone data.

'You work for the local authority in Grenivík. What does your job entail?'

'I'm responsible for all sorts,' he said with a touch of pomposity. Salka thought she could even detect a shadow of a smile. 'I look after maintenance and make sure that the buildings are all in good repair. I'm responsible for the school building, the church, the swimming pool, facilities at the camp site, and loads more. Residents often come to me if they have a problem.'

'Like what?'

'Like what?' he asked, as if the question had taken him by surprise and a note of irritation crept into his voice, maybe because Salka hadn't looked at him for a while.

Salka was satisfied with his response. She knew that she needed to trigger a variety of responses, and the only way to do that was to do things that Skúli wouldn't expect.

'There's always someone who has a problem. Blocked pipes, this and that. All sorts of stuff. And I'd like to be on my way now. I have work to do,' he said, and made as if to rise from the chair.

'What about the church?'

'What about it?' Skúli said, sitting back down.

'You fix things for the church as well?'

'Yes. Now and again,' he said, sounding less secure.

'So you must have known Hróbjartur?' she asked, looking at him.

Skúli held her gaze and rubbed his palm with the tip of his thumb.

'Yes.'

'Well?'

'No, not really. I'd run into him now and then, of course, if something needed fixing.'

'When did you last meet him?'

Skúli thought. He glanced down at his palm, as if the answer could be found there, like a cribbed answer to an exam question.

'That would have been three days ago. That's when I saw him walking through the churchyard.'

'What was he doing?'

'That I don't know. Just looking around.'

'Did you speak to him?'

'No.'

'When did you last have a conversation?'

'Hmm,' he said, puffing out his cheeks and looking up at the ceiling. 'Probably last weekend. He asked me to fix one of the pews in the church. One of the seats had come loose. But we didn't talk much. I didn't want to... we didn't talk a lot.'

'What didn't you want to do?'

When Skúli failed to reply, Salka repeated the question.

'May he rest in peace, and all that, but I've no more to say. I told you I wanted a lawyer, and now I've spoken too much and for too long. And if anything's happened to Húbert, then that's down to you,' he said, pointing a finger at her.

This was the second time that Salka felt a dislike for him, there was something in his eyes that just didn't feel right.

Salka was about to continue when a loud voice and a babble of noise carried into the interview room from the office next door. She hesitated, but as the volume grew, she stood up and opened the door.

Along the corridor, in front of the open door of Valgeir's office, a broad-shouldered woman was wagging an accusing finger through the doorway, while Gísli stood open-mouthed to one side.

'Now you listen to me, Valgeir, and let the lad out,' she barked, glaring in through the open doorway. 'What on earth is all this fuss about? The lad has nothing whatever to do with all this.'

'My dear Alda,' Valgeir protested, appearing in the doorway and placing an arm around her shoulder, which she unhesitatingly slapped away. 'It's just procedure, Alda.'

'Don't give me any of that *my dear Alda* crap. No arguments, and you stay right where you are!' she snarled, her eyes on Valgeir, but her words intended for Gísli who had taken a step in her direction. 'He's your brother's son, Valgeir. I'm telling you right now to hand my boy over!' she ordered, noticing Salka standing in the doorway and taking rapid steps towards her. Now the wagging finger had a new recipient.

Salka stepped out, shutting the door behind her, after

instructing Skúli to stay exactly where he was. Now Alda faced her, and there was no hiding the anger that shone from her dark blue eyes. She was a powerfully built woman, wearing a dark green cardigan over a burgundy roll-neck sweater. Salka wasn't surprised to see beads of sweat on the woman's ruddy face. Her mousy hair stuck out from under the multi-coloured woollen hat and the perspiration ran down from under it and over her forehead.

'You're *that* Salka, aren't you?' Alda said, coming closer, and wiping away the pearls of sweat that threatened to run into her eyes. 'Gísli called me and said my Skúli's been arrested, and you're the one behind all this.'

That, Salka thought, noticing the tremor that passed through the woman's jaw as she ground her teeth.

'I didn't say...' Gísli broke in as he stepped closer.

He must have taken a shower at the station, as Salka noticed a strong whiff of aftershave from him.

'Be quiet!' Alda said, glaring at him, while Salka struggled not to laugh. 'Is he in there?'

'Good morning, Alda,' Salka said with a smile and offered a hand. 'That's right, I'm *that* Salka. I guess you're Skúli's mother.'

Alda had instinctively grasped Salka's hand, snatching it back as soon as she realised what she had done.

'That's absolutely right. And now he's coming home with me,' she announced, in a more measured tone but with the same unmistakeable emphasis to her words.

'We need to speak to...' Salka said, pausing as she noticed the young female officer she had seen earlier that morning approaching, a sheet of paper in her hand. 'Just a moment, Alda,' she said as she stepped past her, exchanged a few words with her colleague and returned to resume the conversation with Alda. 'Skúli is going to be here a little while longer but you're welcome to wait.'

'Wait?' Alda demanded.

'You can wait here at the station. I can't say how long

he'll be here. But this is a search warrant,' Salka said, holding up the sheet of paper that Alda practically snatched from between her fingers. 'We need to take a look at your house.'

'I don't think so. Now, go and fetch my Skúli and we're going home.'

Her finger pointed along the corridor, and if Salka wasn't mistaken, northwards to Grenivík.

13

As she and Gísli arrived in Grenivík, Salka slowed down, and drove past the turnoff for the tarmac road that led down to the church. Quite a few cars were parked on the open ground in front of the old school that had been an imposing building in its day. Salka could make out at least two vehicles in the colours of TV stations. Camera teams and reporters had taken up positions in front of the police tape that had been strung across the road leading to the church. The police officers on duty there had been told to pay them no attention unless they got pushy and tried to get closer – which had already happened. The church was in a fairly open space, so it could be approached from three sides. Reinforcements had been called in to close off access.

They parked in front of Alda and Skúli's house. Alda had given in, agreed to wait at the police station and handed over her house keys. In Akureyri the fog had finally lifted and the message reached Salka that the forensic team were finally airborne.

She inspected the detached house that had been built on conventional lines. It was an understated, white-walled house with a low roof of red corrugated iron. The grass was freshly mown and the hedge around it had been neatly clipped.

'Good morning to you,' said a voice behind them, and Salka turned to find that it belonged to an elderly man.

'Good morning,' Salka replied, taking in the man who stood on the pavement.

'You're from the police, are you?'

'We are.'

'I saw your car by the church this morning. I live in the

next house along,' he said, nodding in its direction.

'I see,' she said, going over to him. 'And when was that?'

'When you drove up to it just before seven.'

'Had you been up long by then?'

'No, I was only just up,' he said, taking a handkerchief from a back pocket and applying it to his nose. 'May I ask what's going on?' he asked with a smile.

'It's difficult to say at the moment,' Salka said, and returned the man's smile.

'This is a small place, as you can see,' he said slowly, and the smile disappeared from his face. 'Somebody mentioned a body in the church.'

'I'm not able to comment right now. Sorry,' she said, about to turn away.

'No,' he said thoughtfully, glancing downwards. 'There's not much goes on around here that makes the news. I don't recall ever seeing a whole pack of newsmen here before, and I've lived here all my life.' He laughed, and the handkerchief was returned to his nose before being pressed into service to polish his glasses, while he squinted at the clear sky above. 'There's a rumour going round that something terrible has happened. What do you want with Alda ... and Skúli?'

Salka noticed a movement at the edge of her field of vision. The man's white-haired wife had emerged from the house next door and Salka could see her eyes wide open as she stretched to raise her chin above the hedge. When she glanced that way, she could see faces in the windows of houses across the street, all of which dodged behind the curtains as she met their gaze.

'As I mentioned, there's nothing I can say at this moment,' she said courteously and turned to walk towards the house.

'No, of course,' she heard the man say behind her, as if speaking to himself.

Gísli had waited silently by the front door, and the dog started barking inside before he had even opened it. Gísli swung the door open and they went inside. A black and

75

white collie stood in the middle of the living room and fell silent as it saw them. As far as Salka could see, its sense of smell was being put to full use. She wondered what the dog would make of Gísli, as it had probably been aware of his aftershave the moment the car door had opened.

'So you must be Húbert?' Salka said, dropping to her haunches.

The dog looked at her suspiciously, and then lay down, which Salka interpreted as meaning she wanted to be scratched. She stroked the dog's belly and head.

'They say that these are the smartest dogs in the world,' Gísli said.

'You seem to know something about dogs,' Salka said, getting to her feet.

'I was brought up in a dogs' home. Which is to say that there were dogs in the household I grew up in,' he explained when he heard Salka stifle a laugh.

'Here, put these on,' she said, handing him light blue latex gloves and matching shoe covers. 'We'd best take care not to touch too much in here. I don't want to upset the forensics guys.'

In the living room Salka looked out of the window, gazing over the open ground at the church she guessed to be around a hundred metres away. She cast an eye around the neat living room with its bland furnishings, a few porcelain ornaments and plastic plants here and there. A hulking leather sofa and a TV chair had been placed in front of the television. There was nothing out of the ordinary other than the cuckoo clock on the wall. Salka inspected it and was startled when little doors in the clock face opened and shut in turn and a bar shot out and in again. The cuckoo itself was missing, even though it squawked thirteen times, indicating that it had to be one o'clock.

Checking the other rooms, Salka found Skúli's bedroom. It was in complete contrast to the tidiness in the rest of the house. The floor was awash with clothes. The bed was unmade and Salka felt that the sour, heavy air was thick enough to cut with a knife. She clicked the light switch by the door several times, then realised that the lightbulb was dead. She gingerly made her way across the room and drew the blackout curtain. She wanted to open a window but decided against it, preferring to touch as little as possible. A desk was strewn with junk, and a laptop. She switched on the computer and saw that a password was needed to get any further, and the same went for the phone that lay on the bedside table. Alongside the phone were the backing strips from sticking plasters and she thought of what Skúli had told her, that he had banged his head badly.

'There's something wrong with her,' Gísli called from the living room.

'Who?'

'Húbert ... Who calls a bitch Húbert?'

'Skúli does,' Salka said, returning to the living room. 'What makes you think there's something wrong?'

'She doesn't want to stand up,' Gísli said, trying to lift the dog to its feet, but Húbert remained lying on her side.

'Look, there's blood,' Salka said and reached down to lift Húbert's tail.

'The poor thing's not well,' Gísli said after taking a careful look.

'Is she miscarrying? Is that what you'd say? A miscarriage?' Salka asked.

'Yes, more than likely. But she shouldn't be bleeding. Something's happened to her. You can see how sore she is when I touch her belly,' he said and Húbert whined as he pressed gently on her middle.

Salka stood up. She looked out of the living room window at the church and thought of Skúli. He must have known about the dog's condition.

'Why the hell didn't Skúli say anything?' she muttered.

'This hasn't happened by itself. Something's happened to her. He... she could have been hit by a car, or...'

'Or what?'

'Or someone could have kicked her,' he said as he stood up. 'We'll have to take her with us.'

Salka's phone rang and she answered without looking at the screen.

'Hello, Salka. Óttar here.'

Salka hesitated. She had the sinking feeling that she should recognise the person on the other end of the phone, but she couldn't. The distinctive voice did sound familiar, which helped her dredge through her memory for a face to go with it.

'Ah. Hello, Óttar. What's new?'

'Everything's fine. We've landed in Akureyri.'

'Oh, you're in the forensic team?'

'I am,' Óttar laughed. 'And I'm leading it.'

She had got to know him in during her time with the police in Reykjavík when they had worked on several of the same cases. But she hadn't seen him since leaving for London.

'That's a step up. Congratulations on the job. Where are you now?'

'On the way to Grenivík. Should be there in half an hour. And you?'

'I'm in Grenivík at Skúli's house. He was the first person on the scene at the church. I'll give you the details when we come over to see you. Looking forward to seeing you,' she said and ended the call.

In the kitchen Salka looked over the pale green cupboards that showed their age. She opened the cupboard under the sink and peered inside. She let the light of her torch play over the waste pipe and couldn't see any trace of blood where Skúli could have hurt his head. She checked the greasy bottom of the cupboard. She picked a couple of plastic bottles of cleaning fluids. Some had clearly been unmoved for a long time, with no grease to be seen where they had been. If Skúli had genuinely had to deal with a blocked pipe, then he would have had to move the bottles and everything else to get to it.

She had no doubt he had lied to her.

Leaving the house was like walking into an ambush through the clicking of camera shutters and reporters' questions to the street. Gísli carried Húbert to the car and laid her tenderly on the back seat. They answered no questions, got in the car and drove away.

Gísli parked in the yard in front of the church next to a black van. Salka got out and saw four forensic technicians in white overalls make their way into the church, while Óttar sat in the open van, pulling on his overalls.

'Hello there, Salka. You look worn out. Can't sleep?' he said with a smile.

Now she remembered. He always got straight to the point. They had always got on well and as she looked at him now she saw that in the intervening years he hadn't changed in the slightest. He was around sixty. While there were maybe a few more grey hairs, he came across as his usual cheerful, amiable self. He was neither slimmer nor fatter than before. The paunch was still there and she recalled him regularly cursing his weight.

'I'm fine,' she said, taking a seat beside him.

'How's it going?'

'Hard to tell.'

She gave him a quick rundown of the situation, including her conversation with Skúli and how he claimed to have received his head injury.

'He lives over there,' she said, jerking a thumb at the house. 'I'd like to ask you specially to take a look at the cupboard under the kitchen sink and check if there's any trace of blood. I know the church takes priority, but any chance you could take a look soon?'

'What for?'

'I suspect Skúli's not telling the truth and it would be very useful to be certain before I talk to him again later today.'

'I'll do it,' Óttar said as he got to his feet. The overall was unwilling to go past his hips and he worked the material back and forth while Salka grinned. 'I understand from Pétur that you were involved in a case concerning Hróbjartur four years ago.'

'That's right. We investigated accusations against him and other priests. We were never able to reach a conclusion. That's the worst of dealing with these cases. You have all the victims' narratives and you can put your finger on what's right and just. At the same time, you have the feeling that it'll all come to nothing, as happened with this case. The whole thing was dismissed.'

'Shit,' Óttar said in irritation.

Salka glanced at him in surprise, and saw where the zip of the overalls had given way as it had been stretched across his belly.

'I took the wrong size,' he said with an awkward smile, pulling the overall off.

'Try this one. It's an L,' she said, stretching behind her for an overall pack, at the same time pulling off the XL label. 'You'll be a good while in the church,' she said, standing up. 'I need to run into Akureyri. Húbert needs to see a vet and I need another chat with Skúli.'

Óttar gave her a surprised look, and Salka explained about the dog.

'I'm wondering if it's all right to take a look at Hróbjartur's place?' she added. 'He lived in Akureyri. I'll be careful.'

'That should be fine. You know what to do.'

'Thanks. Good to see you again, Óttar,' she said, and left him to get into the patrol car with Gísli.

14

Salka went into the interview room and took a seat facing Skúli, who glanced up at her from where he sprawled forward across the desk. Valgeir had already told her that he had offered him a cell if he wanted to lie down, since he had complained of being tired.

'Have you had anything to eat?'

'Yeah,' he said and sounded calm.

Salka switched on the recorder, and clearly stated the date and time, her name and Skúli's, then gave herself time to think things over.

'Is Húbert all right?' Skúli asked, sitting up straight.

'To tell you the truth, I don't know.'

'What do you mean?'

'She clearly wasn't right, so we had to take her to a vet.'

'I told you. This is your responsibility,' he said angrily, rising to his feet.

Looking up at him, Salka told him to sit back down.

'You remember what we talked about,' she said sharply when he stayed on his feet. 'Húbert was like that when we got there. She was in pain and bleeding.'

'Bleeding? Where?' he demanded, sinking back into the chair.

'Her genitals. And her belly is sore. Something has happened to her. That hardly occurred while she was at home alone. Or what do you reckon?'

Skúli stared at Salka, and then his gaze travelled around the room. He leaned back in the chair.

'Don't know.'

'So you're telling me that she was fine when you last saw her?'

'Absolutely. Nothing unusual. Can I go to the vet?'

'No.'

He hunched forward and stared down at the floor.

'Why do you think I'm guilty? I was the one who called about Hróbjartur,' he said as he straightened himself upright again.

'That injury, Skúli,' Salka said, bypassing his question.

'What? Oh, that,' he said, a hand going to where Salka's eyes rested. 'What about it?'

'Where, and how, did you get that cut?'

'I've told you already – twice,' he said with heavy emphasis, tugging a lock of hair down over the cut to his temple.

It was clear to Salka that he was uncomfortable with the subject.

'The forensic team are in Grenivík and they took a look at the cupboard. They called me just now. There's nothing to indicate that you got the injury there. No trace of any blood.'

'That doesn't mean anything. There was so little blood anyway, and I probably wiped it off the pipes when I was messing about with them. And I don't know if I caught my head against the drain or the stopcock under the sink. Those have sharp edges.'

'Nobody has touched those pipes or the stopcocks for a long time, Skúli. That was obvious when the location was inspected.'

'That's total bullshit. Are they plumbers?'

'No,' Salka said, allowing herself a thin smile. 'These are specialists. They see that kind of thing. It was obvious even to me. Nobody has touched that drain for ages.' She leaned forward and continued calmly. 'Tell the truth, Skúli. How did you come by that cut? That was quite a blow. Did it happen in the church?'

There was a long silence before Skúli spoke.

'All right. But you promise not to tell anyone,' he muttered.

'I can't promise that, Skúli.'

'Then I can't tell you.'

'Why not?'

'Because then I'll lose my job!' he barked, taking Salka by surprise.

'Don't you want to get out of here as soon as possible? Tell me what happened.'

'I sneaked into the swimming pool during the night,' he said, after holding Salka's gaze for a long time. 'I wasn't at home, like I told you I was. I sneaked into the pool. I'll lose my job if anyone finds out.'

'How did you get in? Did you have a key?'

'I have keys for all the places where I look after the maintenance.'

'And where are these keys?'

'You took them, of course. Everything was taken off me when I was brought here.'

'I suppose there are cameras at the pool?'

'Yes, but I switched them off while I was there. I do it sometimes and I can't let anyone find out,' he fretted. 'I had a swim and then went in the cold plunge pool. I tripped as I was getting out and that's when I banged my head.'

Salka wanted to let out a sigh of frustration. She was certain that there would be no chance of finding any supporting evidence.

'You were alone?'

'Yes, of course.'

'And did your trip to the pool take long?'

'No. Maybe half an hour.'

'And then? What happened after you left the pool?'

'I walked past the church on the way home and saw the door was open. It's just like I told you before. I found Hróbjartur by the altar, went home and called the cops.'

'Tell me about it one more time.'

After listening again to his account, she sat and watched Skúli, who looked down at his hands. Somehow, she felt sympathy for this lad. She realised there was no reason to keep him at the station, and decided that he could be released.

'Why not?' he asked when Salka told him he couldn't go straight home, explaining that the house was still part of a suspected crime scene.

'Húbert had better be fine,' he said as an ominous parting shot, looking around as Salka watched him go along the corridor. The tone was disturbing. He left the building and got into his mother's car.

She looked in at Valgeir's office, where he was at his desk.

'Afternoon snack?' she asked with a smile.

Valgeir started, placed the pastry on a plate and picked up a serviette to wipe his mouth.

'You'll scare me to death doing that,' he laughed. 'How did it go with Skúli?'

'To be honest, I don't really know. He changed part of his story,' she said and explained about Skúli's night-time visit to the pool.

'I think you're on the wrong track with the lad.'

'Why's that?'

'You've seen the treatment Hróbjartur got. I spoke to Óttar earlier and he told me about the state of the corpse. Skúli could never have done anything like that. It's just not possible. He's not the type to carry out anything on that scale of brutality.'

'More than likely, and I would hope so. And I never said that he was the perpetrator. Do you remember the Grótta murderer?'

Valgeir thought for a moment, then nodded.

'The man's wife swore that he could never have murdered that person. He was nervous, sensitive, afraid of the dark and the type who cried at romantic films. And I agreed with her. When I spoke to him, I was convinced that it was out of the question that he could have committed such a terrible act. But what I know today is that even though it's hidden away somewhere deep, the unlikeliest people have a dark side. And you know this as well. I hope that you're completely right about Skúli and that he's innocent. But until there's evidence to the contrary, he remains a suspect,' she said heavily, and took a deep breath.

'All I'm saying is that I know him so well that...'

'I have to go to the hotel now, and then I'll take a look at Hróbjartur's place,' Salka said as she left his office. 'I'll be in touch later.'

15

The sun shone on this hot August afternoon. People sat outside the cafés on Hafnarstræti with drinks and snacks.

Leaving the police station behind her, it occurred to Salka to stop off at one of the bars for a beer, but this tempting thought was quickly abandoned. It was getting on for five in the afternoon and this was turning out to be a very long day. She decided to go up to her room and take a quick shower before looking over Hróbjartur's apartment, which was within easy walking distance.

Salka wasn't sure how long she had been sitting on the bed. She felt completely drained.

She thought things through. She stood up, fetched a glass from the kitchen cupboard and let the water run cold from the tap before she filled it. Then she went over to the window that overlooked Hafnarstræti, peering out between the curtains.

As she took in the colourful throng of people passing by outside, it was difficult to work out whether the majority were foreign tourists or locals. Mostly tourists, she decided, as most of them wielded cameras as they stood on the sweep of the one hundred and seven steps leading up to the church, or standing by one of the world's smallest turreted houses that was halfway along Hafnarstræti. Otherwise, they posed in front of Grýla and Leppalúði outside the tourist shop just below her window. The locals seemed to stroll past, deep in thought, or else strode with determination on their way from A to B.

Skúli's behaviour troubled her, but Valgeir was probably right. He was unlikely to be Hróbjartur's killer. There was an unbelievable fury behind the crime, some indescribable rage, and she couldn't see Skúli as the person who had castrated Hróbjartur. All the same, she was certain that he wasn't telling her the whole story. When she had asked about his relationship with Hróbjartur, he had said that they hadn't had much to do with each other, apart from the times Hróbjartur had asked for something to be fixed. Just like in their first conversation, Salka had the feeling that Skúli felt uncomfortable every time Hróbjartur was mentioned. Still, it was possible that he could be one of the cunning ones, one of those consummate liars who can spin a complex tale on the spur of the moment, the ones who can do all this untroubled by the slightest guilt.

The air was stifling, and she dropped the towel she had wrapped around herself before lying naked on the sofa. The breeze from the open window above was as gentle as a feather as it played over her skin. Last night she had slept for three hours. It was tempting to shut her eyes for an hour, but her conscience wouldn't allow that. It was time to get back to work. She got quickly to her feet and pulled on some clothes.

Her phone rang and she felt a stab of anxiety seeing an unfamiliar number. She sat on a kitchen stool. Yes, after looking at it for a while, this was a number she recognised after all. Magnús came to mind. She had thought of him while she had sat in the café earlier, and looked him up in the online phone directory. She had toyed with the idea of calling him, but decided against it. She stared at the screen and hesitated. She didn't want to appear too keen.

Hell, she thought, and was about to answer the call when an email alert appeared on her screen. She opened it. The message was from CID, which had forwarded the case files she had requested connected to the previous charges against the priests.

'Hello,' Kolla said when Salka answered the phone, just as she was getting dressed, and confirmed that the email had reached her. 'Unfortunately, I can't be there,' Kolla said. 'I'm abroad at the moment, trying to get my flights changed so I can get back sooner. Thank you for responding so quickly. How's it going?'

Salka gave her a quick status report on the investigation. There were long silences as she described the state in which Hróbjartur had been found. She tried to tone down her descriptions, so as to shield her from the worst of it, but quickly realised that this was irritating Kolla, who wanted the facts of the case.

'How did you know Hróbjartur?' Salka asked after a long pause. There was no mistaking that her account of the circumstances at the church in Grenivík had left Kolla shocked.

'We got to know him many years ago. Probably a good thirty years ago, through a mutual friend. We got on well and have stayed in contact, but at intervals. He was a missionary in Africa for some years. My husband managed a fish sales company for a while, and Hróbjartur helped him establish some business links there.'

'Any idea who could have wanted to harm him?'

'I haven't a clue, but it goes without saying that the accusations that were made against him come to mind. Those people were naturally crushed when the case was dismissed. But this... it's unbelievably brutal. Going by your descriptions, there's something serious behind all this. I can't imagine anyone going to these lengths unless something terrible happened to them in the past.'

'When did you last see Hróbjartur?'

'Last month. We were invited to a dinner party, and he was there as well.'

'And you didn't get the feeling from him that anything was wrong? Anything out of the ordinary? Apologies for the questions, Kolla. I'm trying to make sense of all this,' Salka said, conscious of the oddity of having to pose questions to a senior officer as if this were an interrogation.

'That's no problem, Salka. I understand perfectly. But no. He was just his usual self. Funny and cheerful. We talked about all sorts of things.'

'What about the accusations that were made against him? Is that something he ever mentioned?'

'No. Never. But I can be certain that was a heavy burden for him. As you know, the case was dismissed as it was beyond the statute of limitations, but also because there was precious little evidence. There simply wasn't enough there to make a conviction likely.'

'What about you?'

'Meaning what?'

'Do you believe he was innocent?'

'It's difficult for me to answer that right now. But at the time my opinion was that he was innocent,' Kolla said after pausing for thought.

'You don't sound exactly convinced,' Salka said.

'I don't know. It's always difficult when a case is connected to you personally. It could be that I simply didn't *want* to believe that he could have been capable of anything so vile. But that sort of thinking doesn't count for much, and I've been losing sleep over this,' Kolla said. Salka could hear the anguish in her voice. 'I've not been able to stop going over our relationship in my mind over the years. There's nothing I can put my finger on anywhere that points to anything abnormal or wrong about his behaviour. Or that he could have abused girls... or boys. But what do I know? How do you even notice that kind of thing? Maybe I'm closing that off and can't bring myself to see the whole thing in a clear light. Do any of us know anyone so intimately? Who is capable of such deception?'

Kolla fell silent and Salka sensed the anger in her. She tried to dampen it down.

'We'll see how things develop, Kolla.'

'You can imagine what the media would make of it if they knew we had dinner with him, or if they knew about our acquaintance.' This time there was a longer silence. 'But that's a problem for later. Take a look at the documents I sent through to you. One of those who made accusations lives in the north. You could have a word with him. And I spoke to Valgeir,' she continued, changing the subject. 'He wasn't happy at all that this Skúli is being held. He said you were being...'

'Skúli isn't being held right now, but I suspect I'll have good reason to speak to him again. With respect, Valgeir has to be able to say exactly what he thinks. But he comes across as being dissatisfied with everyone and everything,' Salka said, suddenly aware of how sharp her tone had become.

'I know. He can be cross-grained, but he's a decent man. I hope you can get along with him until I get there, which hopefully won't be long. Do you think that'll work out?'

'I'll do what I can,' Salka said as the call ended.

She dressed quickly, and sent Gísli a message telling him to meet her outside Hróbjartur's place on Lundargata.

Salka inspected the exterior of Hróbjartur's house. It was a small, old detached house with two storeys, in one of the older districts, just to the north of Akureyri's Hof cultural centre. The cladding was faded and white paint was flaking off the window frames.

She had already looked up the details of a Nissan car that was registered in Hróbjartur's name, but there was no such vehicle to be seen anywhere near the house.

On the way there, she had called a locksmith, and found him waiting for her by the door. The sight of the man made her want to smile. He was someone she probably wouldn't have trusted with her house keys. Dyed hair stood up at angles and a devil tattoo peeked over the neckline of his shirt. The letters F U C K were tattooed on the fingers of his left hand. She showed him the required warrant to open the building on her phone, and he set to work with his tools. It took the locksmith a matter of moments to open the door, and she went inside after thanking him, to which he responded with 'have a great day, darling.'

She stepped into a narrow hallway. There were couple of freesheet papers, advertising leaflets and envelopes on the floor behind the front door. She snapped on gloves and crouched down to check the papers. The oldest was from three days before. She stood up and went into the darkness, to open a door leading to the kitchen, bathroom and living room. The air was stuffy, with curtains drawn over every window. Weak beams of evening sunshine flickered between the heavy living-room curtains that were swaying to and fro. She went over to them and saw that the window had been forced. A sound behind her made her start, and she spun around. She saw nothing to begin with, until a quick movement caught her eye. She glanced to one side and looked into the eyes of a black cat that had jumped onto the living room table.

Salka made an effort to bring her quick breaths under control.

The cat miaowed pitifully, and its tail stood up straight. It had to be looking for attention – or food. Salka left it to its own devices and, after checking each of the downstairs rooms, she looked up the steep carpeted steps leading to the upper floor. She couldn't shake off the feeling that someone else, other than the cat, was in the house with her. She went cautiously upstairs and looked into the small bathroom, then pushed open another door to find what seemed to be a study. A few more steps took her to a closed door. She turned the handle and opened it. There was complete darkness inside. She felt along the wall by the door until she found a switch. The light illuminated a scene that made her blanch.

'Hello,' a voice behind her said.

Salka flinched as if she had been punched. In what seemed a flash, and without a moment's hesitation, she jerked her elbow back with all the force she could muster, into the belly of the person behind her.

She turned to see a man bent double in front of her, both hands clasped to his belly as he whined in pain. Salka crouched down to get a sight of the man's face.

'What the hell d'you think you're doing, taking me by surprise like that?' she demanded, placing her hands on his shoulders.

Gísli looked up at her, his face flushed bright red.

'What do you mean?' he asked once he had got his breath back. 'Maybe I should ask what you're up to?' he said as he straightened up gingerly.

'Sorry. I didn't mean to… How was I supposed to know it was you sneaking in here behind me?' Salka laughed.

'Sneaking? I wasn't sneaking,' he said with chagrin. 'Didn't you hear me? I called out more than once when I came in. The front door was open.'

Once Gísli had recovered, they looked into Hróbjartur's bedroom. Dark red letters on the headboard spelled out

Thou shalt not…

Salka went in cautiously. A heap of CDs and video cassettes had been piled up in the middle of the made up bed. On top of the heap lay the video camera that went with them.

She picked up the camera and after turning it over in her hands, switched it on, and opened the screen window. She pressed the *play* button and Gísli leaned closer to see the screen.

Someone holding the camera was pointing it at two boys romping in a hot tub. They looked to be fourteen or maybe fifteen years old. The recording was a little unclear, far from recent.

The one who gets the other one's pants off gets a prize, said someone behind the camera. It was a strong voice, but also had a certain tenderness to it – or not so much tenderness as a cajoling quality to it.

The boys laughed and grappled, taking hold and each trying to rip off the other's swimming trunks. It was difficult to make out what they said as they wrestled with each other.

Careful, boys. Careful, the voice behind the camera said. *Let's not get the camera wet,* it continued as drops of water landed on the lens. The hand holding the camera moved it randomly from side to side, as if trying to avoid any more splashes. Then it was again focused on the two boys.

Sorry, sorry, sorry, one of them said, his face coming closer to the lens.

Judging by his eyes and the way he slurred his words, it was clear to Salka that the lad was either drunk or under the influence of some other substance.

The sequence ended abruptly, cutting to the two boys side by side in the hot tub, beers in their hands. They gazed at the camera as if dazed, their eyes blank.

Shall we? the voice asked.

The sequence again cut and resumed to show the boys entering the dim bedroom, naked.

'Fucking hell!' Gísli burst out, taking Salka by surprise.

'That's the second time today you've almost given me a heart attack,' she smiled.

'Sorry. But do we need to watch this?'

Salka appeared not to have heard him as the sequence continued to play. She stopped it when she noticed that Gísli was looking away, and that he was as white as a sheet.

'I know. It's appalling. Are you all right?' she asked, and there was no reply. 'Gísli?' she said, plucking at his sleeve.

'Yes, fine,' he said, startled.

'Do you recognise those lads?' she asked, without catching Gísli's eye.

'No,' he said, absently.

'And the voice?'

'No. That's not familiar either. It must be Hróbjartur. Or what do you think?' he asked as she didn't reply.

'I don't know,' she said at last, rewinding the tape. 'There's something I want to take another look at.'

She pressed *play* again.

Careful, boys. Careful, the voice could be heard saying, as the camera turned smartly to one side. Salka paused the replay. The image was blurred and far from clear. It was only when she had played and paused it a few times that she found a sharper image.

'Where is this?' she said, and looked up at Gísli, who was on his feet.

He leaned forward and peered at the screen for a long time.

'Not sure. But it's familiar,' he said, sounding breathless.

'Gísli, are you sure you're all right?'

'I'm fine,' he said firmly.

'OK,' she said, surprised at how taciturn he was being. 'That mountain. Where's that?' she asked, pointing at the screen. Only the higher reaches of it could be seen, the lower slopes hidden behind a hedge. His hands shook as he took the camera and held the screen close to his face.

'I'm not certain but it looks like Thengilshöfði.'

'Where's that?'

'It's south of Grenivík,' he said, handing the camera back.

'And where could this have been taken?'

'I don't know.'

'Come on, Gísli. You know the area.'

'It's possible it's taken from a summer house. There's an estate of summer houses at Sunnuhlíð, just north of Grenivík. There's a view from there over Thengilshöfði,' he said after studying the screen again.

'Thou shalt not...' Salka said, looking up and reading the words to herself. 'This refers to the Commandments, I guess.'

'But which one?'

'Not easy to tell. Maybe *thou shalt not commit adultery*. The Commandments hark back to the time they were written down. My best guess is that this refers to the tenth commandment, *thou shalt not covet thy neighbour's house, thou shalt not covet thy neighbour's wife nor his manservant* ... How did it go again? *Nor his maidservant, not his ox, nor his ass, not anything that is thy neighbour's,*' she finished and turned to find that Gísli had gone.

She hadn't heard him leave the room.

16

'Any sign of his phone?' Salka asked as Óttar emerged from the church and sat in Gísli's patrol car.

She was getting tired of all this driving, but the forty or so kilometres between Akureyri and Grenivík seemed to be getting shorter every trip. After watching the recording, they had decided to go straight back to Grenivík.

'No. There was no phone on him,' Óttar said. 'Did you find anything at his house?'

'No phone and no computer. Judging by the newspapers under his letterbox, Hróbjartur hadn't been home for the last three days ... hang on,' she said, leaning forward to pull off one shoe and shake a piece of gravel from it. 'But we found a video that was probably recorded here in the area. Gísli reckons it could have been somewhere up at Sunnuhlíð,' she said, pointing northwards. 'We'll take a look and see if we can identify the location from the background. Anything else you can tell me about Hróbjartur?'

'Not so far. The body will probably be sent to Reykjavík for the post-mortem. He was certainly made to suffer. He'd been restrained, judging by the marks we saw on his limbs and upper body. Those are marks that come from some real tension, so he must have struggled. He was badly beaten about the face, but had been cleaned up. The perpetrator made efforts to clean away any traces of blood.'

'What for?'

'No idea. The genitals were removed with a very sharp implement. Parts were placed in the palm of each hand, and the rest in his mouth. He has stab wounds to the chest made by a large knife. We haven't found the knife,' Óttar said, opening a bottle and gulping down water. 'The only traces of blood we have found were some very slight ones just inside the doors inside the church lobby.'

'Do you know where that came from?' Gísli asked.

'No. Of course, it could be older drops of blood that were already there. We took the samples to the lab in Akureyri to be analysed. Apart from that, we'll be finished here before long,' he said, taking another long swallow from the bottle.

'It's getting on for seven-thirty, so Gísli and I are going to take a look at the Sunnuhlíð district.'

Salka switched on the video camera and stared at the picture frozen on the screen, trying to work out the viewpoint, while Gísli drove slowly along the gravel road leading to Sunnuhlíð. There were a few summer houses each side of the road, but all of them stood on open ground. The place that had featured in the video was clearly surrounded by a thicket of trees.

They were halfway up the slope when Salka asked Gísli to stop. She got out of the car and looked down at a large summer house below the road. A gravel track led down to an elderly Nissan pickup, which looked to be the one that was registered in Hróbjartur's name.

Salka's phone rang. She answered it.

'Thanks for that,' she said, after listening for moment.

'Who was that?' Gísli asked.

'Data. I asked if they could get a register of Hróbjartur's property. He has a summer house right here in Sunnuhlíð.'

Gísli drove down the lane. Salka peered into the silent car. They walked across a broad decking area and saw a hot tub next to the door. Salka went over to it, glanced at the video screen and compared it to the view. Thengilshöfði loomed above the spinney of trees at the edge of the plot. More of the mountain could be seen in the video, back when the trees had been smaller.

'I reckon this is the right place,' she said, handing the video camera to Gísli.

She looked through a couple of windows before going to the door, and pulled on gloves before trying the handle, but found it locked. Salka walked around the building until she found an open window, where someone had unscrewed the window lock. Gísli held the window open wide while she wriggled through the gap. Inside, she stood in the middle of the room and listened. She looked around and saw a washing machine, washing lines strung from wall to wall, and a shower cubicle. It was always uncomfortable standing like this in an unfamiliar place, as if she was there without permission. She had often wondered if this was something that burglars felt. Apart from the occasional drop of water from the shower head, there was complete silence. She carefully pulled the matte shower curtain aside. Water dripped steadily into the wet shower tray, where someone had obviously taken a shower recently – or used it for something.

Salka opened a door and went into the panelled living room that doubled as a kitchen. She stopped again, looked around and listened. She could smell the scent of pines. She hated this kind of silence, the kind of black silence that boded ill.

In the little tiled hallway some coats hung on pegs. Several pairs of shoes had been lined up neatly by the wall.

She opened the door to let Gísli in. As they crossed the floor, they both looked at the living room door. They both recognised the angle. That was where the boys had come in. Salka looked over the tidy kitchen. There were apples in a bowl on the table. There was no dirty crockery anywhere to be seen. She checked the two rooms that were open, and they stopped in front of a closed door. She felt a dark foreboding as she went closer. She could no longer smell the pines. She opened the door and switched on the light. They looked down at the neatly made double bed. A painting of a lake and a mountain surrounded by shafts of sunlight that were reminiscent of burned fingers hung over the head of the bed. The graceful necks of two swans in the middle of the

97

lake formed a heart. Salka's thought was that if this had been painted by a child, then there was a cuteness to it. If it had been painted by anyone with artistic aspirations, then it was simply bad.

'Was that the painting in the video?' she asked Gísli, who stood behind her.

'Yes.'

She stepped cautiously into the cramped bedroom and bent down. She lifted the bed cover and examined the wooden legs at the foot of the bed.

'There are marks here,' she said in a low voice.

'What do you mean?'

'Óttar said that Hróbjartur had been restrained hand and foot, and there are marks that would fit with that at the end of the bed.'

Gísli squeezed past Salka and examined the frame at the head of the bed.

'Same here,' he said, shining the light of a little torch over what he saw.

Salka lifted the bed cover and the duvet. There was no trace of blood to be seen. She went back to the living room. Everything was neat and clean. There was nothing unusual to be seen anywhere, as if nobody had been here for some time. In the kitchen she opened the fridge, which contained a few essentials. The apples on the kitchen table were fresh.

'I don't get it,' she said, after calling Óttar to let him know they had found the summer house. 'It's more than likely he was murdered in the bed that's been made up nicely. Everything here is as spick and span as you could ask for. No sign of blood to be seen, although that could change when the forensic team take a look. The murderer presumably took Hróbjartur from here up to the church and laid him out there in front of the altar. The risks he must have taken … it's all so, well, unbelievable.'

'Salka!' Gísli called. 'In here. Look.'

She went to where he stood in the bathroom. The front

page of a newspaper had been taped to the mirror, where the headline *Church Abuse Cover-Up* could be seen. Some red writing could be seen along one side. Salka lifted it from the surface of the glass and could read what a familiar hand had written.

Face in the mirror, you don't listen

17

The wind had picked up and it was close to eleven by the time she was back in Akureyri and parking the car on Skipagata.

Óttar and his forensics team had been to the summer house and had begun the painstaking process of examining the scene. They agreed that they would be in touch in the morning.

She got out of the car and walked towards the alleyway that led to the hotel apartment. She stopped when she saw a man walking along the other side of the street with someone else beside him.

'*Hæ*,' she called out, but he didn't hear her. 'Magnús!'

This time he stopped, exchanged a few words with his companion who carried on his way, and he came over to her.

Salka felt a flush of heat course through her at the sight of him.

'*Hæ*,' he smiled.

'I thought you were fishing?'

'That's the problem with the drug squad. Never a moment's peace. I was called out on a case that's actually a long-term investigation. I'll be going back tomorrow. In any case, I need to get to the tackle shop in the morning.'

'Is the case dealt with now?'

'For the moment. We've been tracking some big-time dealers and had what was supposed to be a cast-iron tip-off that they'd stashed coke and pills, and had a dope factory behind that restaurant there,' he said, jerking a thumb along Skipagata. 'But all we found was frozen meat and chips,' he added. 'I tried to call you today.'

'I saw that. Didn't answer in time ... it's been busy,' she said haltingly. 'Anything important?'

'Nothing special. Just wanted to hear how things were going. I didn't see you at the fishing lodge at breakfast time and wanted to ask how you were getting on.'

'I guess it's the same as with you. Never a moment's peace. Pétur called me at stupid o'clock this morning, and now I'm working on a case that's...'

'The murder in Grenivík. I heard about that. But I didn't know you'd been called in,' he said.

'Short-staffed,' she said. 'Where are you off to?' she continued, surprised at her own question.

'I'm on the way home.'

'It's been a tough day and I'm going to get myself a glass of red wine. Would you like one as well?' she asked after a moment's hesitation.

'I don't know,' Magnús said, glancing at his watch as he thought it over. 'I have to be up early...'

'No problem. See you soon, then.'

'Maybe one glass wouldn't do any harm,' he decided with a smile.

'Coffee?' Salka asked, sitting on the edge of the bed and holding the mug close to Magnús's face. She had been up for half an hour, and was showered and dressed.

'Thanks,' he said, prising his eyes open as he sat up and took the mug. 'What's the time?'

'Seven-thirty.'

'Ah. You always sleep late on a Sunday?'

'Don't you have to be on your way up to the river?'

'Yes. You're right,' Magnús said, sipping coffee. 'And I need to stop off at the station before I go.'

Salka was about to reply, when her phone rang.

'Status meeting at eight,' a cheerful-sounding Gísli told her. Salka was relieved. She recalled how hard the video recording the day before had hit him. As they parted in the evening, he hadn't been himself.

'Fine. I'll be there before then,' she said, and ended the call. 'I need to be on my way,' she said, about to stand up.

'Hold on,' Magnús said, catching hold of her arm. 'Are you all right?'

'What do you mean?'

'Just … everything that happened. You know.'

They had talked far into the night. The wine bottle had been emptied and after a glass of brandy each, Salka felt her inhibitions slipping away. She wasn't sure if it was carelessness on her part, or simply that she had allowed her subconscious voice to take control. This was the inner voice she had fought so hard against these last few months, the one she had stifled, the voice that whispered to her it would be fine to let her feelings go. The shock… There was no reason to keep it locked up.

She had sat at Magnús's side on the sofa, until she suddenly got to her feet. Listening to what the voice told her, she was perfectly aware of the meaningful look she sent Magnús, as she went to the bedroom and began to undress.

Salka luxuriated in his caresses, on the gentle side for her liking. The extended foreplay he seemed to have in mind was already more than she could stand. They had stood in the centre of the living room as his hands touched and stroked every part of her. But his tongue on her earlobe was the last straw. She pulled his shirt off him and hauled his trousers down, then stripped off what remained of her underwear and turned to the wall, her back to him.

She had no idea of the sounds that came from her and didn't care, and then her hand connected with a picture on the wall that crashed to the floor. They tried to contain their laughter as three heavy blows banged against the wall from the next apartment, and they rolled onto the bed.

'I'm fine,' she said, looking into his eyes. 'And you?'

'I reckon so. Last night wasn't exactly what I had in mind ... maybe the same goes for you?' he said and laughed. 'But if you're happy, Salka, then so am I.'

He ran his fingers through her soft, damp hair. In the morning brightness making its way past the curtains, it was the colour of syrup.

'That's good,' she said, and stood up.

'Are you sure you have to be on your way right now?' he asked, sitting up.

'Yes, absolutely sure,' she said, turning away. She took a last gulp of coffee and emptied the rest into the sink. 'There's a meeting about to start.'

Magnús stood up, went to the bathroom and set the shower to run.

'See you,' she called out.

'All right,' he called from the shower.

She paused in the doorway and listened to the voice.

It's all right, Salka. You've done nothing wrong. You're every right to let yourself off the leash. You don't need to...

From force of habit, Salka silenced the voice. She sighed in irritation and left the apartment.

18

Sunday 24th August 2014

'There's someone asking for you at the reception desk,' said an officer in the corridor at the police station, just as she was about to go into the status meeting.

'Hello, Mum,' Salka said, taken by surprise when she appeared at the entrance to the building. It wasn't just that she looked tired, but she also seemed to have shrunk. Probably it was the sloping shoulders that gave this impression. A brightly coloured skirt could be glimpsed under her light overcoat.

'I was passing. Your phone's always engaged, so I decided to drop in.'

'I'd offer you a coffee if I wasn't on the way into a meeting. Is everything all right?' Salka asked, giving her mother a kiss on the cheek and tucking back a lock of grey hair that had come adrift.

'Yes, more or less. Your father is a little poorly. But I've been out of sorts.'

'What's up?'

'I had a terrible dream.'

'Mum, you know you shouldn't let dreams upset you. When have these dreams ever come true?'

'I know,' she said thoughtfully. 'You're probably right. I shouldn't be bothering with this. Over the years I've dreamed plenty of shit, but never seen any of the money it's supposed to portend.'

'Mum!'

'Yes, I know,' she laughed. 'Last night I dreamed that I'd lost all my teeth and there was blood everywhere. You know what that means.'

'I don't even want to know what that's supposed to mean,' Salka said, hugging her mother and planting a kiss on her cheek. 'Think things over. And now I have to go. They're waiting for me.'

Salka stood still, watching her mother walk from the police station and along Thórunnarstræti, until she disappeared from view. She had no belief in dreams and could rarely remember them. On the few occasions she had tried to recall dreams, they had slipped away from her like ice melting in her fingers. Her thoughts remained fixed on this dream of her mother's. Salka knew perfectly well that the loss of a tooth signified the passing of a loved one.

'Is there something about my voice that means you can't hear what I say?' Gísli called from where he stood on the steps, a smile on his face.

'What?' Salka asked, turning to face him.

'I've called you three times. The meeting's about to start.'

In the meeting room, Salka offered a 'good morning' to those present, and took a seat at the end of the long table. She placed a stack of papers in front of her and went through them. She had started the morning by printing out all the documents she had collected and stored on her computer. She stood up and fixed with magnets three sheets of paper to the white board on one wall.

She had woken up during the night and found herself staring at the ceiling. She slipped as quietly as she could from the bed so as not to disturb Magnús. Part of the night had been spent going through the documents she had received connected to the accusations against Hróbjartur. Then she had switched on her computer and combed through articles and anything else she could find about him online. Only then had she slid back into bed and fallen asleep.

'I don't know if you've had time to look at the material concerning Hróbjartur that I sent through last night. As you know, he was accused, as were several priests, of sexual assaults against young boys and girls. The charges didn't result in the convictions that the accusers had hoped to see,' Salka said, glancing at the group present, Gísli, Valgeir, Óttar and four others she hardly recognised. She pulled a sheet of paper from the stack. 'What we know about Hróbjartur is that he was born in 1948, and was sixty-six years old when he died. He had been a serving priest since his ordination in 1973. From 1985 to 1990, with some intervals, he was involved in missionary work in Ethiopia and Senegal. He regularly attended YMCA meetings. He came to Akureyri in 1991 to serve as a priest and returned to Reykjavík in 1996. I couldn't find much about his activities or travels from that period. That's possibly because that's when the accusations I mentioned were raised against him. He returned to the north five years ago, 2009, when he became the Grenivík parish priest. According to the documents, one of the victims and one of his accusers lives here in Akureyri. Gísli, did you manage to find out where he lives?'

'No, that's been a challenge but I'm working on it. The man is Kristján Rafn. Everyone just calls him Rafn,' Gísli said, looking around the room, and it was clear from the nods of those present that the name was familiar. 'He's a drug user and a dealer, and he's crossed the police's path often enough,' Gísli continued. 'He has impermanent residence, but I've been in touch with the drug squad and they'll ask around to see if they can track him down.'

'What about Skúli?' asked the young female officer Salka had spoken to a couple of times already.

'I've ... I'm sorry, but I don't think I've been told your name,' Salka said.

'Fanney.'

'I have my doubts about him. All the same, he's still a person of interest and I suspect he's sitting on something. Considering the treatment Hróbjartur received, I think it's likely this is connected to the accusations.'

'Could the murderer be laying a false trail to take us down

that route?' Fanney asked.

'Yes, that's a possibility. If that's the case, then he's going to some extreme lengths. You can see the pictures on the board. One shows the newspaper headline accusing the Church of sweeping the abuse claims under the carpet. The killer stuck the headline on the bathroom mirror in Hróbjartur's summer house. As you can see from the two other pictures, the murderer wrote messages or quotes. The words *Face in the mirror, you don't listen* were written under the headline stuck to the mirror. It's not easy to figure out what that means or represents. At Hróbjartur's place on Lundargata the murder wrote *Thou shalt not...* in red. That seems to refer to the Ten Commandments. The writing is poor and almost as if written by a child, and it's possible that was the intention,' Salka said, and paused. 'Of course, I can't be sure, but it appears that the killer wants to make it plain that this involves children. We need a handwriting expert to examine the script and compare it, for example, against Skúli's handwriting. When he was brought in for questioning he filled in forms and provided personal information. So how does this work?' she asked, struggling to connect her computer to the projector unit.

Valgeir offered his help, got to his feet and plugged the cable in. Salka caught his eye as he sat down, giving him a smile and a nod.

'Next we have the pictures of Hróbjartur taken in the church,' she said, and hesitated. 'I'm asking simply because I don't know you all. You're all ready to see these pictures? This isn't for just anyone.'

There was silence in the conference room. Salka caught everyone's eye in turn, and opened the pictures.

'The fact that the killer cut off the genitals, placed parts in his palms and a part in his mouth, seems to me a very strong indication that this is linked to abuse Hróbjartur committed. This may sound far-fetched, but the hands could symbolise groping, and the mouth oral sex. Please feel free to suggest other theories.'

Someone tried and failed to stifle a loud cough, then cleared his throat and shifted in his seat as the others glanced in his direction.

Salka looked at Gísli, who leaned forward, his hands together in front of his mouth and nose as if in prayer. She raised a concerned eyebrow, and as if he understood what she meant, he sat up straight and folded his arms. He smiled weakly.

'Óttar, is there anything you want to add?'

'Yah. We examined the body very carefully and as you can see from the pictures, the victim was given some brutal treatment. There had to be a tremendous anger behind this. No individual could commit this kind of act without some deep-seated fury and there has to be a back story of some kind to it. Of course, we have examples of insane individuals committing terrible crimes on the spur of the moment, but, considering the circumstances, I don't believe that's the case here. There's a certain amount of consideration that has gone into this and it appears to have been very carefully planned. Meticulously, I would say. There's practically no forensic evidence. I know it doesn't sound great, but in my line of business we could say that this is exemplary. In all likelihood, Hróbjartur was murdered in the summer house. The marks on the frame of the bed indicate that he was restrained there. We found blood traces in the bedroom of the summer house which are being analysed now, but apart from that, the place was spick and span. It's most likely that he was alive when he was castrated, so he would have endured terrible pain,' Óttar said, leafing through his notes and taking off his reading glasses. 'There was nothing of significance to be found at his home on Lundargata, apart from the words that had been written above the bed and those videos.'

'Have all the videos been checked?' Salka asked, looking around the room.

'We're making good progress on it,' said an officer from

the analysis department, a middle-aged man.

'We completely forgot to introduce ourselves to start with,' Salka said with a smile. 'What's your name?'

'Thórarinn. Everyone calls me Tóti. There are two of us working through this stuff, me and Andrea,' he said, nodding at his colleague beside him. 'I have to say, the contents are ... simply revolting.' He pressed a pen he held in his hand against the tabletop, so that it clicked repeatedly. 'There were a couple of DVDs that we worked through quickly, and they contain foreign material. These contain child porn with young boys. But the video tapes we're talking about are recordings of Icelandic boys. This is local. Judging by the picture quality, the clothes, the boys' hairstyles, and other stuff that we can see, this is all old material.'

'How old?'

'Difficult to say with any certainty, but we estimate fifteen years, give or take. There are quite a few lads on these tapes who we've...'

'How many boys?' Gísli broke in.

'So far, seven. No, sorry. Eight. Of the videos we have viewed so far, the perpetrator, by which I mean the person holding the camera, is never in shot. There's one recording, or rather, a sequence, that we're examining carefully as reflections of the faces of two perpetrators are visible.'

'What do you mean by reflected?' Valgeir asked.

'Reflections in a window. The sequence isn't very clear and we're sending it to a specialist. We're hoping he can clean it up and make it clearer.' To Salka's relief, he put the pen down. 'We're taking screenshots of the faces of all the boys who appear in the videos, and also of any features of the surroundings that could give us any clues. We're hoping to finish this today.'

'Thanks, Tóti. Óttar, is there anything more you would like to add?' Salka asked.

'No, I don't think so. It's worth bearing in mind that the killer seems to have taken both Hróbjartur's phone and computer. The only phone we have held on to is Skúli's.'

'You have that, don't you, Birna?' Valgeir said.

'Yes. We've been working on his phone and there's not a lot there. It's mostly communications between him and his mother, and other numbers are connected to his work. That means calls from the local authority, the school, the swimming pool, the sports hall, that kind of thing. It's the same with the text messages. He's practically absent from social media. We still have to take a look at the records for the home phone.'

'And Hróbjartur's call history? Have you taken a look at that?' Salka asked.

'We managed to get through that this morning. Or, to be more accurate, during the night,' Birna said, standing up to pass around sheets of paper to all those present, before sitting down again. 'There's quite a number of individuals, organisations and whatnot that Hróbjartur was mostly in touch with, but there are two numbers that crop up regularly that are worth investigating. One is Helgi Alfreðsson, who's a deacon. He lives here in Akureyri. The other is the Reverend Gunnleifur Kristinsson. He was the parish priest of the Glerá church and is now retired. Finally, we're working on which masts Hróbjartur's and Skúli's phones connected through.'

'We need to organise interview with residents in Grenivík, the parish council, parishioners, local authority staff, the mayor, teachers, staff at the Co-op and the café. We also need to track down and interview relatives and friends. Who's going to do that?'

'I will,' Fanney said.

'Excellent,' Salka said, picking up the papers in front of her and squaring them against the tabletop. 'Tóti, please send me the screenshots of the boys when you're ready. I know that many of you are pretty shattered. Some of you have been working through the night. But this all depends now on things happening fast. Anything to add, anyone?' Salka said and stood up as heads were shaken around the table. 'Then that'll do for now.'

19

'Impermanent residence?' Salka said with a grin as she and Gísli made for the canteen. 'Is this delightful new expression something you came up with?'

'All my own work,' Gísli said after a second's thought and with a note of pride in his voice.

After the meeting they had talked over the next steps with Valgeir. Salka couldn't help noticing the change in Valgeir's demeanour, coming across as more amicable than he had the previous day. He offered to speak to the mayor and other figures in Grenivík, adding that he knew these people well.

In the canteen Salka noticed Magnús chatting with Tóti at one of the tables. Their eyes met for a moment as she passed by. She sensed the smile, unsure of whether it could be made out. The feeling was that it was being beamed her way, although it was just as likely that this was just her imagination.

She joined the queue for the coffee machine and looked around the canteen. Tóti stood up and left the room.

Salka went over to Magnús's table and took a seat facing him, saying *hæ* without noticing the awkward silence. She was left with a troubled feeling, verging on discomfort. She was about to say something, but failed to find the words, as if the messages from that part of her brain weren't getting through.

'Is the meeting over?' Magnús asked, and Salka felt a relief, as if the ice had been broken.

'Yes.'

'All well?'

'Just going over the situation,' she said and glanced over to where Gísli stood in the queue. 'So...' she said, looking into Magnús's eyes. She laughed at the sight of the smile that spread across his face, as if he was reading her thoughts.

'You feel it was a mistake, don't you?' he asked in a low voice.

'I don't know. I don't know if it's something that could be called a mistake or not. We're both adults. Our choice, isn't it?'

He said nothing.

'Yes, you're right. Of course what we get up to is our choice,' he said, picking up his cup by the rim with his fingertips, turning it in its saucer. 'I have no regrets, but maybe we should...'

'There's no reason we can't meet again, talk things over,' she interrupted, hoping that she sounded calm and collected.

'We could do that. I have one more day on the river and I'll be back tomorrow afternoon.'

'And?' Salka asked after he had paused for a while.

'Dinner? How does grilled trout sound?'

'I like the sound of that.'

'I got you a cappuccino. Did you want ordinary coffee?' Gísli said, holding two cups of coffee as he took a seat next to Salka.

'The tackle shop should be open by now,' Magnús said, getting to his feet just as Fanney appeared.

'Could I have a word, Salka?' she asked, taking a seat by the window as Salka nodded. Fanney gave Magnús a smile and a cheerful greeting.

'Something new?' Salka asked.

'Could be. You mentioned Helgi Alfreðsson, who appeared in Hróbjartur's call log. The name rang a bell and I thought of a friend who used to live here and was familiar with Helgi. We've just had an interesting conversation,' she said, squinting and reaching out to tweak the curtain, deflecting the sun shining in her eyes. 'She knew Helgi. He was active with young people here in the past and among other things, he ran the amateur dramatics society at Dynheimar. She took part in a couple of productions and he was ... creepy, as she put it.'

'How so?'

'He was very tactile, with a need to touch,' she said, looking down at notes on a scrap of paper. 'But not with the girls. He was all over the boys. There was a lot of talk about it. He was also a deacon, and might still be.'

'I'm sorry, but what's a deacon?' Salka asked, and Gísli seemed just as keen to know the answer.

'You're not the only ones,' Fanney laughed. 'I had to look it up. A deacon carries out some sort of pastoral care.'

'I'm still none the wiser.'

'Deacons are involved in all kinds of church activities,' Magnús chimed in. 'Such as end of life care. They assist those who struggle to help themselves, or have been bereaved. They help people out, visit people,' he said, and fell silent as the others looked at him in surprise. 'One of my cousins is a nurse, and she's also a deacon.'

'That's right. What I found out is that deacons often work with children and are involved in child and youth activities within the Church.'

'And does he still do this?' Salka asked.

'I've no idea. But here are his address and phone number,' Fanney said, handing Salka the piece of paper. 'And she mentioned a particular boy, one who was part of the theatre group. She recalled that he and Helgi had got on badly.'

'When was this?'

'That's what I asked her, and she couldn't be certain of the date, but reckoned it must have been between 1993 and 1995.'

'And who's the boy?'

'Rafn.'

There was no answer, even though Salka had hammered four times on the door and called Helgi's number from where she stood by his front door. He lived in the middle of a row of terraced houses in the Norðurbyggð district.

She had decided to try and track Helgi down after a

fruitless search for Gísli. She hadn't seen him since they had met in the canteen.

Salka tried to peer through the kitchen window, without success, as it was too high up and too far to one side from the steps.

She decided to call Gísli's number again, but there was no reply. *Where the hell is he?* she thought, until her consciousness reminded her that normally he was never far from the phone.

She was on the way down the five steps that led to the front door when the next door along opened. She saw an older woman in the doorway. Salka stopped and sized her up, waiting for a response.

'Can I help you?' the woman asked.

Salka was surprised at this question from what appeared to be a concerned neighbour.

'Good question,' Salka said, going over to her. 'I was hoping to meet Helgi. He does live here, doesn't he?'

'He does. And who are you?'

'My name's Salka. Police. He doesn't appear to be home. And he isn't answering the phone. Do you know where he works?'

'Police. Right. He doesn't work at all,' the woman said, opening the door a little further. 'And he's at home.'

'No. It doesn't look that way. Nobody's answering the door.'

'Oh, yes,' she said, opening the door all the way and peering over at the apartment next door. 'He hasn't been out today. What do you want with Helgi?'

'Just a chat. How do you know?'

'How do I know what?'

'That he hasn't been out today?'

The woman's mouth opened, and she hesitated.

'I know these things. If he'd left the house I'd have heard him.'

'Really? Can I ask how you could have heard? There's a bit of a distance between the doors.'

'These places were built on the cheap. You can hear a mouse in the next apartment.'

'Understood. When did you last see Helgi?'

'That was just yesterday when he went down to the shop. He went out around five and was back round about six.'

'That's quite something. Neighbourhood watch in action. I wish you lived on my street,' Salka said with laugh.

'I'm of that generation, my dear,' the woman replied and finally cracked a smile.

'Isn't he just asleep? It's Sunday and it's not midday yet.'

'Helgi,' she said with emphasis. 'He doesn't sleep late. Let me tell you that, considering I've lived here half a lifetime. He's always up by eight. Spends most of his time indoors and hardly ever leaves the house until afternoon. He ought to watch his health a bit more carefully. Ready meals or baked beans for dinner. Angel Delight and that kind of thing.' Salka smiled to herself, imagining the woman sneaking under cover of darkness to check the contents of the bins. 'Helgi's all right, but this lifestyle's going to finish him off. That's what happens when people stop taking care of themselves and their surroundings,' she said, with what Salka had been waiting for, a snort of displeasure.

'What do you mean by that?' Salka asked, now on the bottom step leading to the woman's door.

'Well, that's what they say. The back garden's a reflection of its owner. You ought to take a look round the back, but you'd never find your way if you ventured into that junkyard.'

'Good grief!' Salka said, laughing at the expression. 'All right, I'll be right back,' she said, ready to set off.

'Won't you take a look inside?'

'What do you mean?' Salka asked, turning back to face the woman.

'We have a key. I was going to ask my old man, Ævar, to check on him when he gets back from the bakery. I'm really worried about Helgi. I haven't heard a thing. There was some man who came around nine-thirty yesterday and hung some pictures for him. His visitor was there for about an hour and I haven't heard a peep out of him since.'

'How come you have a key?'

'Ævar's the chairman of the residents' association. We have one of those … what's it called? Ach, a key that fits all the locks.'

'A master key?'

'Probably. The master that fits everything.'

'All right. Got you.'

'But I don't really know if it was pictures.'

Salka gave her a questioning look.

'Maybe something needed fixing, but those were heavy hammer blows.'

'Let's have the key.'

20

It was a windy night and the falling rain danced in the yellow glow of the street lights.

The couple sat in front of the television, absorbed in Ingvi Hrafn's news digest on the ÍNN channel.

'Shh,' the woman hissed, holding out the palm of her hand to her husband, who thought for a moment she was going to slap him. 'Turn it down.'

'What the hell's that?' the husband grumbled, turning down the volume.

They could hear the muted ping of the doorbell ringing in the terraced house next door.

'I thought as much,' the woman said, discarding her knitting as she shot to her feet. She marched into the kitchen.

'What's the matter with you, woman? Do you really have to run to the window every time someone knocks at his door?'

'Don't be like that. I just want to...' she said, and fell silent, stretching her upper body as far as she could over the kitchen worktop so she could see who had rung next door's doorbell.

'And who was it?' the man asked, without taking his eyes off the screen, as she returned to the sofa and retrieved her knitting.

'Didn't see. Some bloke.'

'You're taking this to extremes. As soon as there's the slightest sound outside, you're rushing to the window,' he said, turning up the TV volume again. 'You'll be wearing out your hips with this Peeping Tom stuff,' he laughed.

'Pffft,' she snorted, giving a dropped stitch her attention.

The signs that greeted Salka as she entered Helgi's apartment were not what she had expected. Her hope had been that she would find that he had simply overslept. But there was also the possibility that something serious had happened.

If that was going to be the case, then her expectation was that it would be neat, and no traces left. After taking the keys from the woman next door, opening the door and stepping inside the place, she felt as if her body went into defence mode, anticipating an unknown adversary.

Coats and a few pairs of shoes were scattered over the tiled floor. A broken coat hook lay in one corner. There was a crack in the glass that protected an embroidered picture of a turf-roofed house and the words *Home Sweet Home*, which hung slightly askew in the hallway.

Salka pulled on gloves and wondered what explanation she could give Helgi if she were to meet him.

From where she stood motionless in the hall, she stared into the apartment, and waited. She listened to the furious, heavy silence.

She could see that the living room was in darkness. The curtains were drawn and the sunlight the colour of cream slipped through the gaps.

Salka took cautious steps into the lino-floored lobby from where the rest of the place opened out. The kitchen could have been tidier, although there was nothing in there that rang any alarm bells. Dirty crockery stood here and there on the worktop. One of the kitchen cupboard doors had been removed to make space for a microwave oven. It was open and on the worktop below stood a ready meal that had been removed from its packaging. The left side of the plastic film had been pierced in a few places. Salka looked around and glanced into the sink, but no knife could be seen, apart from those in a knife block on the table. The wooden handles stood there in a row, with one missing.

To the right was a space where two doors could be seen. Approaching it, she sensed the discomforting smell – not so much strong as pungent. She knew this raw, powerful smell.

She knew that, for the smell to carry like this, there had to be plenty of what caused it.

This was the smell of blood.

She noticed a light switch on the wall and clicked the light on. Looking down, she saw the dark-red, dried-out streaks on the floor and the walls.

The bedroom door stood open. She put a hand inside the door and felt for the light switch.

The trail of blood led along the floor to the bed, which stood in a pool of blood. A duvet and two pillows had been dropped on the floor to one side. To the other lay a pile of clothes.

'Is he home?' called a voice from somewhere behind her. It took Salka a moment to realise that the voice was real. It wasn't until it called out *hello!* that she was wrenched from her thoughts and strode to the hallway, where the inquisitive woman from next door stood.

'Is he all right...?'

Salka marched the woman out of the apartment without a word and shut the door. She turned and looked sadly around the place. She could imagine Helgi going to the door the evening before, opening it.

Helgi cursed under his breath as the doorbell rang. He wasn't expecting anyone. He never had unexpected callers. Practically never, at any rate. He seemed to have reached an age at which visitors took care to call ahead.

He had punched a couple of holes in the plastic film covering the fish ready meal, before putting it in the microwave. He was intent on finishing what he was doing, and then the doorbell rang a second time.

As he went to the door, he realised that the knife was still in his hand. It crossed his mind to take it back to the kitchen, but instead he opened the front door.

Before he could register any surprise, everything turned black. Whoever had been out there had thrown a bag over his head. He could

119

feel himself being shoved back into the apartment, a choke hold around his neck so tight that he could hardly breathe. Every sound seemed to have been turned up to maximum volume. He managed to snatch at a coat that hung by the door, and heard the clatter as the coat hook snapped and fell to the floor.

He remembered the knife in his hand and swung it aimlessly behind him a couple of times. The second time, he was sure it met some resistance. He couldn't be sure if it had caught against clothing or flesh. Or maybe something else. But hadn't he heard the man yelp? He couldn't be sure, as he could barely sense anything around him. The man caught hold of his wrist and Helgi felt the back of his hand slammed with great force against something hard. His fingers turned numb and he dropped the knife.

Everything that happened in the next half-minute unrolled at great speed. He could feel how in the space of a heartbeat, he had been deprived of that which was so important – freedom.

Whoever held him by the neck dragged him into the apartment. His forehead crashed against a door as it opened, and a moment later he was thrown onto the bed.

Helgi tried to fight back, but knew that the battle was already lost. Someone sat on top of him and he could feel strong legs pinning his arms to his sides.

'Is it hard to breathe?' a voice close to his ear hissed as the bag was pulled aside. He felt the hot breath and the scorching pain as he heard the words.

He nodded hard.

A gloved finger searched out the hollow below his Adam's apple. If it had been hard to breathe before, now it was out of the question.

'And now?' the voice whispered.

Helgi opened his mouth in the hope of drawing in a little of the oxygen that he breathed in twenty thousand times every day. He felt the pain in his throat, an inner voice telling him that these would be his last moments, until the grip on his throat was suddenly relaxed and a hole torn in the bag. Air flowed almost uncomfortably and freely in, he was drawing it in too hard. But it didn't last, as something was stuffed into his mouth. His first thought was that it was a sock. The sour smell told him that. His nose worked overtime to draw in air.

The bag was whipped from his head and he looked into eyes that stared back from the holes of a balaclava. They were lively, but dark. If someone had asked him later on what colour they had been, he would have said that they were black. But at that very moment, he had no idea that he'd never be asked that question. He couldn't know that twenty indescribably painful minutes later, he would be dead.

'Frightened, Helgi?' whispered the voice of the man on top of him, as the sock as pulled from his mouth. He adjusted his leather gloves.

'Yes.'

'Fact number one. You don't have long to live. Maybe twenty minutes. Fact number two. If you shout, then that time is significantly shortened. You'll have a minute of life left. Maybe two. You understand that, don't you?'

'Yes,' Helgi said, in the same low voice as the man used.

'And we're going to take care to keep our voices down, aren't we?'

Helgi nodded.

'And we're going to take care to tell the truth, aren't we? Are you the Helgi who likes young boys?'

He said nothing.

'I repeat. Are you the Helgi who likes young boys?'

Still no reply.

'For the last time,' the man said, his finger seeking the point below Helgi's Adam's apple and applying pressure. 'Are you the Helgi who likes young boys?'

He released the pressure as the shade of Helgi's face couldn't be mistaken. Helgi made a sound, as if trying to say something.

'Who are you?' he gasped once he had caught his breath.

'That's not important. What matters is who you are, and who you were.'

'I don't understand ... I'm just ... What do you want?'

'Correct me if I'm wrong. You directed the Dynheimar amateur dramatic society. That's right, isn't it?'

'Good grief, that was years ago!'

'Yes or no, Helgi?' the man said, one finger on his throat, looking for the spot.

'Yes.'

'And today you do youth work and you're a deacon?'

'Yes.'

'And you're still abusing young boys, aren't you?'

Helgi was silent.

The man pulled off one glove, reaching inside the waistband of his own trousers, and then held his fingers under Helgi's nose.

'Familiar?'

Silence.

'No?'

Still silence.

'That's the smell the boys know,' the man said, replacing his glove. 'Open your mouth, Helgi.'

Again, no reply – no response.

'Open your mouth,' the man repeated, gripping Helgi's cheeks, squeezing them together. Helgi's mouth opened and the man again stuffed the sock into it. He took hold of Helgi's forehead as if to keep it steady. One hand was slowly lifted, as if he was pulling back on a bowstring.

Helgi felt everything in his head shaken loose as the gloved fist slammed into his cheekbone. A piercing pain burst out in his temples. A high-pitched whine hissed in his ears.

He was dimly aware of the sock being removed from his mouth.

'Good with names, are you, Helgi?'

Silence.

The man slapped his cheek.

'Names? Yes ... or ... think so.'

'Do you remember...?' the man said, leaning close to him and whispering in his ear.

Helgi stayed silent.

'Come on, Helgi,' the man said, straightening up. 'Of course you remember them. You've only just stopped abusing them. You and your friends.'

There was still no reply.

'But do you remember...?' he said, whispering again in his ear. 'Isn't that right, Helgi?' he continued, coming close to his face, so that the tips of their noses touched. 'You liked him, didn't you? At any rate, you abused him on eleven occasions. Let's say that he remembers eleven times, but there were many more, weren't there?'

The man straightened his back and looked around, puffed loudly. He looked at Helgi again.

'Your whole life has been about getting into jobs and positions that put you in contact with young boys. It's what your life has revolved around. Getting close to them. Building up their trust in you, slow and steady. Murdering their souls. He was the one who had never been able to trust anyone, not even his closest relatives. But he trusted you implicitly. Once you had built up his trust, you all got to work. You stopped seeing him as a person. Isn't that the way it was?' the man said, his face again coming close to Helgi's. He stared deep into his eyes. 'You saw him as disposable trash. But that's what happens with stuff that's supposed to be disposable. You only use it once. Yet, even though he had been ruined after being raped that first time, you used him again and again. That's what you did with those boys. You murdered their souls not just once, but many times. But you're innocent, aren't you? Those boys wanted it, offered it. Tell me, Helgi, when you see yourself in the mirror in the mornings, do you see yourself as good looking?'

There was no response.

'Sure, you do. You look in the mirror and take a look at those grey bags under your eyes,' he said, touching them. 'That dirty, coarse skin,' he continued, stroking Helgi's cheek with a sound that was reminiscent of sandpaper. 'And you believe people think there's gel in your hair when you pull it back into that greasy ponytail. And you really believe that the stink of you is hidden if you squirt on some cheap aftershave? Can you see your dick when you take a piss? You've convinced yourself that they wanted it, that all of those boys found you simply irresistible.'

He stuffed the sock back into Helgi's mouth. He raised a hand and rammed a bunched fist into his temple.

'You know the Commandments, Helgi,' the man said, even though he had lost consciousness. He lifted himself off and sat on the edge of the bed. He took off the balaclava and went into the living room to fetch the backpack he had let fall as he had rushed in. Then he placed it on the table, opened it and examined the contents.

'What on earth is going on?' the woman asked as she brought the plates into the kitchen, where her husband stacked them in the dishwasher.

'He must be hanging up pictures, or something,' he said as hammering stopped.

'A whole load of pictures,' she said, glancing at the kitchen clock. 'Is he allowed to do that?'

'Yes, that's all right. It's only a quarter to ten. Now stop this endless fretting. Shall we take a stroll?'

Half an hour later they stood on the pavement by the front door. A fresh wind blew and the woman supported herself with a hand on the rail as she went down the steps. For a brief moment she caught sight of the back of a man with a backpack who strode from the steps outside Helgi's door and out into the street.

Salka opened her eyes, leaning against the front door she had just closed. She could hear the neighbour making her way down the steps outside.

She went back into the apartment. She looked at the trail of blood across the floor from the bedroom into the dark living room. She glanced around but couldn't see a light switch anywhere and went cautiously into the room.

Salka took a deep breath, held it for a moment, and shone the torch in her phone on the floor, where the trail of blood went to the middle of the room and then swerved to one side. A pair of feet were illuminated by the beam of light. She moved the light up the wall.

She looked at Helgi.

Then she went cautiously to open the bathroom door. The pale light that shone through the frosted matt window was cold.

She switched on the light to read the words that had been written in blood red letters on the mirror.

Farewell with a kiss

21

'Getting him down is going to be easier said than done,' Óttar said, after carrying out the initial examination.

Salka stood next to him in the middle of the living room, struggling with the sight of Helgi nailed to the living room wall, crucified. The killer had used many of the same methods as with Hróbjartur. His arms were spread wide and the broad heads of the nails could hardly be seen. These had been hammered through each hand, as well as through the testicle that the murderer had placed in each of his victim's palms. The feet were crossed, with the sole of the left foot placed on the instep of the right, and a nail driven through them both. There was a wound in his left side and the knife lay on the floor. A white towel, red with blood at the front, had been wrapped around his waist. Helgi's head lolled forward, and his penis had been stuffed into his mouth.

'Is that a knife from the block in the kitchen?' she asked, nodding to the knife on the floor.

'No. I already checked,' Óttar said. 'This one is far too broad.'

'Did you find another knife?' she said, going to the kitchen with Óttar following behind her.

'Not yet. I had a careful look at all the knives in the block and none of them match the stab wound. Look, a small meat chopper, a bread knife, and this little one that's probably for chopping vegetables and doesn't have a point. Then there's the sharpening steel.'

'Could he have used a fork to punch holes in the cover?'

'No. It looks to me like it was done with a sharp knife,' Óttar said, examining the plastic film over the ready meal.

'Helgi had only made holes in it on one side,' Salka said,

opening drawers to search for a knife with a sharp point, without success. 'If he was doing this just as the doorbell rang, then he probably had the knife in his hand as he answered the door.'

'Could be.'

'Where's that knife?'

'Most likely the killer took it with him,' Óttar said, raising an eyebrow,

'Yes. But why?'

'Because Helgi may have cut him?' Óttar suggested cautiously, as if there might be a prize for the correct answer.

'Exactly. It'll be interesting to find out if there are traces of blood from someone other than Helgi.'

Salka went back into the living room and looked around. She stared at the picture on the wall. The print showed a young boy and a girl walking across a weather-beaten wooden bridge as they crossed a raging torrent below. An angel with long fair hair, outstretched arms and unfurled wings watched over them.

'I know this picture.'

'What?' Óttar said, glancing at her.

'The guardian angel,' Salka said, almost to herself. 'This picture hung on the wall of my parents' bedroom. It's not something you see often these days, but when I was a child, it was on the wall in many homes.'

'Yes, I remember it. It's pretty. My grandmother had this on the wall. She'd lost her son,' Óttar said and watched Salka as she muttered something. 'Are you all right, Salka?'

'What? Yes, fine...' she said, wrenching herself up from her own thoughts. 'Do you think Helgi might have wanted to protect someone?'

'Whoever was at work here certainly wasn't looking to protect Helgi,' Óttar said, getting to his feet. 'It's a very different scenario to the first crime scene... apart from the treatment the victim went through. There are signs on the corpse and the legs of the bed indicating that he had been restrained. Then there's the thing with the genitals.'

'Looks like he didn't have the same time to do his work as he had with Hróbjartur,' Salka said. 'The neighbour, the kitchen-sink-generation woman, said that she saw a man ring Helgi's doorbell at around nine-thirty, and she saw him leaving roughly an hour later when she and her husband went for a stroll. So he had one hour... to do all this,' she said, looking around. 'What about the nails? Do you think those were Helgi's?'

'I don't think so. The only tools we've found are in a little toolbox in the pantry behind the kitchen. The only nails there were little steel ones. There was a little dolly hammer in there, and I don't imagine that was used, although we'll examine it anyway. The murderer used a heavier hammer for these,' he said, looking at the palm of Helgi's hand.

'So it was well prepared, but he had to be quick,' Salka said.

'We found footprints. He stepped in the blood as he walked around. There are prints that show how he walked around, here, here, and over there,' Óttar said, pointing at the floor. 'The steps lead into the bathroom. Come and see,' he said and Salka followed. 'It's not easy to be certain, but I suspect he took a shower,' he added, drawing the shower curtain aside.

There was a blood-tinged dampness in the shower tray and on the plastic-lined walls of the shower cubicle.

'We'll check whatever we get out of the shower trap for DNA.'

'How did this pan out?'

'What?' Óttar said, looking at Salka.

'How would I have done this? I ring the bell. Helgi opens the door. Maybe I know him, as the neighbour heard no noise other than the hammer blows, and they thought he was hanging pictures or something. I overpower Helgi. Knock him out. Did you see any signs of violence on his head? Or at the back of the head?'

'There's a wound to the forehead, which could be from a blow. And the face has been badly battered.'

'At any rate, I overpower him and tie him to the bed. I put on fresh clothes, an overall. I put on a hood or a hair net. Then I put on gloves and even shoe covers with no pattern. I beat Helgi up. By then he's almost unrecognisable ... and I castrate him. I drag him into the living room and nail him to the wall. I either stab him with the knife in the bedroom or the living room. Leave him there like Jesus on the cross.' She sighed and thought. 'Jesus was stabbed after he was crucified. Then I come in here to the bathroom, and what? Take a shower wearing the overall and wash it off? Or do I take it off and wash it? That's the more hazardous way, because I don't want to leave any physical traces, such as hair, behind. Anyway, I wash myself, put the clothes into a bag and leave the apartment. All that in just an hour?'

Her phone rang.

'*Hæ*, Gísli ... You'll have to speak slowly.'

She listened.

'I'll be right there,' Salka said and ended the call. 'I have to go,' she said, turning to Óttar, and making for the door.

'Anything wrong?'

'Everything's wrong here. Gísli was calling from hospital.'

'What? Has he had an accident?' Óttar asked, following her out into the passage.

'He's found Rafn.'

'It's nothing serious,' Gísli said with a smile. The words seemed to send a stab of pain through his head.

Salka had driven straight to the hospital and found him lying on a bench in Accident and Emergency.

'We'll have to put a notice out that we're looking for Rafn,' he said weakly.

'What happened?' Salka asked, sizing up the bandage around his head.

'I was at the station and saw that one of our old friends was being locked away in a cell. He's a junkie. So I went to talk to him in the cell. After a bit of a chat and a few promises, he told me where to find Rafn. He's been living with his sister for the last month, and where do you think she lives? Can you imagine where the bastard's been living?'

'With his sister?' Salka said, speaking slowly.

'Yes, but she lives in the block of flats next to the police station. He's been looking in through our windows!'

Salka knew that in moment's hesitation he had held back a few choice curses.

'Don't they say you should keep your enemies close?' Salka grinned.

'What do you mean?'

'In this instance, we're the enemy. But go on. What happened?'

'I went straight over there, took the lift up, and as soon as it opened, he was standing there in front of me. He took to his heels, and on the way down the stairs, well, something happened.'

Salka could see from the look on his face that it was embarrassing.

'Out with it, Gísli.'

He looked back at her for a moment.

'He was one landing ahead of me, and he was like greased lighting. I wasn't far off catching up with him but must have taken too many steps at once. I slipped and fell, banged into the wall and landed against a massive Chinese vase that was smashed to pieces. And I cut myself,' he said, lifting his shirt to show her the dressing on his side. 'And he got away.'

'I don't see why you went alone.'

'Didn't you go on your own to Helgi's place?'

'Yes, and I'd tried again and again to reach you. We don't have good news from there.'

Salka gave him an explanation of what she had found, and what had become of Helgi.

'Anyway, what did the doctor say? You might have concussion. You take it easy and then you can go home and rest.'

'No chance, Salka,' he said, getting up. He picked up his jacket from the chair it had been hung on.

22

It was getting dark when Salka parked the jeep in an empty space in front of the block next to the police station from where they had a view of the entrance.

They watched two men go in through the main door. Twenty minutes later they emerged, got in a grey Toyota and drove away. The man in the passenger seat nodded discreetly to Salka as they drove past.

'They've placed cameras. So we should be able to see who comes to the apartment,' she said, looking to one side at Gísli, who was prodding at a plaster next to the bandage around his head. 'Are you all right?'

'Yeah, fine. I thought in proper police terminology it was called shadowing the area?'

'That's right,' Salka said, opening the app on her tablet connected to the cameras.

'But you don't?'

'No,' she said, her mind elsewhere.

'Exactly,' he said, looking out of the side window.

'There. All connected.'

'What?' Gísli said, leaning over towards her.

'Now we'll see when anyone comes or goes.'

A covert camera the size of a coin had been placed in the stairwell opposite the flat where Rafn had been staying. Salka had already arranged for roads out of town to be watched. Cars were being stopped and checked at the Leira junction and at the turnoff for the Dalvík road. She had asked Fanney to alert the media that the police were looking for Rafn.

'We might have to sit here for a few days.'

'That could happen, yes.'

'And I'm starving hungry.'

'Here you go,' Salka said, reaching for a bag on the back seat and dropping it in Gísli's lap. 'Somehow I don't expect we'll have long to wait. Rafn went running off as soon as he saw you. If he's been staying with his sister for a month, there's a good chance there's something or other in there that he'll need. So that's why we placed the cameras. Either she'll take something for him, or he'll come to collect something from her.'

'Really?'

'Yes, really.'

'No, I mean a prawn sandwich and a can of malt?' he said, peering into the bag.

'Is there something wrong with that?'

'It's just so...'

'Perfect. I suppose you expected a hot dog with red cabbage and chips. A dreadful combination. Everything underneath and the sausage lying there naked on top like the princess and the pea.'

'I'll be nervous about ordering a hot dog after that description,' Gísli laughed.

'I may be a local, but I never got the hang of all that red cabbage, let alone a burger with chips inside the bun,' Salka said. 'Do you have a family?'

'Not yet,' he said, glancing at her in surprise. 'Working on it.'

'Which means what?'

'Early into a new relationship. Doesn't it always start like that?' he said, fumbling to open the packaging around the sandwich.

'Yes. Probably. But not for everyone.'

They sat in silence for a while.

'Why did you choose this as a career?'

'The police? Good question. The classic reasons, I suppose. Wanted to help people. In any case, not for the money,' he said with a smile. 'And my foster father was in the police. That had something to do with it,' he said and caught

Salka's eye. 'I'm adopted.'

'OK.'

'My mother died in childbirth and my father was lost at sea when I was two. Do you want a bite of this?' he asked, handing the sandwich to Salka. 'How about you? You're from here. Do you have much of a group of friends here?'

'My parents live here and I have a few childhood friends. I don't have much contact with them. I was more of a tomboy,' she said, handing the sandwich back to him. 'Never had the kind of friends who share confidences and all that stuff, and we never sang into hairbrushes,' she laughed.

'Someone coming there,' Gísli said. A couple of cars had parked in front of the block while they had been sitting there, but no residents or visitors had gone in the doorway leading to Rafn's sister's apartment. 'I can't believe that car's legal,' he said, and followed Salka's example by sinking down in his seat.

They watched as a beige, rusty Citroën stopped in front of the building. A passenger got out and went into the block.

'Is that him?'

'No. Rafn has dark hair.'

'And the driver?' Salka asked, handing him binoculars.

'Can't see him... No. That's a woman,' he said, once he had caught sight of the driver.

'He's going to the flat,' Salka said, watching the screen of the tablet.

A girl stood in the open doorway of the apartment and a skinny young man with fair hair went in. A moment later he reappeared with a sports bag in his hands. He came out of the door and got into the car, which drove away.

Salka waited for the car to be far enough away before moving off. They followed it out onto Thingvallastræti as it went in the Hlíðarfjall direction. It turned into Miðhúsavegur and past the Roads Administration building. Salka slowed as she saw the car turn onto a gravel road, parking in front of a cluster of sheds close by a spinney of larch trees at the top end of the golf course.

It was almost dark by now. Salka took the binoculars and watched people get out of the car, stepping into the circle of light at the door of one of the sheds before going inside. She drove slowly into the area and brought the car to a halt a little way from the shed.

'He must be in there,' Gísli murmured.

'We'll see,' Salka said, getting out of the car. She walked over to the shed with Gísli following. Windows each side of the door in the middle of the gable wall of the shed stood slightly open. Salka picked up a stub of metal pipe that lay on the ground at the corner of the shed, and went past the end. She peered through the window. It wasn't easy to see anything for the grime on the glass and the darkness inside. A glimmer of light further inside could just be made out.

She went to the door and eased it open as gently as she could.

Inside, there was an overpowering smell of oil. The floor under their feet was slippery with years of filth, oil and grease. An old Toyota and an all-terrain vehicle stood in the middle of the space. The bonnets of both were hooked open. A white canvas sheet had been spread on the floor next to the all-terrain truck, with tools and engine parts laid out on it.

Voices carried from a room at the inner end of the shed where light streamed out from an open door. It looked to be an office of some kind.

Salka stepped cautiously towards it. When she was about fifteen metres short of the door, the fair-haired man came out, the sports bag in his hands, and saw Salka.

'Fuck!' he swore. 'The cops are here!' he yelled, and there was immediate turmoil inside the office.

Salka hurtled towards the man, who did the unexpected, heading straight for her. As she was about to grab hold of him, she slipped on the greasy floor and failed to catch hold of his jacket. She saw him dodge past Gísli, who set off after him. Their efforts to remain upright reminded Salka of people trying to run on a frozen lake. The man jumped over the spread of the all-terrain truck's engine parts, but landed badly, slipped and fell to the floor. Gísli caught up with him and fumbled for handcuffs.

As Salka went into the narrow office, she glimpsed a foot disappearing through the open window.

A young woman stood frozen by the window, staring as Salka went up to her. She flinched, as if expecting Salka to harm her. Fear shone from her eyes. She had been crying, and the make-up around her eyes had run down her cheeks. She was thin and hollow-cheeked. The dark shadows under her eyes were the colour of mussel shells.

'Everything all right?' Gísli asked from the doorway.

'Give me the torch,' Salka said, climbing out of the window,

She jogged towards the larches behind the shed, stopped and listened. She stepped quickly into the wood, but it was difficult to see anything. She switched on the torch, shining it around her. She picked out a path and set off.

She flashed the torch from side to side as she ran, then stopped and listened. There was something there. She left the path and went among the trees. She could feel her heart race, the adrenaline kicking in.

She heard a faint click away to one side. She shone the torch in the direction and cautiously went towards it, then paused to listen.

The silence was complete.

She was about to continue when the shadow of a figure slipped between the trees.

Salka took off in pursuit.

She glanced to one side as she heard something pass through the branches of the trees beside her. She felt that her heart was ready to burst from her chest as she saw another figure running away.

Salka stopped, trying to figure out this unexpected situation.

She set off again, and saw both figures take to their heels as the beam of the torch picked them out.

Salka could feel the burn in her throat and the heat in her legs; she realised that she was out of condition.

Nevertheless, she was sure she was gaining on them, until one of them suddenly changed direction. There was no choice but to take a spur-of-the-moment decision and stay on the trail of the man, who carried straight on. Salka was gaining on him when she heard a piercing cry from among the trees to one side. She stopped, listened and shone the torch around, but saw nothing. Training the beam again ahead of her, she found the man she had been chasing was nowhere to be seen.

She cursed to herself, stepped off the path and into the wood. After a few steps she came to a clearing in the larches. She looked around and felt uneasy when she realised that she had lost her bearings.

Setting off towards the sound, she suddenly found herself standing by the sheds, and saw the red lights of a car driving away.

Salka swore and went into the shed where the skinny man sat on the floor, his hands cuffed. In the office the woman sat in a shabby armchair, the same expression as before on her face, and her wrists handcuffed together.

'Where's Gísli?' Salka demanded.

'Gísli? The guy who was with you? He went out,' the woman said, jerking her head towards the window.

23

Salka handed a glass of water to the woman perched on a chair in the corner of the interview room. She sat at the desk and started the sound and video recording.

'The date is Sunday the twenty-fourth of August and the time is 2215. I am Salka Steinsdóttir and with me is Marta Einarsdóttir.'

She stood up from the desk and sat in a chair next to Marta. She placed the glass on a small circular table between them.

'Are you all right?'

Marta gave an almost imperceptible nod and sipped water. She smoothed back her dark hair and pulled a lock of it behind one ear. That was probably because she saw the red camera light go on.

'Do you want a cigarette?'

Not long before, Salka had taken the fair-haired man to have his details recorded before he was locked in a cell. Salka scanned his blank face, his eyes and the dead expression. She shut her eyes for a second, not looking forward to interviewing him, as she suspected his answers would all be along the same lines. His answers would reflect the expression on his face. *As if I give a shit.*

Gísli had appeared at the shed just after Salka.

'Where the hell did you get to?' she asked in a low, firm voice.

'I went after you.'

'And left these two here? Unsupervised?' she said, jerking her head in their direction.

'I had secured them and ran after you. I didn't want you to be alone out there. What can I say? I was worried about you.'

'And did you see anything? I mean, it's dark.'

'No, not a lot. I found the path once I got used to the darkness and then I heard some shouts.'

Salka shook her head.

'I don't get it,' she said.

'What?'

'Suddenly two people running for it. And I don't quite see what you… Ach, let's leave it. We'll take these two to the station.'

'You're sure you don't want a cigarette?'

'I don't smoke,' Marta said, looking into the glass.

Salka wasn't convinced. The smell of smoke must have clung to her clothes. She recalled that Marta's car had reeked of stale smoke when she looked through it outside the shed. The first thing she had seen was the furry dice. She had seen these in large sizes before, the kind that usually hang in the rear window. But this one broke all records. The car was a mess of dog hair, empty cigarette packets, empty bottles, fast food wrappers of all kinds, and unopened envelopes, some of the bearing the logo of the County Sheriff's office. In the boot were tools of all sorts and sizes. Salka's guess was that these were used for any number of purposes that weren't mentioned in the manufacturers' instructions.

'Do you own the car you were travelling in?'

'No. It's Valur's. I don't really know. It might be stolen or something.'

Salka watched Marta, who lay back in the chair with her legs stretched out from under her long sweater. She wore tight black jeans and her legs were reminiscent of cylindrical table legs. She was thirty-three years old, and had a long record of offences and police cautions.

During such interrogations, Salka liked to step back in time, trying to work out how life had been for these people before everything collapsed around them. At some point this young woman had been the apple of her parents' eye.

Somewhere behind the taut features hid a pleasant woman with happy eyes. But now they were completely blank.

'What were you doing there, Marta?'

'I couldn't say. Valur asked me to drive him. He doesn't have a licence.'

'But you must have known what was going on there?'

'No. All I know is that Valur said he had to meet Rafn.'

'Exactly,' Salka said. 'Marta, I know you'd like to be out of here as soon as possible. It's not the pleasantest place to spend time. So how about you tell me what went on? I have a feeling that your friend Valur isn't going to say much.'

'He's no friend of mine.'

'You were in his company. What are the links? Is he your boyfriend?'

'No. I don't know anything and I told you that we went there to meet Rafn. End of.'

'What were you doing in the shed?'

'Seriously? You just asked me that,' Marta said, looking at Salka.

Salka gazed back impassively, saying nothing.

'Valur said that he had to meet Rafn. That's all I know. I was just with him. I went there with him. There's nothing complicated about it.'

'You must know what took Valur to the shed, why he needed to meet Rafn.'

'No,' she retorted, irritated.

'What about the bag you had with you?'

'I don't know anything about that bag. I drove Valur when he fetched the bag from Rafn's sister, and then he just told me where to drive. That was up to the sheds. Then you turned up.'

'And you have no idea what's in this bag?'

'No,' Marta said firmly. She rubbed her nose with the back of her hand, and sniffed.

'All right,' Salka said, ready to get to her feet. 'You'll be staying with us a little longer.'

'I know there was some of Rafn's stuff in the bag. There must have been some gear in there. He's been dealing.'

'What sort of substances?'

'You must know that. You must have been through what was in there.'

'That's right. There were some substances in the bag. It's being checked out now. And there was a stack of money. What do you know about that?'

'Nothing.'

'Valur collects the bag from Rafn's sister and you go up to the shed to meet him. What happened when you got there?'

'Nothing much. We went into that smelly office.'

'What happened in the office?'

'They talked for a while.'

'Who?'

Well, Rafn and Valur.'

'Was there anyone else there with you?'

'Anyone else? Nah.' She sounded offended. 'I fucking hate this,' she said, loudly and lifting her hands as she spoke.

'What is it that you hate, Marta?'

'Just, everything. Everything about this fucking life. And you.'

Salka stayed silent. She didn't take Marta's professed hatred personally. She knew that she was simply a symbol for the police as a whole, for authority. She allowed Marta to stare out of the window, and up at the ceiling. She closed her eyes again.

'Listen to me. Tell me everything and this can all work out a lot better than you think,' Salka said finally.

'You listen to me. If I tell you everything I know, then I'm dead meat,' Marta retorted, glaring at her.

'We can protect you...'

'Protect me?' she said and laughed. 'You've no idea how often I've heard that. It means just as much as it does in politics. Sorry. Although politics isn't something I know much about. But there are all kinds of people who have said they'll protect me. I've been betrayed by every one of them. And most of all by you.'

'Come on. Let's go and have a smoke.'

Marta looked doubtful.

'It's no problem. Nobody can see us from the street,' Salka said when she realised where Marta's doubts lay.

'You know Rafn well?' Salka asked as they stood by the wall, in the shelter of the waste containers on the south side of the police station.

'Yeah,' she said after a long silence, opening the can of Coke Salka had picked up on the way. 'We've known each other a long time.'

'When did you get to know each other?'

'This is the point where I'm supposed to open right up? You act friendly and I give you everything on a silver platter? Forget it.'

'When did you get to know Rafn?'

'You don't give up, do you?' Marta laughed, blowing smoke into the still air. 'I don't remember exactly. We were teenagers. Problem teenagers,' she said with an introspective smile. 'We were together back then, but these days we're just friends.'

'What about Valur?'

'He's a waste of space. I've known him for a long time and don't want anything to do with him. Trouble follows him around. Just like now. Another fucking mess,' she said, tapping ash from her cigarette. She watched it fall to the ground, until a draught that sneaked around the corner of the building whipped it away. 'Is your name Salka?'

'Yes.'

'And is that your real hair colour, or is it dyed?'

'It's real,' she said, laughing at the unexpected question.

'I'd have liked to have had red hair. Are your kids redheads as well? You do have children, don't you?'

'My daughter has red hair,' she said with a smile.

'And your husband? Does he have red hair as well?' she asked, as seriously as if she were collecting data for a thesis on genetics.

'He has fair hair. Tell me about Rafn.'

'Hey, you like to change the subject fast. Rafn, yeah,' Marta said and paused for thought. 'I reckon he had a bright future ahead of him. He's amazingly talented. He could play all sorts of instruments and he was a fantastic actor.'

'Really?'

'Yeah. We were both in the Dynheimar theatre group. We took part in a few performances,' she said and fell silent. She seemed to withdraw into memories of the past, standing motionless and staring into space.

Eventually she returned to the present as the glow of the cigarette reached her fingers. 'Ach, I don't know. I don't want to remember all that.'

'What makes it so tough to remember?'

'It was a crazy time with the theatre group. I mean it was all supposed to be part of helping us, getting us problem kids back on the straight and narrow. It was fantastic to start with. I mean, we were on a stage. We were the centre of attention. The youth committee crowd, or whatever it was called, was there to get us back on an even keel in life. We were all teenagers and most of us came from lousy homes, with parents who were drunks or scroungers, all sorts. Everyone had some kind of baggage. The magic youth crowd were going to stuff us so full of bright blue happiness that we'd be able to dance and sing our way through life like star-spangled elves in an adventure,' Marta said, adding a few theatrical gestures of her own.

Salka couldn't help warming to Marta when she saw this spark that suddenly appeared in her. It was as if her eyes filled with a smouldering passion and her face brightened with her heartfelt laughter. But without any warning, a bank of black cloud seemed to overshadow her.

'That crowd ruined us. If some of us hadn't already

ventured into all kinds of temptation, then that was where we encountered it. And that bastard Helgi, he was notorious.'

'Was he the director?'

'Yeah,' she said, glancing at Salka. 'You know him?'

'No. I've only heard his name mentioned,' Salka said, trying to sound neutral.

'He was a complete bastard. We kids realised far too late what was going on. He abused the boys, the fucker,' Marta said, a sob developing in her throat. Tears trickled down her cheeks, and Salka turned to her, and put an arm around her shoulders. 'But nobody said anything. It was all dust that the wind blew away.'

'Stay strong,' Salka said, arms around Marta, who laid her cheek on Salka's chest and wept.

'Rafn was never the same after his friend disappeared.'

'Which friend?' Salka asked.

'Anton. They were close friends, and somehow something more than that.'

'What do you mean?'

'I don't mean like *that*. They weren't a couple or anything. Sometimes it was like Rafn was his dad. He looked after him and took responsibility for him. Anton had terrible parents who didn't look after him at all. Maybe because he had been adopted. In any case, they drank like fish and he was like a stray cat. He knocked around and stayed here and there, spent a lot of time at Rafn's house.'

'Was he adopted?'

'Yes, or so Anton said, anyway. His parents never admitted it. But he was certain of it and used to talk about it with Rafn. I think Anton had started to look into it not long before he vanished. And then it was as if the earth had swallowed him whole.'

'When was this?'

'The Dynheimar years. I don't remember exactly. '94 or '95. It was investigated. He was last seen in the Glerá church, and that was it. People here talked about him having thrown himself in the river, but Rafn always said that he had been murdered.'

'Murdered? By whom?'

'Well, the priest. You know Rafn went public with his accusations,' Marta replied with a sharp sideways glance.

'Yes, Hróbjartur and Helgi.'

'And Gunnleifur,' Marta said and Salka gave her a surprised look. 'Yeah, I knew the case against Hróbjartur and Helgi made some progress through the system before it was all dismissed. But the case against Gunnleifur never went anywhere.'

'Why not?'

'No idea. Politics, I guess,' Marta said, her smile twisted.

Salka was about to say that she had never known there had been a case against Gunnleifur, but she kept quiet.

'Why did Rafn think that Hróbjartur had murdered Anton?'

'I didn't say that. It was the one at the Glerá church. The Reverend Gunnleifur. Rafn was sure that he had murdered Anton. And he said that he could prove it.'

'How?'

Marta sighed and caught Salka's eye before she continued.

'When we were there at the shed, he was really anxious to get a look inside the bag. I thought it was because of the dope, or the money. But no. There was a diary in there he said he could sell for millions, if not more. His face lit up when he saw the book was there in the bag.'

'So what diary is this?'

'Anton's diary.'

24

Salka immediately sent a patrol car to Gunnleifur's house. After her conversation with Marta, she called the SÁÁ rehabilitation centre, where a counsellor agreed to collect her and to provide secure shelter. On the way out, Salka looked in on Valgeir and asked for temporary access to the LÖKE system, the inner circle of the police intranet.

'What do you need that for?'

'It's part of the investigation.'

'Yes. But why?'

'Valgeir, I'm in a hurry. Would you please sort this out for me? It's important,' she said, trying to sound patient.

She didn't hear his reply as she was already halfway along the corridor, heading for the car.

Salka parked in front of Gunnleifur's house. Curiosity had brought the neighbours out, and a knot of them stood on the other side of the well-lit street.

She got out of the car and stooped under the yellow police tape that a uniformed officer was using to fence off the drive. She walked up to the darkened house. She could see the full moon, which seemed unusually large on this starlit August night.

'Are we too late?' she asked the officer she met on the patio by the house.

'No, I don't think so. There was nobody home.'

'Really?' she asked. 'So why the crime scene tape?'

'There's been a break-in. One of the windows has been forced.'

Salka went into the house, a handsome building like most of those among the beeches above the golf course.

'Has the whole place been searched?' she asked the first

officer she saw inside.

'We've looked everywhere. But I heard some movement when I came in.'

'So where's Gunnleifur?' she asked in annoyance, before realising she had spoken out loud.

'He's not here. We've tried to call him and he's not answering. Birna has been called in and...'

'Who's Birna?' she asked, and felt how wrong the question sounded. She felt awkward for not having yet figured out the names of everyone involved in the investigation.

'She handles anything concerning phones and computers. She's working on locating his phone.'

'Ah, yes, Birna. Of course,' Salka said, before he finished speaking. 'Where's Gísli?'

'I'm not sure. In any case, I haven't seen him here.'

Salka quickly went from room to room until she found the bedroom. She checked the double bed, which appeared to be immaculately made up. It was disturbing that everything seemed to be in order. She stooped to check the legs of the bed, and saw no marks.

She walked around again, and went to the bathroom. The mirror was clean and she looked into the shower cubicle, where she squatted down and ran a finger over the shower tray to find it was bone dry.

'You've checked every room? And the garage? Is there an attic?' she asked as she returned to where the uniformed officer stood in the living room.

'We've looked everywhere, and there's no attic space,' he said, looking at Salka in some confusion.

'No marks anywhere?'

'Nothing at all. Maybe he took him away.'

'What do you mean?'

'Maybe he took Gunnleifur away with him.'

'Could be. Where's Gísli? Sorry. I already asked that,' she said, irritated. 'I really want you to go over the whole house again. Check under every table, bed, and in every cupboard.

Check the toilet as well if you like. Whoever came here was no fucking ghost. Someone could be hidden here. Was this door unlocked?' she asked, turning the handle of the patio door.

'I can't be sure,' the officer said, as he went over to her and looked at the locking mechanism that had a black button on top. 'Was this up?'

'It was,' Salka said, feeling for a light switch behind the curtains beside the door. She pressed it and the lights outside came on. She opened the door, went out onto the deck and stopped at the end where a neat lawn began.

'Are those footprints?' she said, pointing to a patch where the grass looked to have been flattened.

'Looks like it to me. Looks like someone went over there to the shrubs.'

'Do you have a torch?'

'It's not much good,' he said, handing it to her.

Salka pressed the button but it wasn't until she had smacked the torch twice against her palm that the light shone. She stepped out onto the grass to one side of the prints as far as the redcurrant bushes at the edge of the garden and squatted down. She played the light around their stems and looked down at the footprint with no pattern in the damp earth.

'He's been here in the house. The man who murdered Hróbjartur and Helgi. He heard you come in, made a break for it and went this way through the bushes.'

Salka looked to one side when there was no response and realised that the police officer hadn't followed her. She could see him talking to a colleague in the living room.

She stood up, shone the beam of the torch between the branches, and squeezed through into the next garden.

The light of the torch showed faint but definite tracks leading to the back of the next house. She followed them as far as the sun deck behind the house. She stopped and switched the torch off as she noticed a movement behind the living room window. The house's occupant sat at the living room table and opened a laptop. The reflections on the inside of the windows meant that he had probably noticed nothing.

Salka saw barely discernible prints on the decking left by feet that had been through wet grass. They tracked at an angle across the deck towards the corner of the house. Salka cautiously followed them. She peered around the corner of the building and looked into the gap between the house and the garage. There was a small window on this side of the house and a dim light found its way into the gap, but not enough to illuminate the complete darkness at the far end.

She felt for the torch switch, knowing she was taking a risk turning it on.

When she pressed the button, nothing happened.

She slapped it hard against her palm and a narrow beam appeared.

The first thing she saw was the wood wall that closed off the gap between the house and the garage.

The light went off. She banged it against the flat of her hand, but nothing happened.

The next thing she saw was the man who rushed at her from the darkness.

He grabbed her by the neck, and threw her to the ground.

25

Salka left Gunnleifur's house, sat in the jeep and slammed the door shut behind her. She leaned forward against the steering wheel and stared out at the brightly lit street in front of her. Looking up into the black sky, she hoped to see the moon.

It was nowhere to be seen.

She adjusted the rear-view mirror and examined her neck, left red by the attacker's grip.

She was dazed and annoyed. No, not annoyed. She was angry with herself for having allowed the man to take her unawares for the second time that day.

She began to suspect that maybe she simply wasn't in great emotional shape. Maybe she was far from prepared for an assignment such as this one; she needed more time.

It wasn't clear in her memory. The man had rushed at her like lightning and she hadn't had a chance.

Hell, she thought. She should have known, or at least expected, that there could be someone hiding there in the darkness. She recalled fighting for breath as the man's fingers locked around her throat, and as she smashed the torch against his head.

She saw once again the attacker raising a fist, ready to punch her. But he hadn't. He hesitated, held back.

Why on earth did he hold back? Salka thought, slapping the steering wheel with both hands.

She was sure she had been close to blacking out when he had decided not to hit her.

Was that it? Did he hold back? she wondered, and felt her own head with her fingertips.

There was no pain.

Yes, he held back.

He had quickly stood up straight, staring into the darkness.

Had she sensed a smell? She couldn't remember exactly. Yes, there had been something. She tried her best to force vague, confused recollections into some sort of order. As soon as Salka felt that things were becoming clearer, they would slip beyond her grasp again, like elusive dreams.

She was startled from her thoughts as a neighbour walked past her car.

She started the engine and drove away.

Back at the hotel apartment, Salka tried her best to get to sleep. But there were too many negative thoughts coming at her from every direction for her to get any peace.

Sitting up in bed, she opened her laptop and saw that Valgeir had given her access to the LÖKE intranet. She logged in and searched for the case files referring to Anton's disappearance. She had to search for a while, but was finally able to track down the file and open it. There was a basic outline of the case, and that was it. She decided that this was probably because the LÖKE system hadn't been around until a good ten years after Anton's disappearance in 1995. Or was it? She was sure that work had been done to upload older case files to the system.

She closed the computer and dressed. She decided to jog around the centre of town to help clear her mind, thinking back to her poor physical condition when she had to run through the woods earlier. It was still and cool outside, and she enjoyed the feel of the fresh breeze around her neck.

Salka ran through the alley and out onto Thórunnarstræti, then stopped in front of the police station. As she caught her breath, she noticed that there were lights at many of the station's windows. At reception the officer on duty let her in.

A group of officers were chatting in the canteen, and she went past them up to the second floor. It seemed that Sunday night was a quiet time. The upstairs offices had glass walls, so it was easy to see inside them. One of these was a large office with many desks, where Salka saw one of the staff sitting in front of an open laptop.

'Good evening,' she said, and introduced herself. 'Do you know where I can look up old case files?'

'How old?'

'1995. I have access to LÖKE, but there's not much there.'

'That's odd. Sure you searched well enough? I believe that all cases back to 1994 have been uploaded to the system, with all the documents scanned in. What case is it?'

Salka knew the number.

'It's 4850/1995. And yes, I spent quite some time searching, but only found a case summary that isn't much use.'

'Yes. I can see that here. That's strange,' he said. 'Come with me.'

Salka followed him out of the office to a set of locked doors which he opened by punching in a four-digit code. He switched on the lights and they went into a room where document boxes and folders had been arranged in numerical order on heavy steel-grey shelves. The man sat at a computer by the door and used it to look up the case number.

'It should be here,' he said, stepping between the shelves and scanning the contents. 'Aha.'

He triumphantly took down a folder and handed it to Salka. She opened it, riffled quickly through the contents and saw that it contained a number of documents and some photographs.

'What are you doing in here?' asked Valgeir, appearing in the doorway, looking along the passage between the shelves.

Salka walked purposefully towards him, suspecting that he was deliberately blocking the way, as she sidestepped past him and out into the corridor.

'Case notes I need to look at,' she said with a smile.

'What case?'

'Ach, an old case connected to Hróbjartur and Helgi. I just

need to take a quick look. I'll see you in the morning,' she said, setting off along the corridor.

'You mustn't take that out of the station, Salka,' Valgeir said firmly.

'Of course not. Don't worry. I'll look through it here.'

It was almost one in the morning when she returned to the hotel apartment with the stack of photocopies of the case notes that she had run off before leaving the station.

She was exhausted by the time she sat on the bed with a glass of wine to look through the documents. She had forgotten to take her phone with her when she had gone out for a run, and when she looked at it she saw that Gísli had called – four times,

'*Hæ*, Gísli. I saw you'd been trying to get hold of me.'

'Yeah,' he said, his voice hoarse. 'That was... Salka, it's almost one o'clock,' he yawned. She was about to tell him not to be so fussy when he continued. 'We've located Gunnleifur. He's in Hveragerði.'

'Hveragerði? What's he doing there?'

'He's been at a health spa. I got hold of one of the staff. He's been there two weeks and tomorrow's his last day. He's getting the midday flight home.'

'That's grand. You'll have to meet him at the airport. Be discreet about it and make sure you take an unmarked car. Bring him straight to the station,' she said, glancing over the paperwork she had distributed across the bed.

She picked up one of the sheets, saw the signature at the bottom, and sighed. Valgeir had been the officer in charge and she was already dreading the morning.

'Is that all?' she heard the voice on the phone ask.

'Sorry, Gísli,' she said. She had forgotten he was still on the line. 'No, one thing. Where were you while I was at Gunnleifur's place?'

'A group of us went up to the sheds to carry out a search and bring the cars down to the station. We went through the woods as well, the place I reckoned we heard a scream.

153

Didn't find anything.'

'All right,' she said thoughtfully. 'On whose instructions did you do that?'

'Valgeir's. I thought you knew that.'

'Ah, yes. Maybe. I must have forgotten,' she said, and ended the call.

But she hadn't forgotten a single thing.

26

Monday, 25th August 2014

'Did you take those case files away with you?' Valgeir thundered as he stood on the landing between floors of the police station.

This Monday morning had got off to exactly the start that Salka had expected.

'Yes, I did,' she said without looking at him. She marched past him into the office that had been allocated to her on the upper floor. She could hear Valgeir's fast steps behind her as he followed. 'I took photocopies.'

'Photocopies or whatever. Taking case files off-site is strictly forbidden. Can I ask exactly why you're digging into this case concerning Anton?' he asked, following her into the office. He shut the door behind him.

'How did you know it was the Anton case? I thought I told you it was an old case concerning Hróbjartur and Helgi.'

'I checked the search log,' he said awkwardly, after a pause. 'Salka, I want to know why you're snooping through these old documents.'

'What do you think happened to Anton?' she asked, taking a seat at the desk.

'What do you mean? Nobody knows what happened to him.'

'The last sighting of him was by the Glerá church, talking to Gunnleifur, then *pffft*. He's gone.'

'I went through all this in great detail and nobody knows what happened,' Valgeir said, taking a seat by the desk. 'I spoke to Gunnleifur many times, and other witnesses. Nothing at all came out of it.'

'What about the kids?'

'Kids? What kids?'

'According to the documents, Gunnleifur had a confirmation class at the church on the day Anton disappeared. He was seen talking to Gunnleifur by the church. I can't see anything in the files that indicates they were all interviewed.'

'Yes. I spoke to them. It's all in...' he said, pointing at the stack of papers in front of Salka.

'Yes, it's here. You spoke to three of them.'

'That's right. I did, and...'

'There were fourteen of them, Valgeir. Fourteen kids in the confirmation class. Why didn't you speak to the other eleven?'

'There was no need to,' he said, after glaring at Salka. 'It was clear that Anton came up to the church, as drunk as a lord, and in a proper state. The children were terrified. He swore at Gunnleifur and left. He walked away, and that was the last that was seen of him.'

'These three kids you actually spoke to had nothing to say,' Salka said, opening the folder and leafing through it. 'In broad terms, it's all *I don't know*, *I don't remember*, and *maybe*. Reading through the transcripts, I can't see much other than that they were frightened. Were they, Valgeir? Were they frightened?'

'Damn it, they weren't frightened,' he said, standing up and going to the door. 'I did everything I could to get to the bottom of this case, but, unfortunately, that's the way it turned out. There was nothing and nobody you could pin down. Why are you digging this up now?'

'I think this is connected to the murders of Hróbjartur and Helgi.'

'How the... And how have you figured that out?' he said, hands spread wide.

'Did you talk to Rafn when you were investigating Anton's disappearance?'

'No. Why would I?'

'Because they were childhood friends. He and Anton. Rafn is sure that Gunnleifur had something to do with this.'

'How do you know?' he demanded, and Salka began to have concerns about the colour Valgeir's face was taking on.

'I spoke to Marta.'

'Marta? You know her background, Salka? And Rafn's? To put it mildly, he's a troublemaker. I remember he had some outlandish theories that never stood up to scrutiny.'

'You know he was one of those who had charges brought against Hróbjartur, Helgi and Gunnleifur for sexual abuse?'

'It's my experience that there's no point taking notice of anything that boy says,' Valgeir said, as if reading from a book. 'He tries, and has always tried, to extort money and that was one of his many attempts to do that. He's a wastrel who has destroyed himself with long-term drug abuse. Everyone here knows that. You can go through the whole Anton case with a fine-toothed comb, and I can tell you right away that there's nothing to be found.'

'Do you have any idea why the charges Rafn brought against Gunnleifur didn't get any further?'

'No,' he said. His response was so fast that it made Salka wonder, as if there was no need for thought.

'We need to find them,' she said.

'Find who?' he asked, his irritation crystal clear.

'The kids who were in that confirmation class. We need to talk to them.'

27

'Good morning,' Salka said, introducing herself and shaking Gunnleifur's hand as he was brought into the police station.

'Yes, good day to you,' Gunnleifur said with a broad smile. 'That was a very unexpected welcoming committee at the airport. I don't remember her name, but the police lady didn't want to say too much. Maybe you can inform me of what is going on.'

Police lady, Salka thought. It wasn't just Gunnleifur's old-fashioned choice of words that troubled her, but the fact that she had given Gísli instructions to meet him.

'Yes, I can do just that,' Salka said, gesturing for him to take a seat in front of the desk. 'I imagine you've already heard about what has happened to Hróbjartur and Helgi?'

'I most certainly have,' he said and the smile faded from his face. He laid a drab coloured raincoat over his knee as he took a seat. 'It was deeply shocking to receive such dreadful news. Have you made progress?'

'I'm right in thinking that you knew Hróbjartur and Helgi?'

'I did. They were gentlemen in every way. True to the Lord in word and deed.'

'Exactly,' Salka said, examining this man of seventy-three who looked to be ten years younger. There was hardly any grey to be seen in his dark, but thinning hair, combed to one side. She wondered if it was dyed. The skin of his narrow face was smooth, with sharp lines that formed at the corners of his mouth and on his forehead. His ears were large, prominent, somewhat out of proportion to the rest of his head, although that didn't seem unusual as ears often seemed to experience a spurt of growth once their owner reached a certain age. His lips resembled a blueish line. His deep-set eyes were clear blue and had an almost benevolent look in them.

'Do you have an idea who could have wanted to harm them?'

'No,' he said with emphasis. 'That is something that is completely beyond me.'

'Were you in frequent contact with them?'

'I wouldn't say so.'

'And in the past?'

Gunnleifur stared at Salka in surprise.

'What do you mean by that?'

'Just whether you have been in contact with them over an extended period, or...'

'Our dealings have always been in connection with our work; Hróbjartur and I in our functions as priests. Helgi was a deacon and assisted me with a number of things over the years.'

'Helgi was also active in youth activities. Were you also involved with that?'

'No,' he said, drawing the word out. Salka had the feeling that he was on the defensive.

'Nothing to do with the YMCA or such activities?'

'That was very limited,' he said with a smile, and Salka wondered if that indicated an untruth. 'I am not entirely sure what this is about. I fail to see what that has to do with anything at all.'

'Maybe not. I'd like to discuss the disappearance of Anton.'

'Hmm?'

'Anton Hermannsson. He disappeared without trace in 1995.'

'Yes,' Gunnleifur said, looking serious. 'And what do you wish to discuss in that connection?' he asked, almost with a note of caution in his voice.

'According to the case files, when he disappeared, you were the last person he spoke to.'

'That's right.'

'Tell me briefly about that meeting.'

'I am sure that all this is in your case files, my dear Salka.'

My dear Salka, she thought, instinctively suspicious of this smooth, oleaginous tone. The smile returned to his face.

'I often spoke with Valgeir around the time that the lad disappeared,' he continued. 'I did my utmost to shine a light on the matter, but my participation in this was marginal. I met the boy for just a moment.'

'Good friends, are you? You and Valgeir?'

'I wouldn't say that. We are acquaintances.'

'Really? Nothing more than that?'

'No. Nothing more than that.'

The smile appeared again.

'Valgeir has three children. You baptised all three. You confirmed them all and officiated at the wedding of one.'

'Yes. I have been able to share in this family's happy moments. Delightful children, all of them. Intelligent, and perfectly good people, every single one. Of course, it's a long time since all this happened, my dear Salka. One's memory develops some gaps,' he said once the silence had hung uncomfortably long in the air.

'That's right. Nineteen years. But there are always certain special events in anyone's life that stay with them, and don't fall through the cracks,' Salka said with a smile of her own. 'You knew Anton well, didn't you? As I mentioned just now, you are the last person known to have spoken to him. After that he was never heard of again. That could hardly have slipped your mind.'

There was silence. Then another smile.

'No, you are quite right. It was a dreadful matter and a tragic one. I held a prayer meeting for the boy's immediate family once it was obvious that he was ... that he would not return.'

Salka noticed that Gunnleifur never spoke Anton's name. Experience told her that people avoided saying out loud things with any painful association. That would trigger bad memories that would become increasingly acute.

'You still haven't answered my question.'

'What question?'

'I asked if you had known Anton well.'

'I wouldn't say that. Of course, I became acquainted with a great many young people through my work as the parish priest. But I remember him well, that lad had demons of his own.'

'How about Rafn? Did you know him?'

The silence and the smile were repeated.

'I remember him, yes,' he said cautiously, as if every word were fragile. 'Could I ask, my dear Salka, where you are going with this?'

Salka leaned slowly forward over the desk. She looked into his eyes and smiled.

'I'm not your dear Salka. Just like you're not my dear Gunnleifur. Tell me how you know Rafn.'

'Do you know, Salka? I have other fish to fry,' he said in a condescending tone, once he had stopped laughing. 'I've just come from a health spa and now I intend to go home. I was advised to take things easy and avoid unnecessary stress. Which is precisely what this meeting is. It has been a pleasure to meet you,' he said, and this time there was no sign of the various forms of the smile that had flickered across his face since his arrival. He made to stand up.

'He had charges placed against you.'

'Who?' he said in surprise and sat down again.

'Rafn.'

'Now you can hear me out,' he said in a tone that bordered on anger. 'That was the most appalling slander and it was dismissed. There was nothing in his accusations that was any basis for a prosecution.'

'That's fine. But for security reasons we unfortunately can't allow you to go home.'

'Why on earth shouldn't I do that?'

'For your own safety, we can't take that risk. There's a murderer on the loose and we believe that the murders could even be connected to Anton. And I would very much appreciate it if you would start by telling me the truth. You ought to know how that's done. You knew Hróbjartur and Helgi and were in considerably closer touch with them than you seem inclined to admit.'

'This is unacceptable,' Gunnleifur said, rising to his feet. 'Is Valgeir here?'

'He is,' Salka said calmly. 'Would you like me to take you to him?'

'No, thank you,' he snapped, and stormed out.

28

Gunnleifur had protested furiously at not being allowed to go home. Valgeir had given way, on the condition that he agreed to police protection.

'We found fingerprints on the knife that was used to stab Helgi,' Óttar said, placing a sheet of paper in front of Salka. 'The dimensions of the blade also fit the stab wound we found on Hróbjartur's body.'

He had called and asked her to come down to the technical department's office.

Salka took the sheet and scanned it. Unconsciously and out loud she spoke the name that appeared on it. Skúli Pálsson.

'This isn't possible,' she said, staring at Óttar.

'What isn't possible?'

'I don't know ... But this doesn't add up. Sometimes you can just smell evil, and that's not the way it is with Skúli. He doesn't fit with this at all. He's not capable of carrying out what we have seen. Unless there was someone with him,' she said thoughtfully.

'His alibi isn't strong. There's nothing to corroborate that he was there at the pool the night he found Hróbjartur,' Óttar said.

'Yes, I agree with that. But there's something here that isn't right. I know he wasn't telling the whole story, and I know there's something he's keeping back. But to my mind him being the killer doesn't ring true.'

'Then what do you make of this?'

Salka looked over a second sheet of paper Óttar placed in front of her, showing the analysis of the blood found in the church.

'Blood from a dog?'

'Yes. It's blood from Húbert. You mentioned that Skúli's dog had lost blood. Something certainly went on there in the church.'

Salka's phone rang, and Gísli's name appeared on the screen.

'They're here,' he said.

'Who?'

'Confirmation kids. You know, people who were in the confirmation class back then.'

'Good. You'll have to send someone to Grenivík right away to fetch Skúli,' Salka said, and explained what Óttar's conclusions had been. 'We'll need an arrest warrant straight away, but I'd like you with me when I talk to the confirmation group.' There was silence on the line. 'Are you there?' she said.

'Yes, of course. I'd prefer to go out to Grenivík to fetch Skúli.'

'Why?' she asked in surprise. 'I'd be a lot happier to have your support with the group.'

'You know what Skúli's like. And Alda. I reckon it would be best if someone familiar goes to bring him in.'

'Fair enough,' Salka said, after a moment's thought.

'Good afternoon and thank you for coming at such short notice,' Salka said to the group that had been waiting for her upstairs. The look Valgeir had given her in the corridor had been far from friendly.

She looked from face to face of the group seated around the long table, and took a seat at the end, with the case files in front of her.

Fanney had made a considerable effort to track down the 1995 confirmation class, but only eight of the fourteen were present. These were the ones who lived in Akureyri or close by. Others had moved south to Reykjavík, some lived overseas and one had died in an accident.

'I remember it like it was yesterday,' one of the group said when Salka asked for someone to take the initiative and make a start. 'We were all in the confirmation class when Anton turned up. We were all scared stiff.'

A mutter of agreement went through the group.

'What was it about him that made you afraid?' Salka asked.

'He was somehow completely out of it,' the woman said.

'Not sure I agree entirely,' said a man with a beard. 'He may have been drunk, but there was something about him. Something in his face,' he added thoughtfully, and fell silent.

'What was that?' Salka asked, after having allowed him a moment's reflection.

'A terrible depth of sorrow,' the man said, catching her eye.

'Yes, I agree with that. He was desperately unhappy,' another woman added. 'Of course, we were just kids at the time and we laughed at him. Even though we wouldn't have dared do it openly in front of him. But his appearance was dreadful.'

'In what way?'

'There was make-up on his face and he was wearing a white robe. And ... y'know, genitals ... had been drawn on the robe.'

'A cock and balls,' someone said.

'Yes, and the wings.'

'Wings?' Salka asked.

'That's right,' said the one who had spoken first. 'We thought he'd been at a graduation party. He had angel's wings on his back. Then we heard later that it was to do with a play that had been performed at Dynheimar the evening before he disappeared. He had been the costume designer. There had been a party somewhere near the church and he had come straight from there.'

Salka had seen in the case files that Valgeir had spoken to party guests and the one who had invited the revellers home.

He had also spoken to several people who had taken part in Helgi's performance. Some of them had taken part in the celebration, but said that they hadn't seen Anton after that.

'I understand he didn't spend long in front of the church,' Salka said.

'Didn't spend long?' the bearded man said. 'You could say that, because he went into the church with Gunnleifur.'

'Precisely,' Salka said, making an effort to remain calm. Nowhere in the files had it been mentioned that he had gone inside the church. 'Go on, please.'

'Well, as a kid you see things in a different light. But looking back, it was obvious that Anton was terribly upset. He was in a very bad way and he was angry with Gunnleifur.'

'Did it come to blows?'

'No, nothing like that. But without being able to recollect any precise words, he had plenty of unpleasant things to say.'

'That's right enough,' said a man who had not so far spoken. 'He accused Gunnleifur of something, and so he looked really awkward and told us all to go home. Most of us did that, but two boys – who aren't here today – and I stayed and played by the church.'

'You spoke to the police back then, didn't you?' Salka asked, leafing through the notes.

'Yes. I was asked to come in for an interview.'

'Here at the station?'

'Yes.'

Salka wanted to shake her head in disapproval. It wasn't the done thing to bring children under sixteen to the police station to be interviewed, not even back then.

'Was there an adult with you?'

'Yes, my parents. But they weren't there in the room when Valgeir questioned me. It was all pretty terrifying and I just remember being shit scared,' he said with a laugh.

'Same for me,' said the woman who had spoken first. 'It was all a bit strange.'

'And the rest of you? Weren't you asked for your versions

166

of what happened?'

There was a chorus of no, accompanied by shaking heads.

'Tell me more about when Anton went into the church while you played outside.'

'We messed around out there for a while after Anton went inside with him. I don't remember for how long, but then Gunnleifur came out.'

'Alone?'

'Yes. He drove away.'

'And you didn't see Anton?'

'No. I mean, he could have left without us noticing. At any rate, we didn't see him.'

'Were the two boys who were with you ever interviewed?'

'No.'

'And you don't know how long you were outside the church before Gunnleifur appeared?'

'No, I don't remember. I think I said something to Valgeir. Isn't it there in the records?' he said, pointing at the folder of case files.

Salka leafed through them, pretending to be looking it up. Almost everything they had told her was nowhere to be found in the files.

'Yes. It's here. Half an hour, it says. I must have missed that,' she lied.

The last thing she wanted was for it to become clear how poorly the investigation into Anton's disappearance had been carried out. That would attract attention and would inevitably find its way to the media.

'Half an hour? We were there much longer than that,' he said. 'As I said, I can't be certain, but it was certainly longer than half an hour. We built a massive igloo there and that must have taken more than an hour, if not longer.'

29

'Valgeir!' Salka called after him as he marched across the car park on the north side of the police station, heading for his car.

He opened the car door and looked up at her.

'We have to talk,' she said as she approached.

'It'll have to wait,' he said dismissively. 'I'm in a hurry.'

'To go where?'

'Grenivík. I have to discuss things related to the case with some people there,' he said, getting into the car and shutting the door.

He started the engine.

Salka tapped on the window.

He looked up at her for a moment before pressing the button, and the window hissed open.

'What kind of investigation was that into Anton?'

'What do you mean?'

'Really. Valgeir, are you going to play that game? You know who was here just now.'

'Yes, I saw that,' he said, shifting uneasily in the driver's seat.

'I could request an inquiry into your investigation.'

'Salka. I don't know what you're talking about and I won't tolerate...'

'Valgeir, you're no longer competent to have an involvement in this case.'

He stared out of the windscreen, and loosened the knot of his tie.

'I'm going to discuss matters, and we'll speak later today,' he said, slipping the car into gear.

'No, Valgeir. You've no business talking to these people in

Grenivík. We have to talk now,' she said, grasping the edge of the window.

'Salka!' someone called from behind her.

'Valgeir. Turn off the engine, and we can talk over a coffee.'

'Salka!' the voice repeated.

'What?' she demanded, turning round. She saw Fanney at the doorway, gesturing to her. The moment she took one step back from the car, Valgeir closed the window and drove away.

'Valgeir!' she called after the departing car. 'What the fuck is going on?' she cursed. She felt the soreness in her throat intensify, from the hold she had been caught in the night before.

'He's disappeared,' Fanney said, hurrying towards her.

'Who's disappeared?'

'Skúli.'

Salka leaned forward and arched her back, hands on her knees. She felt her breath coming fast, as if she had run a marathon. She also felt an overwhelming urge to yell with every ounce of strength she had.

Salka stood at her office window, watching a heavy bank of cloud that lay over Eyjafjörður, looming over Grenivík.

She hoped it wouldn't pass over the town, as she could see that grey shadow of a downpour beneath it. She decided it would be no surprise if they were heading her way, both the shadow and the downpour. She felt that, considering the progress the investigation was making, far too much was piling up on her shoulders.

She saw a patrol car pull up outside by the back entrance. Gísli and another officer got out, opened the back door and helped Alda to get out. As they made for the door, Gísli looked up, saw Salka and smiled.

'You've scared my boy away with your unfounded allegations,' Alda snapped, standing as if gearing up for a fight in front of Salka's desk.

Gísli looked awkwardly at Salka, and shrugged, standing as he was behind Alda. He mouthed a sentence that Salka tried and failed to understand.

I couldn't hold her back...

'Alda,' Salka said, standing up and coming around the front of the desk as Alda sat down. 'We really need to speak to Skúli.'

'What on earth for?'

'I can't tell you at this moment,' Salka said, taking a seat by her side.

'Is this to do with Hróbjartur?'

'Alda,' Salka said firmly. 'We're running an investigation and there are all kinds of angles that we need to examine. That includes talking to Skúli. When did you see him last?'

'Just before dinner yesterday.'

'And what time's dinner at your place?' Salka asked impatiently.

'On the dot of eight o'clock. Someone called and he said he had to nip out quickly.'

'Who called?'

'He didn't want to tell me. The home phone had rung twice before Skúli came home. He had been fixing something at the pool. I answered the phone but whoever it was hung up both times. And there's no point asking what number it was, because it showed up on the screen as a withheld number.'

'And what happened when Skúli answered?'

'He spoke quietly and I couldn't hear what he was saying. He put the phone down and said he had to go out quickly. I wasn't pleased, because dinner was ready,' she said, staring into space with sorrow in her eyes.

'Does he have the use of a car?'

'Yes. My car.'

'Did he take it?'

'No.'

'Could he have been collected?'

'At least not at the house. I watched him walk away,' Alda

said with concern in her voice.

'What about friends? Or a girlfriend?'

'Neither. My darling boy's pretty much a loner.'

'Does he have any enemies?'

'No, certainly not. He's well liked, as he's always helpful.'

'What if he wants to be alone? Is there any place he can go?'

'There's just his room,' she said with a smile. 'Or the sofa in the living room, which he shares with Húbert.'

'Why didn't you get in touch with us earlier?'

'I can see now that was a mistake,' she said after a pause. 'I thought he'd just come home. I thought of contacting you, and then each time I thought I'd wait a little longer. Every time I was about to call, I had the feeling he was about to walk in. You have to find him,' she said, looking at Salka imploringly. She took her hands, and Salka could feel how cold they were.

'Is there anything else you can tell us?' Salka asked, sensing that Alda had something on her mind. 'I've had the feeling that Skúli wasn't telling me the whole story. Do you know anything?'

Alda held Salka's gaze for a long time before she sighed and looked down at her hands.

'If there's anything you want to tell us, then I would encourage you to do so right now,' Salka said quietly. 'Of course, I hope he's fine, but that might not be the case. It's important that you tell us everything, and it could make all the difference. We want – and you want – him to be found as soon as possible.'

'He was spending more time that I was happy with in Hróbjartur's company. I never did like that man.'

'How so?'

'He had a sneaky look in his eye. I know the type. I was married to one like that.'

'Tell me about their dealings.'

'I don't know exactly what they got up to. If I asked, he'd

blank it out. Skúli isn't like most people. More than likely you've figured out that he has his own ways of dealing with people. He's easily led, sometimes on the simple side, and he's too trusting. And he always means well. I've tried my best to shield him, but there are always people ready to abuse his trust. Thank you,' she added as Gísli brought her a glass of water. 'Grenivík is a wonderful place to live,' she continued. 'There are good people there, all of them. Or, most of them at least. It's a small community and everyone knows everyone else.'

That was something Salka had seen as she had driven around; she had noticed that neighbours greeted one another. She had dropped in at Jónsabúð, the Grenivík grocery store, and every customer had enjoyed an extended chat with the cashier. There were questions about health and prosperity, and the queue for the till was longer than it needed to be.

'We don't need a local paper. Everyone here is almost a reporter. You go out to walk the dog and come back with all the news of what's going on and how everyone is. That's the way it has always been and I suppose it's nothing unusual. And you get questions. People were asking me if Skúli was working for Hróbjartur. He'd been seen at his summer house at Sunnuhlíð. He had been seen getting into his car. He'd been seen in the church. To begin with it was nothing odd, but when I started hearing this kind of thing daily, then I started to pay more attention. And I didn't like what I saw,' she said thoughtfully, and put the glass of water down on the desk. She wiped away a few drops of water that had landed on her leg. 'I found an envelope full of cash in his room.'

'Was it unusual for him to have cash?'

'Yes. That's unusual. He works for the local authority and his wages are paid every month, direct to his account.'

'But hasn't he been doing all kinds of extra jobs? Fixing this and that?' Gísli asked.

'Yes, but that was just pocket money. Like I said, there were always people ready to take advantage of his good nature, that he's so straightforward. There was far too much money in that envelope for it to be that.'

'How much was it?' Salka asked.

'Three hundred and eighty thousand.'

'And I take it you asked him about it?'

'Yes, and he just got angry. Didn't answer. There have never been secrets between Skúli and me, never. That's why I found it so strange that he'd hidden this under his mattress. And then I caught them.'

She looked at them both, and passed a hand across her eyes.

'Where?'

'In the church.'

'When was this?'

'I don't remember exactly. Maybe a week, ten days. Yes, exactly a week ago. I'd just come home from the sewing circle. I could see from the living room window that Hróbjartur's car was parked outside the church and some people went in.'

'Who?' Salka asked once the silence had been held for too long.

'I didn't see properly. It was getting dark. Except that I recognised the silhouettes of Skúli and Hróbjartur. So I went over there and into the church. Of course there were my Skúli and Hróbjartur ... and that Helgi. I'd never seen him before and didn't realise who he was until I saw his picture in the papers after...' she said, and stared blankly into space.

Salka and Gísli caught each other's eyes.

'And what did you see, Alda?'

'There were more of them,' she said, glancing at Salka. 'There were three lads there.'

The anguish shone from her eyes and she wiped away the tears that trickled down her cheeks.

'Please go on, Alda,' Salka said softly.

'When I opened the door I saw them standing behind the boys who knelt at the altar rail. I asked what on earth was going on, and I could see they were all taken by surprise to see me there. The boys got up and ran past me and out of the church. I told Skúli to come and he followed me home.

'Who were the boys?' Gísli asked.

'I didn't see them. I know practically every face in the village, but it all happened so fast and it was quite dark. I just didn't see them. But they must have been around twelve, maybe fourteen. I couldn't be sure.'

'And what did Skúli say?'

'All I could get out of him was that he was assisting. Hróbjartur and Helgi were setting up a YMCA branch here in the village,' she said and fell silent. She shook her head. 'That wasn't true. I asked around, and nobody had heard anything about that. I even tried to ask about those boys, and that came to nothing. I was going to find Hróbjartur and ask him, but that didn't happen. And now it's not going to.'

30

From where she sat in the canteen, Salka could see along the corridor to where two uniformed officers escorted Gunnleifur up to the second floor.

He noticed her and smiled. She nodded back, expressionless. She had been unable to agree with Valgeir's decision to allow him to go home, even with police protection, when she knew the man was in danger. There was a certain satisfaction in having found that Gunnleifur had gone with Anton into the church. That gave her a pretext for bringing him back in for further questioning.

Salka had asked Valgeir to organise two groups. One would go to Grenivík to search for Skúli and the other would look into Rafn's whereabouts. She had also asked for them both to be listed in the media as persons of interest, and she had stepped up checks at the airport and on the roads leading out of Akureyri. She had gone herself to the Hlíð old people's home to talk with Fríða, who had been Gunnleifur's assistant at the time of Anton's disappearance.

'She's awake for the moment, but she dozes off now and again,' said a young nurse who showed Salka to Fríða's room. 'I'm not sure you'll get a lot out of her. There are gaps in her memory. And her hearing isn't great. Could I ask what this is about?'

'I'm looking for some information in connection with an old case we're following up.'

'How old?'

'Around twenty years,' Salka said, surprised at the question.

'In that case, no problem,' he laughed. 'She drops in and

out of connection, but if you'd wanted to ask her about something that happened yesterday, then you could have saved yourself the trouble.'

'Hello, Fríða. My name's Salka and I'm from the police. Could I have a word with you?' she asked, pulling a chair over to Fríða's bedside. She moved a vase from the edge of the bedside table to the middle, and could smell the aroma of lilies.

'That's perfectly all right, young lady,' the old lady said, turning her head towards Salka and tugging at her ear as if that would let in more sound. 'What's the news?' she asked, smiling and squinting at her.

'I'll just sort you out, Fríða,' the nurse said with a smile, as he rearranged a pillow behind her head.

'Thank you, my dear Dóri,' she said as he left the room, after fixing her snow-white hair, hooking the hearing aid behind one ear and putting her glasses on her nose.

'Everything's fine,' Salka said, shifting her chair closer to the bed. 'Tell me, you were a deacon for the Reverend Gunnleifur, weren't you?'

'You have such beautiful red hair, my dear.'

Salka thanked her for the compliment and repeated her question.

'Yes. I did. I was a deacon at the Glerá church for twenty-two years.'

'And how long since you stopped?' Salka asked, reaching for a birthday card on the bedside table.

'When I turned seventy. That was enough.'

'I see yesterday was your birthday. Congratulations.'

'Thank you,' Fríða said contentedly.

'So you were working back in 1995?'

'Yes ... 1995 ... I expect so. I'm so bad with dates and years. So, what happened that year?' she said, half-apologetically. 'It's sometimes fine to get older. You see, you can say that you don't remember things, with some justification,' she added.

'It was the year of the avalanche in Súðavík,' Salka said,

after having thought it over.

'Good Lord, yes. Who could forget that? Those poor people. We had a prayer meeting at the Glerá church.'

'Yes, it was a tragedy. So you were...?' Salka said, leaving the question hanging when she saw Fríða's eyelids droop.

'What did you say?' she asked, her eyes still shut.

'You were working at that time?'

'I was.'

'Do you recall a lad called Anton?'

Fríða opened her eyes and looked at Salka.

'Yes. I remember him. I presume you're talking about the boy who disappeared?'

'Yes.'

'Well,' Fríða said on the in-breath, thoughtfully, gazing out of the window. 'That was all rather strange. Look at this,' she said, smiling. 'She comes every day to see how I am,' she continued, meaning the wagtail that had perched on the windowsill. It flew away as soon as Salka turned to look more closely.

'Was there anything in particular that you found strange?' she asked, taking out a notebook.

There was a long silence.

'I don't know. It was wonderful to work with the Reverend Gunnleifur and all those good people who were part of the church. But I remember those days at the time of that event, because so much changed after Anton's disappearance. They came into the church to talk. I saw them take a seat on one of the pews. The boy looked dreadful,' Fríða said, looking up into space. 'But that was the last I saw of him, because I had to go and fetch flowers and other things for the service that was taking place in the church later in the day.'

'And were they speaking calmly, or was Anton making trouble?'

'They were both very calm. But when I came back that day ... and for days afterwards, I found that Gunnleifur was very absorbed. He wasn't his usual self at all.'

177

'In what way?'

'He was just distant, and he was apt to be easily annoyed, which was most unlike him. It became worse as time passed. I was quite simply frightened of him. And then he asked me go down south to Reykjavík.'

'Why did he do that?' Salka asked, when she realised that Fríða had stopped her narrative.

'He encouraged me to go and stay with my son who lived there at that time. Up to then he had never taken any interest in whether or not I saw my son. That was a little strange.'

'And did you go south?'

'Yes, I did. There was nothing else for it, as Gunnleifur had bought me a ticket and drove me out to the airport. It was as if there was some urgency to get me to go to Reykjavík.'

'Do you remember when this was?'

'It was on the Tuesday. Two days after Anton was last seen.'

Salka remembered that Valgeir had interviewed Gunnleifur that Tuesday.

'Did you ever speak to Gunnleifur about this? About what had become of Anton?'

'I tried, but that only made him angry. And he said there was no need for me to talk to the police, even though I had already told him that I wanted to report the disappearance of the candlestick.'

'A candlestick?'

'Yes. The one that couldn't be found anywhere.'

'The same day Anton disappeared?'

'Yes,' Fríða said. 'Gunnleifur gave the impression that Anton had stolen it. I didn't have any doubts about that, as I knew the poor boy had been in all kinds of trouble.'

'So the police never spoke to you?' Salka asked, looking up from her notebook.

Fríða's eyes were closed, and this time she seemed to be asleep.

Salka waited for a while and stood up, ready to leave the

room.

'You have the same beautiful red hair as my mother had,' Fríða said in a voice that was faint.

'And you have beautiful hair as well,' Salka said, went to the side of the bed and took her hand. 'You look lovely.'

'Thank you. I try to look after myself,' Fríða smiled. 'It's a little difficult getting old. I can tell you that here and now, with a clear conscience.'

In the corridor Salka met the nurse.

'She's asleep now,' she said.

'Yes, like I told you, she drops off every now and then. But she's particularly tired now … she was very upset after the visit she had earlier in the day.'

31

Salka checked carefully through Valgeir's case notes and her suspicion was confirmed. There was no mention there of any missing candlestick.

She glanced at the clock and saw it was a couple of minutes after five. She had kept Gunnleifur waiting for two hours. She went into the corridor, saw Gísli at the far end and called to him.

'Why didn't you collect Gunnleifur from the airport, as I asked you to?' she asked as he came closer.

'Had a bit of trouble,' he said, sounding awkward.

'What sort of trouble?'

'Girlfriend trouble. I had to meet her and asked my colleague to fill in for me.'

'Fine. But you should have said something to me,' Salka said, her tone serious. 'Everything all right now?'

'With what?'

'You and your girlfriend.'

'Yes. I think so.'

'Good. And what are you up to right now?' she asked, going up to him.

'I was going to get myself a coffee. I didn't get a chance earlier and...'

'Well, that can wait. I'm going to talk to Gunnleifur. I want you to sit in on this.'

'Gunnleifur? Really?' Gísli hesitated and he saw the look of surprise on Salka's face. 'I mean, I've never been part of an interrogation.'

'You don't need to say a word. We need to apply some pressure and we can do that by there being two of us. You just need to sit, watch and listen,' she said, laying an arm across his shoulders. 'So, come on. It's no problem. There's no delicate porcelain for you to smash.'

'Good afternoon,' Salka said as they stepped into the interview room and sat opposite Gunnleifur. 'You two probably haven't met,' she said as she prepared the recording. 'This is my colleague Gísli.'

Gísli nodded at Gunnleifur, but it was hard to discern whether he returned the greeting, his movements were minimal.

'Are you ready?' Salka asked, looking at Gunnleifur. 'Can I get you anything to drink?'

'No. Thank you. I have had more than enough time to prepare myself,' he said reproachfully.

'It's unfortunate that it has been necessary to bring you in again. But there are a few aspects of this that weren't clear when we met earlier.'

There was no response other than him crossing his legs and adjusting the raincoat folded over his thighs.

'For example, that Anton went with you inside the church.'

Gunnleifur glared at Salka. She joined in the battle of wills, staring back at him in silence, and making sure that she allowed herself a glimmer of a smile. She reckoned that would serve to irritate him.

'That is correct,' he said at last.

Salka wasn't ready to look away and maintained her gaze for a long time.

Finally, she opened the folder in front of her and leafed through it.

'I have corroborating witness statements from several individuals who all say that they saw you together inside the church.'

'Who are these individuals?'

'That doesn't matter at this stage. But these are individuals who saw the two of you walk inside.'

'I'm speechless,' Gunnleifur said in disgust. 'This is

nonsense that...'

'Has no basis in reality?' Salka said, finishing the question for him. 'I know. But what about Fríða?' she asked, and saw his prominent Adam's apple bob up and down as he swallowed, and then cleared his throat.

'Who?'

'Gunnleifur. She was your deacon for many years at the Glerá church.'

'What about her?'

'What did you have to say to her when you visited her this morning?'

'Nothing out of the ordinary. I pop in to see her occasionally. She worked with me for a long time and we are the best of friends.'

'The best of friends,' Salka said, as if to herself. 'It's a wonderful thing to have good friends, but what you say isn't correct.' Gunnleifur was about to speak, but she continued. 'According to the nurse at Hlíð, he's never seen you before in all the time he has worked there. That's quite apart from the fact that you had to ask as you went into the place if Fríða lived there.'

Gunnleifur leaned back in his chair and crossed his arms defensively. He glared at her with loathing in his eyes.

'Fríða saw the two of you talking inside the church. You sat on a pew together and chatted. What did you have to discuss?' Salka asked, keeping her eyes on him.

He said nothing, but she noticed that he was watching Gísli.

'Don't you think it might be best to come clean and tell the truth?' she said, leaning forward over the table. He made no reply and she continued. 'What about the candelabra?'

His Adam's apple worked again up and down, but his gaze remained on Gísli.

'Have we met?' Gunnleifur said, the question meant for Gísli.

Salka could see in her peripheral vision that he shifted

awkwardly.

'No. I don't think so,' he said, his voice low and uncertain.

Salka wondered if she had done the right thing by asking him to be present during the interview. He was far from ready for this.

'What about the candlestick, Gunnleifur?' Salka repeated.

'What candlestick?' he replied calmly.

'The one Fríða said disappeared the same day as Anton was last seen. She wanted to take the matter to the police, but you didn't want her to talk to us. Why was that?'

He made no reply.

'I may as well carry on, since you don't seem inclined to answer questions. Why did you rush Fríða down south to Reykjavík?'

'What are you talking about?'

'You know exactly what I'm talking about.'

'No. I don't know what you are on about. Fríða remembers next to nothing and she doesn't know what she's babbling on about. She's very elderly and her memory is failing. You saw her,' he said with conviction. 'I fail to understand how a person in your position can regard her as in any way reliable.'

'I understand what you mean. But I think you are as aware as I am that elderly people can sometimes struggle to remember what they were doing yesterday. But events that took place as much as fifty years ago are still as clear as day to them. They are able to recollect incidents in fine detail.'

'Well, that may well be,' Gunnleifur said, and paused in thought. 'But many of those incidents can become confused as the years pass. I know this from my own experience as older parishioners have come to me and recalled painful episodes in their lives, even going back to childhood. Their accounts can be highly convincing, but there have been occasions when I have been aware of the facts of those cases. Memories can become distorted, but for them those remain absolute truth.'

Salka knew that there was little to be gained from

contradicting this. The man was right. She had experienced the same for herself when her father had recalled events from her childhood. Most of these were largely correct – but not entirely so.

She couldn't resist the temptation.

'And your memory hasn't been distorted?'

Gunnleifur said nothing. He smiled, and his eyes went to Gísli.

'You deny having sent Fríða to Reykjavík?'

'Absolutely.'

'And the candlestick?'

'I have no idea what you are talking about. Are you sure we haven't met?' he said, again addressing Gísli. 'There's something familiar about you.'

Gísli said nothing.

'And what about you going inside the church with Anton?'

'An outright lie,' he said, raising his voice and fidgeting, as if brushing specks of dust from his coat.

'This isn't just Fríða's account,' Salka said, taking note of his theatrical tricks.

'What the h...' he said and fell silent. He sighed and glared accusingly at Salka as if she alone bore the blame for having almost made him swear out loud. 'Who else is saying this?' he asked after shifting in his seat.

'You had a confirmation class that day. Fourteen youngsters. I've spoken to some of them,' she said. He glared back at her in silence. 'They saw you go inside with Anton.'

'I don't believe this,' he said in a low voice.

'Are you contradicting them as well?'

'If I recall correctly, I sent them all home. I didn't want them to see the state Anton was in. Least of all be witness to his manner of speaking, which was improper and hostile in the extreme.'

'Was he angry?'

'He was upset.'

'About what?'

'I have no idea. He was dead drunk. That boy had always been trouble.'

'I have no reason to disbelieve the accounts of these people, Gunnleifur. It's entirely reliable and there are no flawed memories. You accompanied Anton into the church. It's high time that you told the truth.'

'I think it's high time that I spoke to a lawyer.'

There was a knock, and Óttar put his head around the door. Apologising, he asked Salka for a quick word.

'Wait here, Gunnleifur,' she said, gesturing for Gísli to follow as she left the room and shut the door behind her.

'Skúli has been found,' Óttar said heavily.

'That's good.'

'No. Unfortunately it's not good. He's dead, found floating in the dock at Grenivík.'

32

Devastated by the news about Skúli, Salka went back to the hotel apartment. She made a start clearing up and making the bed.

After questioning Gunnleifur, she had gone to the legal department and asked that he be held in custody on the grounds that he had lied, tried to exert influence over a witness and refused to speak. After some resistance, since the prosecutor wasn't convinced that there were sufficient grounds, he agreed for Gunnleifur to be remanded in custody for forty-eight hours.

Salka was relieved, as she was not only convinced that Gunnleifur had played some part in Anton's disappearance, but she was also certain that he was in real danger. At least he would be safe in custody.

She was finishing the washing up when her phone pinged an alert. The message was from Magnús, letting her know that dinner would be ready at seven and asking gently if she was coming. She wondered if a message in such a neutral tone was deliberate on his part. She was startled when she glanced at the clock and saw that she had less than an hour.

She sighed and started to tap in a reply, apologising that she wouldn't be able to make it. Then she hesitated. She recognised the symptoms – when you feel the spark, the warmth that flows through every part of your body. She remembered how it had been when she first met Eysteinn. She felt that such feelings were tied to him, and how they broke out whenever she thought of him. She could also hear the inner voice telling her that there was no point hanging on to those emotions, that she'd have to let them go. She had every right to breathe new life into new passions and to go in new directions.

She continued to tap in her message, then hesitated once more. Skúli came to mind. She wasn't in the best frame of mind to enjoy food and drink after receiving the news of what had befallen him. She put the phone aside and thought of Alda.

One of the local fishermen had noticed a body floating face-down between the quay and a boat. Gísli had been at the hospital when the body and then Alda had arrived. He had called Salka, telling her that Skúli had a deep wound to the back of his head. He had added that Alda needed support. Salka was about to call Óttar when there was a knock at the door.

It took her a moment to realise who it was after she opened the door.

'Hæ ... come in,' she said, and Eysteinn stepped inside. 'I wasn't expecting you. But it's good to see you,' she said with a smile.

'And you. I'm here on business,' he said in a flat voice, and sat at the kitchen table. 'I stopped at your parents' place. I thought you'd be there, but there was nobody home. They told me at the station that you were here,' he said, looking around.

'You could have called,' she said cheerfully.

'Yeah. I know. How's your dad?'

'Hard to tell. He's withdrawn and doesn't say much. But the treatment will hopefully start soon. Would you like coffee or anything?'

'No, thanks. This is a flying visit. I'm getting the evening flight, I have to be in London tomorrow.'

'Everything going well?'

'Yes. Fine.'

'You're not heading home?' she said, pretending to fetch something from the bathroom and taking the opportunity to glance in the mirror and straighten her hair.

'No. There's even more work than ever over there. I'm not stopping. I was going to ask...'

'Sure you don't want something to drink? I was going to treat myself to a glass of red.'

'No ... Salka, I was going to ask if we can deal with this paperwork. You received all this the other day, didn't you?'

'Yes. I did,' she said, taking a seat at the table and looking at him. She longed to adjust the knot of his slightly skewed tie, to stroke his smooth cheek, to breathe in the aroma of aftershave. She wanted to kiss his eyelids as she had done so many times in the past. 'I meant to call you,' she said, and felt her hands tremble. 'I've been so wrapped up in the investigation, and...' she said and fell silent.

'The investigation into the priest?'

'Yes. And the deacon.'

'I've been thinking of you. It's a dreadful case. It was even mentioned on the BBC news. How's it been going?'

She smiled at the words *thinking of you*.

'It's complex. I don't know...' she said, and her thoughts unconsciously went elsewhere. 'What did you say?'

'I asked if you had the paperwork.'

She could hear the undertone of irritation in his voice.

'Yes,' she said, and stood up. She fetched the envelope, placed it on the table and sat down again.

They both stared at the envelope.

She realised how nervous she was as she noticed herself tapping a rapid beat on the table with her index finger.

'Isn't this something that can wait, Eysteinn?' she said at last.

'No, Salka,' he said, looking straight at her. 'It's best if we deal with this right now. I can take the paperwork with me and hand it in tomorrow.'

'Give me some more time. Please,' she said slowly. 'Let's give ourselves a chance. We owe it to ourselves.'

Eysteinn looked aside and took a deep breath.

'Salka. It's too late. You know how things were. I did

everything I could to work things out. I was ready to sacrifice everything to keep us together...'

'You mean you did all that from your desk at this irreplaceable company that was supposed to provide eternal happiness...' She fell silent and immediately regretted her words. She wanted to snatch them from the air and stuff them somewhere far out of sight. 'I'm sorry,' she said and felt the tears welling, ready to roll down her face. 'I didn't mean to...'

'We've been through this a hundred times, Salka. You shut yourself away. You didn't speak to me for weeks on end, months, even. You wouldn't accept any help, neither for yourself nor for us. You can't accuse me of not trying. It was tough for both of us. I looked for help. I needed help as well. That's what I did and at a certain point I had to move on. Move on with my life.'

'You always blamed me for how things turned out. How was that supposed to help me? You said that out loud more than once, Eysteinn.'

'Salka, I didn't come here to argue.'

'No. Because it was all my fault.'

'Salka. Stop.'

'Are you still with ... whatever your colleague's name is ... Emily?'

'Evelyn. Yes. And we're planning to ... you know.'

Salka straightened her back and looked him in the eye.

'Get married.'

Eysteinn nodded.

Salka said nothing. She opened the envelope and took a pen from the jacket that hung over the back of the chair. She signed her name on several of the sheets of paper and folded them back into the envelope. She pushed it across the table to Eysteinn.

'I'm so sorry, Salka,' he said as he stood up. He placed a hand for a moment on her shoulder as he passed. He left the apartment.

She sat motionless and stared out of the window. For the first time in her life, she had found his touch unpleasant. She stood up and dabbed at the tears that continued to flow down her cheeks. Picking up the phone, she recalled the message she had begun to Magnús. She looked at it for a long time.

Then she erased it and wrote a new one.

I've been held up. See you in half an hour.

33

'Dinner is served,' Magnús said as he carried in the dish of grilled trout, placed it on the table and took a seat facing Salka. He poured white wine into glasses while 'Hotel California' played in the background.

'Cheers. Great to see you.'

'Cheers,' she said, in a drier tone than she had intended, then smiled.

'Everything all right?'

'Yes. Sorry. Just tired.'

'Understood. It takes its toll. That's definitely bad news about Skúli. Any idea what happened there?'

'No. Nothing so far. I'll check with Óttar in the morning.'

'And Rafn? No news of him?'

'No. He's most likely left town.'

'I've had dealings with him over the years. I can ask around among a few people he knocks around with to see if I can get anything out of them.'

'That would be much appreciated.'

There had been doubts in her mind all the way, right up to parking the car outside Magnús's neat detached house, whether she was doing the right thing or not. She had spent a long time gazing at the house. She hadn't come to a decision, and then Magnús had opened the front door and beckoned her to come in with a smile on his face. She got out of the car and walked to the house.

She had noticed on the way that there was no sign of the police presence she had requested at the Leira junction.

All I know is that residents and travel operators are really unhappy with the checks. There are some massive queues at rush hour, Salka had been told when she called the station. She had meant to speak to Valgeir, but he had already left. She was not kindly disposed towards him.

Once they had eaten, Magnús cleared the crockery from the table, refusing any help from Salka.

'Is what Pétur said right? That you investigated Hróbjartur when you were down south?'

'That's right.'

'I remember it back when it was all over the papers. Terrible.'

'What was?' she asked absently, looking around the living room.

'That the case was dismissed,' he said, appearing in the doorway.

'Well, quite a few of them wriggle out of it that way. There's a trampoline in the garden,' Salka said, almost without realising that she had changed the subject.

'Yes,' he said and was silent for a moment. 'I have a daughter who's thirteen. She visits sometimes.'

'Were you in a relationship?'

'Yes and no,' he said and disappeared back into the kitchen. 'It was a short one. It was sort of ... accidental.'

Salka noticed a picture of the two of them in which the girl looked to be around five years old. She picked up another picture and examined it. The faded photo was of a smiling couple of around thirty. They sat on a blanket that had been spread over grass somewhere in the countryside. A lad with a serious look on his face sat between them.

'Is that you?' she said, glancing towards the kitchen. She was startled to find Magnús standing behind her.

'Yes. That's Mum, and Dad. They're both dead.'

'I'm sorry to hear that,' she said, catching his eye. 'Long ago?'

'Five years,' he said, thoughtfully.

'Both of them?'

'Yes. One soon after the other.'

Salka sensed that he wasn't comfortable talking about

this.

'How old are you there?' she asked, looking back at the picture.

'Fourteen.'

'You don't look like you're bursting with joy there,' she laughed.

'True. I don't remember why I was so sulky. Maybe just being a moody teen.'

'Somehow I think I've seen that look before,' she said, looking carefully at the youthful face.

'Is that so?' he asked, taking the picture from her hands and putting it in its place. 'Come on. There's something I want to show you.'

He took her hand and led her out onto the decking.

'That's quite something,' she said, catching sight of the steam rising from the hot tub in the corner, sheltered by windbreaks. 'You've certainly made an effort.'

Magnús had placed a tray of champagne, cheese and grapes by the side of the hot tub. The light that emanated from the outdoor candle was in a corner of the windbreak, where it was overshadowed by the evening brightness, failing to provide the romantic atmosphere he had tried to conjure up.

'I didn't bring a swimming costume with me,' she said, unsure how to react. 'Ach. I'm sorry. I really don't want to spoil the moment, but I hadn't intended to drink either. I need to be up early.'

She went over to him and reached out, touching his cheek and meaning to run her fingers through his hair. She was taken aback as he withdrew from her.

'Yes, I know,' he said seriously. 'Me too. I'm sorry. Trying too hard, maybe.'

'No, not at all. It's very romantic ... and tempting,' she smiled.

'Let's leave the champagne out. I thought you'd enjoy the heat and it would freshen you up.' Their eyes met. 'It'll do you good,' he said cheerfully. 'You can use my trunks and I'll find myself something.'

Salka stood on the decking, perched on the edge of the hot tub and dipped her fingers in the water.

'Where's the bathroom?' she asked, taking the clothes Magnús brought her. When she returned, he was already in the water.

'These trunks are on the large side,' she said, trying to sound casual.

She lowered herself cautiously into the water to allow herself to get used to the heat.

'I decided to allow myself a small one,' he said, holding a champagne flute. 'Sure you won't have a drop?'

'Just a drop,' she said, wrinkling her nose and holding up a hand, a narrow gap between thumb and forefinger.

They sat in silence for a while and Salka felt a wave of wellbeing pass through her.

'So how did you get on at the river?' she asked.

'Finished at lunchtime today. I'll show you,' he said, picking up his phone from where it lay under a towel. 'I hooked this one the day you left,' he said, scrolling through the pictures.

Some showed fish lying on the grass next to the reel to show the size. He had also used the camera to take pictures of himself holding fish, and Salka noticed that he held the catch out, away from his body, a common way of making the fish look bigger.

'This one was on Saturday evening. A real battle and I was in trouble with this one.'

'How so?' she asked, pretending to be excited.

'I went flat on my face. Caught on film,' he said, handing her the phone.

He had selected a video sequence that began as he walked along the bank of the unruffled river, the lens directed at it. Fish jumped here and there. Then there was a sudden whirl of grass and sky, and Magnús cursing.

'What happened there?' Salka asked.

'Tripped and fell. Banged my head on a rock, and have a swelling to show for it, pulled a muscle and picked up a scratch,' he said standing up. He pulled his trunks down an inch and showed her a red wheal above his hip bone.

'It's a dangerous sport. You were lucky to survive,' she laughed, and was rewarded with a splash of hot water.

They spent more than an hour in the hot tub and she knew that if the body language had been right, Magnús would have taken the opportunity to move closer, to touch her, kiss her. It hadn't escaped her notice that this was what he would have wanted, but she didn't allow him an opening to make a move.

It wasn't until they emerged from the water and stood by the bathroom door that he put his arms around her, kissed her and led her to the bedroom.

'You've been a bit distant. Are you sure you're all right?' he asked as they lay naked side by side.

'You think so?' She mulled it over. She felt that she had forgotten herself, caught up in the moment. She had listened to the voice. Hadn't she? Now she was having doubts. 'Maybe,' she said. 'There's a lot on my plate at the moment.'

'Are you sure this is what you want?'

She looked at him and she didn't feel that she had nodded agreement. But she must have done, as he kissed her long and passionately, and rolled on top of her.

Salka was startled from sleep by the sound of something hitting the window. She cautiously slipped from the bed, moved the curtain aside and peered out. A blackbird lay motionless on the grass.

She put on a white shirt that belonged to Magnús and went outside. She could feel the chill nibble at her skin and gooseflesh appeared on her legs, even though the sun was already high in the sky and there wasn't a cloud to be seen.

She tiptoed to the back of the house and looked down at the bird, which looked to be dead. Another blackbird chirped raucously in a nearby tree. Salka wondered if they were a pair.

She picked up the blackbird and held it in her hands. Suddenly it came to life. It looked around as if trying to work out what had happened, shook itself, straightened its feathers and flew away.

It vanished into the distance.

Salka smiled to herself and went back inside. She glanced into the bedroom where Magnús was snoring softly.

She went to the bedroom, dressed and went to the kitchen where her jacket was. Checking her phone, she saw only fourteen percent battery capacity remained, and she remembered that there was no charger cable in the car. She opened a few kitchen drawers, but no cable was to be seen.

She remembered seeing an open door next to the bathroom, and a computer and printer. In the little room she looked around, and opened the top desk drawer. Nothing.

She opened the next drawer down.

A matt folder lay there in front of her. It was closed with bands stretched over the corners.

Salka picked it up.

She glanced out into the corridor as she heard a movement. She watched for a long time, and then looked again at the folder. Even though the cover was matt plastic, she could more or less make out the image beneath it. She slipped the bands off and opened the folder.

She looked at the sheet of paper at the top of the pile.

It was an article cut from a newspaper.

She was about to leaf through the pages when she heard movement, and quickly replaced the folder as it had been.

34

Tuesday 26th August 2014

Salka sat in the jeep. She couldn't get the sight of the article out of her mind. She was startled when someone tapped on the side window.

'Sorry, I didn't mean to take you by surprise,' Magnús said, standing by the car in his dressing gown. 'You're off? You don't want some breakfast?'

'No. I need to get myself to the station. Thanks all the same,' she smiled.

'No problem. I'll let you know if I hear anything about Rafn.'

'Thanks,' she said, and pulled away.

She was close to the Leira junction when she noticed a red car coming the other way at speed. The car took the Leira road and for a second she saw the driver's face. It was Rafn. He put his foot down on the straight stretch of road crossing Eyjafjörður.

Salka followed. In the mirror she noticed a black Skoda Fabia with a flashing light on its dashboard catching up with her. It was still some distance away and she couldn't see the driver.

She put her foot down when she realised that Rafn's car was gaining distance, overtaking another car. He swerved back across the road, narrowly missing a car coming the other way.

Experience told her that it was better to maintain a distance so as not to cause an even more dangerous situation.

Although Salka was driving at 120 kilometres per hour, the Skoda hurtled past her. Another car was coming the other way and she had to brake sharply to let the Skoda onto the right side of the road. A collision had been avoided by a hair's breadth.

'What the hell's going on?' she said out loud, having recognised Gísli behind the wheel.

She again put her foot down, picked up her phone and called, but Gísli wasn't answering. She swore to herself as the phone pinged an alert, telling her the battery was almost dead.

Rafn shot past the turnoff for Eyjafjörður. The road curved to the right at the bottom of the fjord and Salka could see Rafn manoeuvring to overtake again. This time a truck coming the other way was forced onto the gravel verge to avoid a crash. Rafn snatched the car back across to his lane, and just managed to keep it on the road. The wheels on the nearside churned a cloud of dust from the loose gravel at the side of the road. Rafn swerved back onto the tarmac, and seemed to lose control as the rear end of the car lurched to one side. In a flash, the car twisted so that it was side on and spun into the air. As it hit the ground it rolled more times than Salka could count and finished up off the road. Salka saw the windscreen shatter, the shards scattered like diamonds as they caught the sunshine.

Salka pulled up on the verge and ran. She saw Gísli hurrying towards where Rafn's car had come to rest on its roof, next to a line of bushes. She saw him look into the car, and then step back from it.

'How is he?' she asked as she stopped next to Gísli, standing over Rafn, motionless on the grass.

'I don't know,' he said in confusion.

'Call an ambulance,' she ordered, opening the medical kit she had brought from the jeep. She crouched down on all fours next to him and looked carefully at Rafn's pale, blood-streaked face. There were pieces of glass embedded in his forehead and she didn't dare move them. There was a deep cut to his neck. She pressed a dressing to the wound and held it closed with her fingers.

She gently slapped Rafn's cheeks, called his name and was relieved when he came to.

'Where am I?' he asked, his voice faint.

'You're all right,' she assured him, checking his eyes, which were dazed. 'Look at me, Rafn.'

'What happened?' he asked, trying to look around, and coughing so that blood oozed from the corner of his mouth.

'Nothing happened. Just take it easy. Look at me. No, no. Don't close your eyes,' she said as Rafn's eyelids drooped as if he were about to fall asleep. 'You'll be fine. But you'll have to be strong.'

'Do you have the diary?'

'Diary?'

'Yeah.'

'Anton's diary?' she asked after a moment's thought.

'I need it. He mustn't take it...' Rafn slurred, his eyes closing.

'Rafn!' Salka called, listening for his breath.

She looked up at the road, where a row of cars had pulled up. She saw Gísli stretching to reach something inside Rafn's car.

'He mustn't have it,' Rafn muttered, squeezing Salka's hand.

'Who mustn't have it?' Salka asked, crouching close to him.

Rafn was about to say something, but couldn't. She saw a patch of blood had formed on his white shirt and was spreading. She gingerly pulled his shirt away and saw an open wound in his belly. Both of his trouser legs were tattered and bloody.

'Keep back!' she heard Gísli shout.

She looked up to see a middle-aged man trotting towards her with a case in his hands.

'I'm a doctor!' the man yelled back, and he asked Salka to move aside as he dropped to his knees next to her and looked

Rafn over. 'Doesn't look good,' he muttered, after checking the neck injury, and asked Salka to put pressure on it. He gently moved Rafn's head from side to side and listened to his breathing.

The doctor took scissors from his case and Salka watched as he snipped at Rafn's clothes.

'Is he going to survive?' she asked, and immediately regretted the question. At this point, nobody would be able to tell.

'He's lost consciousness. It doesn't look like the injuries are too serious,' he said, trying to turn Rafn so he could see his back. 'But there could be internal injuries and he needs treatment as soon as possible,' he continued, taking another look at the injury to his neck.

She went over to Gísli, still standing next to the wreck of Rafn's car.

'What did you pick up from in there?'

'What do you mean?' he asked, looking surprised.

'Inside the car. You were looking for something.'

'Yes, I was looking to see if there was anyone in there.'

Salka squatted down and peered inside. There was blood on the passenger door, probably from when Rafn had been thrown clear. She heard the wail of a siren in the distance.

'Did you notice a book?' she said, opening the glove compartment and rooting through it.

'No. I don't understand.'

'Rafn said something about a diary. Marta mentioned it to me as well,' Salka said, going behind the car and looking into the open, empty boot. She scanned the things that had been thrown from the car as it had rolled.

The sound of sirens was closer and Salka saw the ambulance appear in the distance along with two patrol cars from Leirunesti.

'You chased him pretty hard,' Salka said, going up to Gísli.

'You think so?' he said, surprised.

'Yes. I thought you'd be aware of the rules for pursuit.'

'I thought I did everything right.'

'You were going way too fast. You were pushing him to go faster instead of matching his speed and staying with him. How did this chase come about?'

'I was coming out of BSÓ, the taxi station...'

'I know what BSÓ is, Gísli,' she snapped in irritation.

'Well, I was coming out and saw him getting into the car. He saw me, and I followed.'

'Why didn't you answer when I called?'

'I'm sorry, Salka. I was too stressed out.'

'You're to go to the station now, Gísli,' she said, not looking at him.

'Don't you want me here to...?'

'No. I'll be there shortly. I need to take a closer look at the scene.'

'You don't need me to help...'

'Gísli,' she said firmly, catching his eye. No more words were needed.

She watched as the ambulance departed, taking Rafn to Akureyri, and then asked the uniformed officers still at the scene to check the area for anything that could have been thrown clear of the car.

'Were you looking for this?' asked one of the officers, handing Salka a book. 'It was in the scrub over there.'

'Is he all right?' Valgeir asked as soon as he encountered Salka on the police station's second floor.

'Don't know. He's been taken to intensive care. He'd more than likely have been fine if you'd given a green light to the road blocks out of town,' she said and was about to continue to her office. She stopped and caught Valgeir's eye. 'I found this.'

'What's that?'

'It's a diary.'

'Sure,' he said, looking at the book in her hand. 'And what about it?'

'Didn't anyone mention Anton's diary when you were investigating his disappearance?'

'Not that I recall,' he said thoughtfully. 'Where did you find that?'

'It was at the accident scene. It was very important to Rafn, so it'll be interesting to look through it. You're sure nobody said anything about this?'

'Never heard it mentioned,' he said firmly.

'Fair enough,' she said, shutting her office door behind her.

She took a seat and opened the diary. She saw the names of Helgi, Hróbjartur and Gunnleifur flash past as she read through the dated entries. There were other names that weren't familiar. His descriptions of the abuse he and Rafn had been subjected to were unnervingly precise. Sometimes there appeared to be improbably short intervals between sessions.

Salka's heart jumped as she stopped at an entry that appeared to have been written three weeks before Anton's disappearance. It described a visit to the police station to make a statement accusing the three men of gross sexual misconduct. He detailed the interview and ended the entry with a few stark words.

That bastard Valli didn't believe a word I said.

Anton's final diary entry had been written just five days before his disappearance.

Went to meet Gunnleifur who said he had to see me. I went to the church hall and got Rafn to wait outside for me to be on the safe side. Gunnleifur was his usual smarmy self and said he regretted everything and wanted to apologise. He offered me money and that was tempting because he offered half a million. I said no and he went crazy. Then Hróbjartur and Helgi appeared from nowhere. I managed to run for it. Those bastards were definitely going to rape me. Or kill me.

Salka turned the page to the next entry and saw that this one was different as the handwriting was unlike Anton's. Someone else had written this, and she guessed it had been Rafn.

There were just three lines.

Face in the mirror, you don't listen.
Farewell with a kiss.
An angel dies today!

Salka stared at the page and the first two lines that had been written on the mirrors in Hróbjartur's and Helgi's homes. The last one should have been for the mirror in Gunnleifur's house, she decided.

At the back of the diary a few photographs had been stuck to the pages. One showed two boys. Salka guessed they had to be around twelve years old. She opened the drawer and took out the folder containing the case files for Valgeir's investigation into Anton's disappearance. There was a picture taken of Anton at around fifteen. Comparing the two, there was no doubt that he was one of the two boys, and the other resembled Rafn. The next picture was a wedding photo of a young couple. Salka felt that the faces looked familiar, but couldn't place them. On the back had been written, *Mum and Dad*. They looked happy, sitting side by side, clasping each other's hands. Salka thought there was a sadness in the woman's eyes. The third picture was of a young girl and Salka recognised her instantly – Marta. She wondered why there was a picture of her in the book. She decided that these pictures must have been important to him, considering he kept them in the book.

She took the fourth picture, a postcard-sized image of a handsome group dressed in their best, standing on a lawn in beautiful weather, and not a coast to be seen. Children in short trousers could be seen running around with a puppy at their heels. The picture had been taken when the group wasn't posed for the photographer. They stood chatting, some with wine glasses in their hands, others holding cups of coffee. Some held plates of cakes and pancakes. A family reunion or a birthday, Salka thought.

She examined the foreground and made out Anton's parents chatting to other guests. A few years had passed since the wedding photo. Again the suspicion returned that she recognised these people. She scanned the faces and the further they were from the lens, the less sharp the focus became. She passed her fingertips over the photograph and the people's faces. After passing by two individuals, she slid her finger back to them, and looked hard.

This can't be.

She wasn't sure if she had spoken the words out loud or not. She pulled open a drawer and rooted through the contents, but couldn't find what she was looking for. That was no surprise. She needed a magnifying glass.

She put the picture down and used her phone to take a picture. She opened the image and spread her fingers on the screen to enlarge it.

This can't be.

This time she was sure she had spoken out loud.

'*Hæ*,' said a voice from the doorway, and Salka jumped.

'*Hæ*,' she said, looking up at Magnús.

'I heard about the excitement at Leira.'

'Yes,' she said absently.

'How's Rafn?'

'He's in intensive care.'

'I see you're busy. Just wanted to see if I could ask you to lunch.'

Salka looked at him wordlessly.

'Hello?' he laughed. 'Anyone home?'

'Ach. I'm sorry,' she said, shaking her head. 'I'm up to my ears in this case. Can we do a late afternoon lunch?'

'Sure,' he said slowly. 'If that's a thing, then I'll give it a go,' he said, leaving with a smile.

Salka returned to the pictures. The last one showed a group of children and teenagers posing for the camera. She knew the building in the background: Dynheimar. There were fifteen of them who had lined themselves up in three rows and she instantly made out Anton, Rafn and Marta, plus Anton had written their names next to each of them. It wasn't until she saw the face and the name of the lad at the end of the back row that her heart sank.

She buried her face in her hands.

35

'Kolla wants a word,' Valgeir called out as Salka passed his office.

'She's back?' she asked, stopping and looking in on him.

'She is,' he said cheerfully, and with what seemed to be a faintly malicious undertone.

Salka knocked at Kolla's door and opened it.

'Good morning, Salka,' she smiled. 'Take a seat.'

Salka was about to take a seat facing the desk, when Kolla ushered her to the better chairs in the spacious office.

'How are things?' Kolla asked, after placing cups on the table between them.

Salka took her in for a moment before answering. There had been none of the usual introductory small talk. The polite stuff.

'Things are not bad. A lot has happened.'

'That's an understatement,' Kolla said, smiling after having sipped her coffee.

Salka was baffled by the smile, and felt that the atmosphere was dangerously pressured.

'What's the real situation?'

Salka had got to know Kolla slightly before she had moved to London, and liked her. She had also heard that she was no soft touch and didn't shy away from difficult decisions. She had a reputation for being agreeable on the surface, but tough when she needed to be.

'It's not clear,' Salka said cautiously. 'So far. Of course, Skúli was under suspicion as the likely perpetrator. As was Rafn, who is now unconscious in intensive care. I'm meeting Óttar later and I hope he has some results that could clarify things.'

'Salka,' Kolla said, moving closer to the edge of her seat.

She looked down at her hands before raising her eyes. 'I have had some conversations during which I have been told that the investigation is disorganised. That's to say, that there is nobody with an overview of the case as a whole. There has been only one team meeting with everyone concerned. Is there any particular reason for this?'

'Yes, there's probably a good reason for that,' Salka said after pausing for thought. 'There are individuals here who are not inclined to be co-operative,' she said and wasn't sure if saying this out loud had left her relieved, or with an added concern.

'And who are these individuals?'

'Could I ask about these conversations concerning the inefficient running of the investigation?'

Kolla looked back at her with no expression, and Salka wondered if she had been caught up in a game, the one that she often played herself and which was reminiscent of poker, when the slightest change of expression, movement or alteration in body language could give away your thoughts.

'Valgeir came to see me earlier,' Kolla said.

'Yes. Valgeir. It goes without saying that he has been complaining. I need to have words with a few individuals ... and I'm wondering if we could postpone the rest of this conversation?'

Salka went to Valgeir's office and shut the door behind her as if it was something delicate.

'No, you're not going anywhere, Valgeir,' she said, as she saw him stand up and open his mouth to speak. 'I won't keep you long. Just a few items to run past you,' she said, seating herself in front of his desk.

Valgeir looked back at her questioningly and lounged in his chair, which she knew was a pretence. He knew what was coming.

'Kolla sent her regards, Valli,' she said, the emphasis on the diminutive of his name. 'I didn't know people called you

Valli. That's right, isn't it?'

'What?' he asked, sounding less than amiable.

'That you're sometimes called Valli.'

'It's rare. Just a few close friends call me that. Why do you ask?'

'I was wondering if we could allow each other a little honesty. Maybe even a little respect,' she said, sidestepping the question.

'What are you getting at?' he demanded, the look in his eye one intended to show self-confidence, but the opposite shone through.

'I have been through Anton's diary and I'd like to ask you if you imagine that there's anything in there that might concern you.'

He stayed silent.

'Valgeir, you heard what I said, didn't you?'

'Yes. I heard you,' he said, shifting in his seat.

'I understand your reasons for going to Kolla and complaining about me. You feel that I'm disturbing your comfort zone and you're concerned about your position. Am I right?'

There was another silence.

'I have zero interest in the police pecking order. I couldn't care less where you are, where you're heading or what happens to me. If I'm sacked today, that's fine. The only thing I have in mind is to do my job and do it well. And I expect that those who work with me think along the same lines,' she said, her eyes fixed on Valgeir, who stared back at her, his face stiff.

Salka stood up and went over to the window with its view over Vaðlaheiði. She turned and perched on the windowsill.

'You tried to get rid of me today. You reported to Kolla that the investigation is going badly and that I have little or no contact with those concerned. And you told her that I don't listen to you,' she said, returning to the chair and sitting to face him again. 'There's a lot in that. I could have done better in keeping everyone informed. But are you prepared to do the same?'

There was silence yet again.

'Valgeir, how about you say something? Answer me?' she said in a low voice as she leaned forward over the desk. 'I'm trying to help you. Do you see that?'

Valgeir looked as if he had been turned to stone.

'This is a photocopy of a page from Anton's diary,' she said, sliding a sheet of paper across the desk to him.

Valgeir took it and placed it back on the desk after reading it. He said nothing.

'I could initiate an internal investigation into your work and particularly in connection with Anton's disappearance. As this shows, Anton came to you with allegations of abuse. That conversation is nowhere to be seen in the archives. Why, Valgeir? And soon afterwards, he disappeared. I'm going to hold off putting this in the right hands,' she said, picking up the photocopied sheet. 'Maybe I won't do it at all. I'm also going to wait before asking you what the reasons were for conducting your investigation as you did, and what links you have to this priest and the deacon. I'm fully aware that you and Gunnleifur know each other well. You might well be close friends, which would naturally have precluded you from investigating back then. So you find all this uncomfortable and you'd prefer to prevent me from blowing the dust off this old case. But now you need to help me, Valgeir.'

'How?' he murmured.

'The next step. I have an idea.'

'Are you free?' Salka asked, appearing in the doorway of the room Óttar had been allocated at the station.

'Absolutely. Sit yourself down.'

'There's a team meeting later, and I need to ask you to do something for me.'

'And what might that be?'

'I need to ask you to lie.'

36

Salka greeted all those involved in the investigation as they entered the meeting room. She heard Gísli say hello, but didn't look up. She had called Magnús and asked him to join the meeting so he could provide more information about Rafn, considering he had often appeared on the police's radar over the years.

She went through each item at a time, and it emerged that the analysis team had not been able to extract anything more from the videos. Salka was promised screenshots of the abuse victims who appeared in them. Óttar spoke, giving an overview of the main points from the crime scenes and going over the results from the biological samples and other evidence.

'Then I think we will simply have to wait and see how things evolve,' Salka said. 'As I see things, taking into account the material we have, Skúli and Rafn were participants in these murders. We will have to look more closely into how they achieved this together. As Óttar mentioned, the footprints we identified on the lawn and the decking at Gunnleifur's house match Rafn's shoe size. We have Anton's diary, and judging by the contents, he had strong reasons for wanting to be revenged on these men. While we can't be certain if Skúli was also abused, we know that they used him to get what they wanted. They used him to bring them young boys,' she said and fell silent as she looked over those present, who gazed back at her silently. 'We continue the investigation and wait for Rafn to regain consciousness, although one of the doctors reported earlier that they aren't overly hopeful. I've interviewed Gunnleifur again and nothing more has emerged that justifies continued custody.

So he'll go home later today and doesn't need a further police presence at his house. He's leaving the country tomorrow...'

'Leaving the country? Is that allowable while the investigation is in progress?' Gísli asked.

'Yes, it's acceptable,' Salka said. 'He's in poor health and is going to Denmark for a PET scan. That'll do.' She stood up. 'If there are no more questions, I suggest we get back to work and meet again tomorrow.'

'I thought you wanted me to be there in case you wanted some background about Rafn?' Magnús said, following her into the corridor.

'Yes. I'm sorry about that. I was a little too quick wrapping things up. We'll have to wait and see what progress he makes, and hopes he come around. If he does, then I'd like you to be part of it when we talk to him,' she said, and smiled.

'Of course,' he said, slipping an arm around her shoulder. 'Shall we get a bite to eat?'

'Now?' she said, glancing at her watch. 'It's not five yet.'

'Yes, certainly. I just wanted to eat together. I have to go to Húsavík this evening and I'll be there overnight.'

'Sure. What are you doing there?'

'I have to meet a friend. Planning a fishing trip.'

'I see. Let's go for tomorrow, in that case. I said I'd drive Gunnleifur home and my parents asked me to dinner tonight. It's a while since I spent much time with them.'

'No problem. See you tomorrow.'

'Let's do that.'

'You're leaving?' Gísli asked as Salka went down to the ground floor.

'Yes. I'm driving Gunnleifur home.'

'Want me to come too?'

'No, it's all right. But, hey,' she said, and looked up. 'It's been a tough day. There's no reason why you shouldn't go home. Go and give the girlfriend a cuddle,' she said with a grin.

'You're sure?'

'Right now, yes. If I were you, I'd make tracks quick before I change my mind.'

In the holding area she opened the cell door.

'Well, Gunnleifur. Let's be on our way.'

'About time. You can expect to hear complaints. You can be certain of that.'

'Really? From St Peter?'

Gunnleifur glared and snorted as he left the cell.

Salka went into the room and placed a chair against the wall. She sat down and waited.

She checked the news on her phone. Most media complained that the police were remaining tight-lipped about the investigation. Eysteinn had been right. The case had been mentioned on the BBC and on most media across the Nordic countries.

She waited.

She stood up and massaged her hips. Her back was sore after sitting in the chair for, how long? She checked the time. It had been three hours. She sat on the floor, opened a bottle of water and sipped.

She started, glanced at the time and thought. No, she probably hadn't fallen asleep, but could have dozed for a moment. An hour had passed since the last time she had checked, and it was now ten-thirty. She stood up and went to the window, peering out between the thick curtains. It was dark. She heard the occasional creak or click, and at first had been on the alert. But she had figured out that these sounds were either the hot water pipes or else branches brushing against one of the windows in the freshening breeze outside.

Salka heard a light drumming sound that accelerated swiftly, and realised that this was rain hammering the steel sheets of the roof. The window where she sat had to be sheltered from the wind, as no drops appeared on the glass. She looked around the darkened room at the many photographs that hung on one wall. Most were black and white pictures of elderly people who she assumed had long passed away. She examined the shelves that were filled mainly with books, apart from one that had been reserved for ornaments, little porcelain figurines, an old fountain pen and an etching of a bird. In the darkness she couldn't be sure if it was a whimbrel or a redshank.

She sat down again on the floor and was about to check the internet, when she noticed that Magnús had sent a message fifteen minutes before. With her phone set to silent, she hadn't noticed it right away.

Thanks for last night.

Likewise

Still with your parents?

Yes. I'll stay at their place tonight. Dad's not good. And you? In Húsavík?

It was a few minutes before a reply popped up.

Yes. Having a beer. Soon time for bed. Good night.

Good night.

Salka leaned her head against the wall and looked up at the ceiling. Her eyes closed.

She waited.

She was startled and took a sharp breath. She wiped a sliver of saliva from her mouth, glanced at the clock and swore to herself. She had fallen asleep and it was one-thirty in the morning.

She moved forward onto her knees and listened.

Had some sound woken her? It was still raining and she could hear branches brushing against a window somewhere in the house with even more force now that the wind had picked up.

Salka got slowly to her feet.

She stood still, listened and heard a knock.

Going on tiptoe to the door, she listened without looking through the gap.

Someone opened a door.

She felt her heart hammer so hard that she could almost hear it. She took a deep breath in the hope that it would calm her.

She heard footsteps approaching beyond the door. She backed away, moving to stand behind the door as someone eased it open.

Salka held her breath. She saw that she had forgotten to pick up the phone from where she had been sitting on the floor.

She could hear the breathing of the person on the other side of the door, with just three centimetres of wood separating them. She exhaled as carefully as she was able.

Suddenly the door was pulled to and she heard the footsteps retreat. Doors elsewhere in the house creaked as they opened.

Salka peered through the gap between the door and the jamb. She could see someone going into a room further along the corridor.

She dipped a hand into the pocket of her jacket and pressed the emergency button.

Then she opened the door cautiously and went along the corridor to the open bedroom door she had seen the figure go through.

She heard a rush, and imagined that the intruder had snatched the duvet from the bed.

She took one more step, and stopped, wincing as the parquet creaked under her feet. She waited for a moment, and continued, focused on the door.

As soon as she looked inside, hands grasped her shoulders, hurling her into the room, where she landed hard against the wall.

She kicked at the wall and threw herself at the man who was about to run out into the corridor. Salka managed to get a grip on the man's neck and clung to his back.

She received a punch to the face, but the anger and surge of adrenaline deadened the pain. She tightened her grip on the man, who stopped in the passage and was ramming her repeatedly against the wall.

Salka lost her grip and tumbled to the floor. She looked up and saw that the man was wearing a black balaclava. She was determined to stand up, narrowly managing to dodge a kick that had been meant for her head. On her feet, she felt a sudden pain in her arm. Something had cut her. The man was about to run when she fought to grab hold of his feet, so that he fell forward. He twisted around as she was about to throw herself at him.

She saw the drops of blood on the blade of the knife.

There was a deafening crash as the armed response unit burst into Gunnleifur's house, with shouts and yells.

The man in the balaclava froze as he was bathed in beams of light from the armed officers, and the knife fell to the floor.

One of the team clicked handcuffs into place and shoved him into a sitting position.

'What the hell took you so long?' Salka yelled from where she lay on the floor, holding her arm.

'Delay in the system,' one of the team replied.

'Don't do that,' she called out, as one of the team reached to pull the balaclava from the man's head.

Salka hauled herself up and onto her knees, looking through the eyeholes and into the eyes that appeared almost black, and which she knew well.

Salka looked down and shut her eyes for a moment.

She opened them and stared into the man's eyes.

She pulled the balaclava off him.

37

Salka sat at the desk in the interview room and switched on the recording. She hadn't slept and could feel her fingertips were numb with fatigue. She took a deep breath and lowered her head, gazing into her lap for a long time, until she had summoned the courage at look at the man seated opposite her.

'Did you manage to organise the fishing trip?' she asked, and looked up.

After a minute's silence she continued.

'You were certainly in a hurry to murder Gunnleifur. And you had everything you needed in your backpack. Tape, carpet knife, restraints, rope, overalls and whatnot. And you were ready to murder me, Magnús.'

There was silence.

'You were the one who jumped me in the garden behind Gunnleifur's house the other night, weren't you?'

Magnús made no reply.

'If I were to run my fingers through your hair, right there,' she said, pointing. 'I'd find a bump. Because you're the one I cracked over the head with the flashlight.'

Magnús inclined his head in a slight nod.

'You didn't fall while you were fishing. That video was acted out. You recorded it afterwards. Just to be sure. Helgi managed to give you a scratch with the knife he had in his hand when you attacked him in the hall at his house.'

'You know what this is?' she asked, placing a small bag on the table in front of him.

He looked at it and shook his head.

'It's dog hair. We haven't checked yet, but I know perfectly well it'll match Húbert. And guess where I found this? I can't hear what you're saying,' she said as Magnús mumbled something.

'No.'

'This is from the tread-less shoes you were wearing at Gunnleifur's house. This was in a crack at the toe of one shoe. Look at me, Magnús. It's the least you can do,' she said, as he continued to avoid looking her in the eye.

'Why did you murder Hróbjartur and Helgi? And Skúli? You murdered him as well, didn't you?'

'Yes. I murdered him,' Magnús said, looking up. 'And Hróbjartur and Helgi.'

'Why Skúli?'

'He would have blabbed.'

'Did you know him?'

'No. He didn't know me. I knew through my work that he was caught up in with Hróbjartur's and Helgi's network. He was the enabler. He caught young boys in their net.'

'So how did your paths cross?'

'He appeared unexpectedly in the church, with that mutt of his making a racket.'

'You had already murdered Hróbjartur?'

'Yes.'

'Where?'

'In the summer house. I took the body to the church, and then Skúli turned up.'

'Did he see your face, or was it covered?'

'I didn't have the balaclava on when he turned up, but then I pulled it on. I don't know if he saw my face. I asked, of course. He said he hadn't seen anything. I'm sure he lied. We talked and I let him handle the knife. He said he hated Hróbjartur. He stabbed the body.'

'Did he do that on his own initiative?'

'I encouraged him. Told him he'd feel better. That made him guilty as well. I wanted to ensure he would keep quiet, in case he had seen me. His fingerprints were on the knife, and I also used it for Helgi,' he said, and fell silent.

'Go on,' Salka said gently.

'I threatened him.'

'How?'

'Said I'd use the knife to prove he was the guilty one, and that I could harm his family. Then he attacked me, but he didn't have much of a chance, and I smacked him in the eye with the handle of the knife. How about taking these off?' he said, lifting his cuffed hands.

'Why did you want to meet him by the dock in Grenivík?' Salka asked, as if she hadn't heard his question.

'I kept wondering if he'd seen my face. Couldn't get it out of my mind. I wanted to make sure he knew I meant it. I told him I'd kill his mother, and reminded him of that. Then he flared up and was going to attack me. It was an accident. He shouldn't have died. I was just going to frighten him into keeping quiet,' Magnús said, his eyes dropping to the floor.

'I'm not so sure,' Salka said.

'What?' Magnús said, eyes on her.

'I suspect that you went to the dock intending to murder him.'

Magnús made no reply.

'But why murder Hróbjartur and Helgi? What had these men done to you that was so terrible that they deserved such cruelty?'

Magnús said nothing.

'I have a couple of pictures here, Magnús,' Salka said, conscious of how painful it was to speak his name out loud. 'I'd like you to look at these with me,' she continued, placing them on the table. 'This is a wedding photo. Anton's parents. Did you know them?'

There was no response.

'This picture here,' she said, placing the next one on the table. 'It's clearly taken at some occasion. That's Anton's parents here at the front, but you see the people here in the background? Recognise them? Look at the picture, Magnús,' she snapped, and he jumped.

He looked up, and at the picture.

'Do you recognise these people? These are your parents,' she continued when he said nothing. 'I saw the picture at your home, with you between them. How come they're in this picture?'

He said nothing.

'What about this?' She placed in front of him a photocopy of the newspaper item she had found in the drawer at his house. 'There's a house here that's in flames. This is the place that went up not far from your place in Hrafnagil. The picture is of the couple who lost their lives in the fire. Anton's parents, weren't they?'

Salka stood up, went to the window and looked out.

'Magnús,' she said when she had sat down again. 'You have to give me some answers. Anton's parents. And this is Anton,' she said, snapping the picture of him onto the table. 'Look at him, Magnús. That's Anton. Tell me about him.'

'He's my brother,' he said, his voice loud, and Salka was taken aback to see his face flushed and furious. 'He's my twin.'

Salka leaned back in her chair and took a deep breath. She felt a surge of relief that hid a great burden. She wondered if the relief was for Magnús having said those words out loud.

'Tell me about Anton,' Salka said quietly, and poured water into a glass for him. She stood up, unlocked the handcuffs and placed them on the table.

He sipped water and rubbed his wrists.

'I never knew him. I only found out seven years ago that we were brothers. That was long after his disappearance. I was looking into family affairs and found that our fathers, or rather, our adoptive fathers, were closely related. I couldn't ask my parents about anything as they were both dead.'

'How did they die?'

'They went quite close together. Dad had Parkinson's and my mother had a heart attack. Mum had been very ill. She tried to tell me something just before the end, but I didn't understand what she was driving at. In fact, after that I started digging through this and found that our fathers had adopted us through a not entirely legal process. Hróbjartur and Gunnleifur arranged this through some network of friends and contacts. Our mother had been seriously unwell, locked away in an institution and had no family to speak of. It was unbelievable how all this was allowed to be discreetly rubber-stamped. But isn't that how so many things get done here in Iceland? It's about knowing the right people, having authority behind you,' he said and fell silent.

'What were you able to find out?'

'That Anton's adoptive father was a complete bastard. He had a dreadful upbringing. I spoke to any number of people who all told the same disgusting tales of violence, and the booze and drugs in that household. The worst of it was that they practically sold my brother. To this and that pervert. At a certain point these God-fearing men became part of the picture. His parents didn't care what they got up to, because these men gave them money. As long as they could fund their habit, they didn't care what Anton had to suffer.'

'What about the fire?'

'I made sure they had a bunch of pills and burned the place to the ground,' Magnús said, and he seemed to shrivel up in front of her, as his tears flowed.

For a second it occurred to Salka to go to him, to take him in her arms. She stayed where she was.

'I ran into them a few times,' he said as he seemed to recover himself. 'Gave them some booze and some of the dope I managed to filch every time we nabbed some small-time dope baron. At a certain point they forgot who they were talking to, and told the whole story. They said it started when he was five.'

The tears continued to roll down Magnús's cheeks.

Salka sat in silence. She was struggling to hold back tears of her own.

'There were two respected citizens here in the town

who also abused Anton,' he said. Wiping his eyes and coughing. 'If those two hadn't been six feet under long ago, I'd have finished them off as well. I made a point of going one night to the graveyard and pissed on the grave of one of them,' he said with a shadow of a smile. 'After that I took the decision that I was simply going to murder these men. I often wondered what would have happened if I had found myself in their hands. I had wonderful parents who gave me love and warmth. But I could just as easily have ended up with those people. I can't imagine that it was anything but coincidence that dictated where each of us finished up. All the same, I can't help thinking that my parents must have known of my brother's circumstances but did nothing. That picture... the one you showed me of that gathering. I found out that they had managed to get together somehow at some point and we played together for a while, Anton and me. Just think... We met as small children. I can't forgive my parents for not taking a stand. In that respect, they were no better than Anton's family. I didn't feel the slightest sympathy when I watched the place burn down around them, and I watched it from a safe distance. I knew they were in there and the flames were licking at them. I wanted to hear their screams, but the roaring of the flames drowned that out,' he said, and looked into Salka's eyes. 'You must hate me, Salka.'

She wasn't sure what to think, whether or not to reply, or what she could say.

'What about the gunshots that were heard, that the rapid response unit was called out for?'

'The electricity had been cut off a long time ago. They used gas to cook, and it was one of the bottles that exploded in the fire.'

'And Rafn. How did he get caught up in this?'

'Rafn,' Magnús said thoughtfully. 'No doubt there was a time when Rafn was a decent guy, but he isn't one now. It's been a long time since he lost his way, and it's certainly not his fault. That's down to those men. But I've had to deal with him more times than I could count. He sells drugs to children and he causes endless trouble. Once when we were searching a place where he lived, I stumbled across the diary. Back then I hadn't figured out the connections, didn't know that Anton and I were brothers. Once I knew that, I did everything I could to lay my hands on the diary. Somehow, he figured out how important it was to me and he wanted an astronomical amount of money for it. I gave him some money, but he cheated me. After he was arrested with some dope, I had a hold over him. I'd get the diary and he'd get a lighter sentence. That was supposed to happen up at the sheds, and then it all went wrong when you and Gísli turned up.'

'That was you running through the woods with Rafn?'

'Yes. I saw you and didn't know what to do. Like I said, everything went wrong. All I could think of was getting hold of that book.'

'What made it so important?'

'Rafn told me during the interrogation, after I found the diary at his place, about the party he had been at with Anton. That was the last time Rafn saw him. When he woke up, Anton was already gone and he saw those words on the mirror. *Face in the mirror, you don't listen. Farewell with a kiss. An angel dies today!* He said that he had written them in the diary that Anton had kept at his place. He said that at first he thought it was something Anton had dreamed up and then taken his own life. Then he talked about how they had been abused by those men, Hróbjartur, Helgi and Gunnleifur.'

'And you didn't believe him, any more than anyone else had?'

'I don't know. To begin with I thought he was lying. But there was something that told me he was being truthful. Maybe you get this as well. Sometimes you just know when people are or aren't lying. Even so, it was pretty rare that there was the slightest grain of truth in anything Rafn said. For whatever reason, those lines somehow were fixed in my mind. I wrote them on the mirrors in Hróbjartur's and Helgi's houses, and afterwards it occurred to me that this had been a mistake. That kind of mistake could lead to me, because those lines were in the diary. I had a photocopy, but Rafn kept the original. If the media got wind of this, then Rafn would see it. He'd know at once it was me, because he told me he hadn't allowed a soul to see the book. And the strange thing was, I believed it when he told me that.'

'We'll take a break now,' Salka said.

They watched each other. Salka smiled.

'What about us?' she said and Magnús's gaze dropped. 'It was no coincidence that we met by the river, was it? You knew I was there. Pétur had told you that he and Kolla wanted me to work with them because I had investigated Hróbjartur in the past, so it would be likely that I'd take on the case. You wanted to be as close as you could to the investigation. You used me. How could you do that?'

'No, Salka,' he said, looking up to meet her gaze. 'I never meant to...'

'After we parted by the river, you went straight to Grenivík...'

'No,' Magnús said in a low voice.

'No, what?'

'First I went to Akureyri because I thought he'd be at home. He must have been watching those videos and forgotten them, as they were on the table in the bedroom. I looked through some of that shit, and left it all on the bed. I knew about his summer house, and went straight there.'

Salka half-closed her eyes. She sighed almost inaudibly.

'You murdered Hróbjartur, and then went back to the lodge late in the evening. Offered me a glass of wine and chatted as if nothing had happened. How is that even possible? What sort of person has such a vile character? You were perfectly normal. And in reality, what you did to me was nothing short of rape, Magnús, mentally and physically. And you'd have carried on using me. Tomorrow, and the next day, and the next...'

The tears trickled down her face.

She looked around, as if searching for answers that were nowhere to be found. She couldn't stop herself from twitching, and could no longer hold back as she sobbed openly. She felt the energy drain from her body.

The door opened and Kolla came into the room. Salka realised that she had not switched off the recording. Kolla went to Salka, who looked at Magnús, and was about to get to her feet. She dropped back into the chair as she felt her legs give way.

Kolla helped her to stand up, and led her to the door.

'I'm so sorry, Salka. I know you must hate me...'

She turned to face him. His ruddy face was awash with tears. His lips trembled.

'I don't hate anyone, Magnús. But I'm dangerously close to feeling that emotion now that I look you in the eye. I feel your pain. I genuinely do. But I can't forgive you,' she said in a whisper, and left the room.

Gísli was waiting beyond the door, and held her in his arms for a long time.

38

The sky cleared towards morning, with just an occasional white cloud to be seen. Salka drove past Leira, over Eyjafjörður, and parked the car in a lay-by near the Veigastaðavegur turnoff.

Kolla had not wanted to allow Salka to take any part in questioning Magnús. She finally gave way after Salka hammered on her desk three times, demanding an informal interview.

Then she had searched Gísli out and asked him to come for a drive.

It was half past nine and the morning sun was already high in the sky. She switched off the engine and looked across the golden, mirror-smooth fjord at the town of Akureyri on the other side, just as it was coming to life.

She wound down the window. There wasn't a breath of wind. There was little traffic and just a few gulls swooped over the fjord.

'How's your arm?' Gísli asked.

'Fine. It wasn't deep. They glued it together,' she said and gave him a smile. Then she twisted to face him. 'Gísli. I'll be completely honest. I need to go over a few things with you.'

'That's fine.'

'You're obviously not aware, but I was equally expecting that you could have appeared at Gunnleifur's house last night.' Gísli stared back at her without a word. 'I know it sounds terrible, but I was starting to suspect you.'

'I'm hugely grateful to you,' Gísli replied. 'For the opportunity to work on this investigation with you, and for the faith you put in me. I had the feeling towards the end that there was something up. I just couldn't work out what it was.'

'I understand… And I don't understand. You haven't been entirely honest with me,' Salka said, and they were both silent for a moment. 'I saw the picture of you outside Dyrheimar.'

'What? What picture?'

'Gísli,' she said in disappointment. 'You know Dyrheimar, don't you?'

'Yes, of course I do.'

'There were a few pictures in Anton's diary that were among the items Rafn had with him. There was a group picture of some children and teenagers who had taken part in a production. And you were in the picture.'

'I see,' he said, gazing into the distance. 'I didn't think that picture was still in existence. I remember when it was taken.'

'Why didn't you tell me that you had been part of this group?'

'To start with, I thought it wasn't relevant,' he said after pausing for thought. 'Later on, I thought it might complicate things, that you'd take me off the case. In fact, it's not relevant. I turned up for two or three rehearsals and knew right away that I wasn't on the same path as those kids. Back then I was big into football, so I didn't go there more than a couple of times.'

'Understood,' she said, catching his eye. She sighed, and turned to look out through the windscreen.

They were both startled as a truck roared past, so that Salka's car shook.

'That's the cat out of the bag,' Gísli laughed. 'But it can hardly be just that one photo?'

'Meaning what?'

'It can't be that single picture that made you suspicious about me.'

'No, there was more. You were distant and absent-minded. Sometimes it was difficult to reach you. So when I put things into context, you could have been at the scene when the murders were committed. I know, I know,' she said when she saw the look of astonishment on Gísli's face.

'You were the first officer at the scene of Hróbjartur's murder. Your hair was all over the place, like you'd been in a scuffle. Looking back, I thought that was suspicious, considering your hair is always so neat.'

They both laughed.

'I can admit here and now that I parked up in the woods and had a nap. I was asleep on duty and woke up when the call came in to go to Grenivík.'

'Yes, but there were just so many things that led to questions and from there to suspicions. I told you right at the start that I was going to be completely honest, Gísli.'

'I think you've already been honest,' he said with a perplexed smile.

'It's very difficult to talk about this, but I must.'

'Go ahead.'

'I saw more pictures.'

'Oh.'

'You were one of their victims, weren't you?'

'Whose?' he said, and Salka didn't like the innocent tone of his voice.

'Hróbjartur's. Helgi's. Gunnleifur's.'

'How on earth... How do you come to that conclusion?' he asked, and fell silent.

'The group photo from Dynheimar. It was taken around the same time as the video.'

'Which video, Salka?'

'The one we looked at together at Hróbjartur's house. You were one of the boys there in the hot tub.'

Gísli turned away, facing the side window. It wasn't until she saw his shoulders shake that she realised that he was weeping.

'It's all right, Gísli,' she said, placing a hand on his shoulder. 'I have no choice but to mention this because I must know if you had any part in this.'

'How do you mean?' he asked, stifling his sobs.

'With Magnús. Do you have any connection to these killings?'

He sniffed hard and sat up straight. He rubbed his eyes and stared out through the windscreen.

'I had forgiven them all.'

'Did this happen many times?'

'Yes. But I don't recall any video being recorded. That's why it hit me so hard when I saw it at Hróbjartur's house. They pumped us full of booze and some other stuff. I don't know what it was. Then I woke up, with a pain in...' he said. The tears were rolling down his cheeks again.

'It's all right, Gísli.'

'It's not all right. I can't maintain any relationship, and this latest one has fallen apart. Yet another one who couldn't bear me for more than a month. All the same, this one set a record. A month and seven days,' he said and laughed through his tears. 'They killed something inside me, but at least I got away from them.'

'How?'

'I disappeared. Made myself scarce. Nobody at home knew, but I had a wonderful grandmother who helped me through everything. It was our secret. She protected me and helped me find forgiveness. I know now that I should have done the right thing and gone to the police. But maybe she knew there was no point. She was of the generation that swept anything awkward under the carpet. But she helped me get back on track. I never expected to encounter these men today. And certainly not in this way.'

'After what you've been through recently, I believe that you ought to talk to someone who can help you regain some peace of mind,' Salka said. 'I think you've lost some of that. There's no point approaching this from the point of view of seeking payback. I'll help you find the right person to speak to.'

'Thanks,' Gísli said after a long silence. 'What about Gunnleifur? Is he leaving the country?'

'No. Never,' she said and grinned as she glanced at him. 'He's as strong as an ox. I imagine you're wondering about the PET scan?'

'You could say that.'

'I called a team meeting and asked Óttar to alter his narrative. As he did concerning the footprints. They were actually closer to your shoe size, and Magnús's. I had my suspicions about him as well. But I couldn't pin anything on either of you. It's easy to be wise after the event, and from much of what Magnús told me, I should have figured things out earlier.'

'He was maybe too close to you?'

'Could be,' Salka said, with a shiver of discomfort. 'Anyway, I wanted to be sure that both of you knew Gunnleifur was being sent home and there would be no police presence at his house. I made it clear at the meeting that I considered Skúli and Rafn to be the most likely perpetrators. Then I drove Gunnleifur home and went inside with him, just in case you or someone else were watching. Once we were inside, two officers took him out through the back door and to the next street. They took him to the hotel apartment where I've been staying and were there with him all night. I knew it was a bit of a grey area and that I could have been wrong. But I had to take the chance. Valgeir owes me a favour and he persuaded Kolla to give all this the green light. Once the two uniformed guys had taken Gunnleifur away, I went down to the station, and then went back to his house to wait for whoever would show up. I waited there in one of the rooms, wondering what would happen. The rapid response guys were in an unmarked car down the street. I had practically given up hope that anything would happen, and then Magnús arrived, expecting Gunnleifur to be fast asleep, and determined to murder him. Gunnleifur is back in a cell now and the warrant to remand him in custody will be issued today. We're going to nail him, Gísli.'

'What'll happen to Valgeir?' Gísli asked.

'I couldn't say,' she said thoughtfully. 'But I imagine his investigation into Anton's disappearance will be re-examined.'

'I have to say, it's a strange feeling, and not a pleasant one, to be under suspicion,' Gísli said seriously. 'But I appreciate you taking the time to talk, Salka.'

'Likewise, Gísli.'

.

39

Salka parked outside the Hlíð care home and went inside.

'Since you came to see her the other day, she's hardly slept, and keeps repeating the same thing,' said the nurse who had called Salka and asked to meet her.

'What's she saying?' Salka asked, following the nurse to a bright communal area and taking a seat.

'It's all rather confused. She talks about funerals and pallbearers, a great weight, and that some woman was a terrible burden, and she mentions Anton. To be truthful, it's getting irritating to listen to the same thing on a loop,' the nurse said and smiled. 'Then, when I came in to see her this morning, it was as if there was a new spark in her eyes. I've never seen her so ... focused and wide awake, as if she'd had an epiphany. She asked me to fetch the church diary.'

'Church diary?' Salka asked, putting down the cup of coffee he had brought her.

'This one,' he said, handing her a dog-eared exercise book. 'She asked me to find the 1995 book.'

'And where was this book?' Salka asked, leafing through what seemed to be a diary Fríða had kept to record timetables and her working hours.

'It was in the wardrobe in her room. She has a box of oddments, and a lot of these exercise books. I found the one she had asked specially for, but when I went to ask her about it, the spark had gone and she was asleep. I had the feeling that this was important to her, and as she said you had been asking about Anton, I thought the best thing to do was to call you.'

Outside in the car, Salka went through the pages and found the date of Anton's disappearance. Fríða had recorded everything faithfully, including the times taken for each specified piece of work she had done. She had been there at eight that morning to prepare for the day ahead with one of the boys. He had helped her find the right paperwork, and then she had prepared cocoa and doughnuts for the children who were supposed to be there for the ten o'clock confirmation class. An hour earlier a coffin had been delivered, ahead of a funeral booked for two in the afternoon. She had written the deceased woman's name in the margin. At the bottom of the page she had written

Anton came.
Altar candlestick missing.
Ask Gunnleifur.

Salka decided to go the Glerá church. She went into the open, airy lobby. The doors stood half-open into the church itself. She walked unhurriedly into the church itself. Sunshine streaming through the windows threw patches of colour onto the white walls from the stained glass windows. The roof soared high above and the lights hanging down from it reminded her of candlesticks. A simple but large wooden cross hung on the wall behind the altar.

Salka wasn't sure of her own feelings. The tranquillity of the place reminded her of when she had been in this church two years before.

'Can I help you?' said a voice behind her that verged on being uncomfortably pompous.

Salka turned to see a thin, neatly turned-out middle-aged man. She hadn't heard him enter the church, probably because he had on soft-soled slippers. He wore drab trousers and a light roll-neck sweater of a similar hue. As if that wasn't enough, his thin hair was carefully combed and was much the same colour as his clothes.

'Yes, good morning,' she said, introduced herself and explained what had brought her there.

'Old church records, you say. Strictly speaking, I should

ask for permission to show you those, but as the Reverend Gunnleifur is ... well, indisposed, we can do this ourselves,' the man said with the same pompous air, having shown Salka to an office, quaking strangely with every step he took. He pulled open a drawer of a large filing cabinet. 'I'm here in the Reverend Gunnleifur's absence, and I'm not entirely certain where things are kept. But I'm fairly sure it should be here somewhere,' he said, going through the folders arranged in order.

He muttered under his breath as he counted through them.

'Which month in 1995, was it?'

'It was March.'

'Here it is,' he said, with a smile.

Salka took the folder, sat down on the sofa and opened it. She found the day the funeral had taken place and the rather detailed information that had been recorded. This included the name of the deceased, a death certificate, the weight of the coffin, and the name of the organist. Gunnleifur had officiated and Fríða named as the deacon present, and the pallbearers were all named.

'Why are the pallbearers named?' Salka asked. 'Weren't they relatives?'

The man perched next to her and looked at the entry.

'No. Probably they were volunteers who were brought in to carry the casket.'

'Why volunteers?'

'I don't know the circumstances, I mean concerning this particular funeral, but if there are only a few or even no relatives, then we have people we can call on to serve as pallbearers. You can see here,' he said, his finger travelling down to the bottom of the page. 'There were only four relatives who attended. There wasn't even a choir.'

'I see,' Salka said. 'Can I take this with me?'

'Ah, I don't think that's a good idea. But you're welcome to take pictures of the documents. Why the interest in this?'

Salka took pictures with her phone and stood up.

'Thank you very much for that. You've been extremely helpful,' she said, and left the church.

40

Four days later

Salka sat at the deck and switched on the recording in the interview room. She hoped it wasn't obvious how distressed she was at the sight of the man facing her.

'The date is the 31st^t of August. I am Salka Steinsdóttir and I am questioning Gísli Guðmundsson.'

It was cloudy and cool that Sunday morning. The sun, still low in the sky, managed occasionally to break through the clouds to warm for a moment those who stood around the grave.

The scoop of a mini-digger sliced through the grass over a poorly-maintained grave.

'I hope you're right on this one,' Kolla muttered to Salka, who stood there with Gísli, Óttar and the churchyard's gardener.

After twenty minutes, the digger stopped and the gardener measured the depth. He had said that the lid of the coffin ought to be around a metre below the surface. Two municipal workers clambered into the hole and shovelled earth until they reached the coffin lid. They cleared earth from around it, then fastened straps around the coffin that were hooked to the digger's scoop so that it could be gently lifted and placed on the ground.

The men swept clean the lid of the coffin, which was unmarked. They used crowbars in an attempt to free it, but the rotten timber gave way without the lid moving. They worked together on one corner, and finally managed to free it.

They carefully lifted the lid and placed it beside the coffin.

They were faced with a diminutive woman whose earth-brown skin seemed to have been glued to her bones. Her hands were at her sides. Her clothes, which Salka assumed had been white when she had been laid to rest, had turned turmeric yellow. The lower part of her body was hidden as another body lay over her at the end of the coffin. A decayed, yellow cowl hid the person's earthly remains and a tattered pair of yellow wings lay on top as if on a dead swan. Next to the head lay a gilded candlestick.

Óttar took the candlestick and placed it in a bag.

'Hello, Gísli. I would like you to recount in your own words the series of events that took place in the Glerá church on Saturday 25th March 1995.'

Salka didn't realise how many minutes ticked past before Gísli raised his head and looked back at her. Neither did she count how many minutes passed before he began his narrative.

'I was thirteen years old and I often helped out in various ways at the Glerá church,' he said and it was as if someone broken the silence with a bang. 'Fríða had called my mother and said that I would have to be there early as there was a lot going on at the church that day. There was a confirmation class in the morning, and I was out the back to wash up after morning coffee, while Gunnleifur took the class. I recall I was excited as he had chosen two of them.'

'What do you mean, chosen them?' Salka asked.

'Two boys. He had spoken to me that morning and said that if he could get two boys to come to him, then I'd be paid.'

'Explain more clearly, please.'

'I was the boy hunter. Gunnleifur let me know which kids he and his pals...'

'Which pals?'

'Hróbjartur and Helgi.'

'Go on.'

Óskar Guðmundsson

'Well, he'd let me know which kids he wanted me to win over and come to him.'

'What do you mean by that?'

'To the *Christian* meeting that was held in the evening,' Gísli said, making quote marks in the air with his fingers. 'But there was nothing Christian about those meetings. They were grooming sessions, tailored to their needs. I was supposed to bring the kids and they'd praise them to the skies a few times. Then there would be sweets. Then money. And finally booze and dope. I knew perfectly well what was going to happen to them, because I had been through it as well.'

'Through this ... grooming process?'

'Yes. But I have no idea how it's possible to convince anyone that at the time I thought I was doing the right thing when I brought in these kids. I genuinely thought I was doing good. I got a reward in the form of money every week, and they told me I was coming closer to Christ. No, that's not it. They told me I was further from Hell, and that I was something special. That was what they said. I was special and they were able to enjoy me. And I'm not sure, but at the time, I think I felt that was fine. I know today that I was totally brainwashed.'

'What happened when you were out the back and heard Gunnleifur come in?' Salka asked, surprised at how dispassionate he sounded.

'I was washing up and expected the whole group would come back into the church. Then I heard Gunnleifur come in and he was talking to someone. Just then Fríða came in and said she had to run an errand. I got on with the washing up, and then I heard raised voices. I went into the church and when I saw that scruffy-looking angel, I froze. I had no idea what was going on. I thought the devil himself had appeared in some disguise. Gunnleifur tried to calm the angel, but he got more and more agitated, and made threats. He talked about mistreatment and abuse, and I didn't know what he meant. All I could see was that Gunnleifur was in danger. I know it sounds ridiculous,' he said, and Salka watched a tear make its way down his cheek.

'Go on, Gísli. What happened after that?'

'I remember that I went quietly into the church to where they were by the altar and the angel ... Anton, had his back to me. And I went closer,' he said and sighed. He wiped away a tear.

Salka kept her eyes on him. She needed to be strong, and hadn't bothered to mop any of her own tears as they flowed down her face. With the tip of her tongue, she could taste the salt on her lips.

'Gísli, continue, please.'

He took a deep breath.

'I remember how frightened I was as I came closer.'

'Why?' Salka asked after Gísli had paused for thought.

'He was four years older than me and much bigger. I remember looking around for something I could use as a weapon, and the candlestick caught my eye. The only thing I could think of was to protect Gunnleifur, my abuser. Then Anton grabbed him by the throat with both hands and squeezed, and I ran, grabbed the candlestick and smashed it against his head. I still haven't been able to forget... the terrible sound of it,' Gísli said and put a hand to his forehead. 'I stared at his head as he stood still. There was blood coming from the back of his head and I was ready to strike again. But then he fell. He lay before me, completely motionless. He was dead. I had killed him.'

'What happened after that?'

'Gunnleifur was beside himself. He grabbed me and shook me... and I wet myself. He paced around the church and babbled nonsense. Then it was as if he had been given an inspiration. That morning a coffin had been brought to the church for a funeral later in the day. We opened the coffin and I remember how small the woman in it was. We put Anton and the candlestick in the coffin. They were buried later the same day.'

'Were you at the funeral?'

'No. Gunnleifur took me to his house and had me stay there during the day. He didn't dare let me stay at the church, nor send me home. Later that day all three of them came and talked to me. They talked about the way the Lord works and that I was their guardian angel. After that they always called me the guardian angel,' he said, and Salka saw that he was trembling.

'Do you want to take a break now?'

'Yes. That would be good. But first there are two things I'd like to mention.'

'Which are?'

'When Gunnleifur said that he doesn't remember some things, then that's true. He didn't remember. He doesn't remember everything.'

'What do you mean?'

'He has Alzheimer's, although it's at an early stage. Memories of the past and everyday things are starting to escape him. I spoke to the director of the health spa he was at in Hveragerði, and he told me this. That's why he didn't recognise me when we questioned him. He was sure he'd seen me before, but didn't know who I was.'

'And the other thing?'

'I'm so sorry, Salka. I hope that one day you'll be able to forgive me.'

Salka had no idea how long she sat motionless in the chair after Gísli had been led from the room.

She sat and stared into space, and thought about forgiveness.

41

Fourteen days later

'...earth to earth, ashes to ashes, dust to dust; in sure and certain hope of the Resurrection to eternal life.'

Many people had made their way to stand in silence on Höfðagata outside Akureyri's churchyard where police officers ensured that only those with a reason to be there went inside.

Salka stood by Anton's open grave as the coffin was gently lowered into it. In one hand she held two white roses, while her other hand clasped Marta's. Rafn sat to one side in a wheelchair. Opposite stood two plainclothes police officers with Magnús between them.

The priest spoke a few words about Anton and his turbulent life.

'... Anton was the victim of much human evil. Not evil that arises from social conditions, not due to poverty. This wasn't even of God's doing. This was an evil stemming solely from human forces. We who stand here together will never forget the words he wrote. *Face in the mirror, you don't listen. Farewell with a kiss. An angel dies today.* We should have listened. But today we say farewell to him with a fond kiss. He was lost to us all, but we found him. And now he has finally come home.'

Salka saw that the two officers opposite had to use all their strength to keep Magnús upright. She would have welcomed their support herself, but all her energy was going into keeping Marta on her feet.

She glanced over at Rafn, hunched forward in a wheelchair as if he were asleep. She knew he wasn't, and that he was weeping tears from the depths of his pain.

Salka remained alone by the graveside as the others left the churchyard.

She took a deep breath and let one of the white roses drop into the grave. She smiled as she looked down at the white casket below, a pair of wings on its lid.

She took the path in the opposite direction that led to the older graves. The tears began to flow as she approached one of them. She stopped in front of one and looked out towards Grenivík, out over Eyjafjörður, and to where Vaðlaheiði was bathed in sunshine.

'It's not right that you need to work until midnight every day of the week and every single weekend, Eysteinn. Is this the future we saw ahead of us when we moved abroad?'

'You knew we'd have to make some sacrifices. And what are you complaining about? We have everything we could want,' Eysteinn said, arms outstretched to indicate the huge house that had come as part of the package when he signed the contract to join the company.

'We have everything?' Salka said, and looked at the time. María would be home soon and she didn't want her to find them arguing. So far she had managed to hide that from her. She had kept her unhappiness under wraps.

'What do you need to be happy, Salka?' he asked.

'You know what, Eysteinn? I think you're at a point in your life at which you think money validates your opinions, regardless of how ludicrous they might be. Look around,' she said. 'All this junk here in the living room. All this was here when we arrived. It's all prefabricated crap that has no connection with us. None of it's ours, not a single one of these things. You got this house and you got the car and you got a fat pay cheque. But we don't even go on holiday together. You're travelling without me all the time. We grow further and further apart with every day that passes. When did we last do anything together? When did you last do anything with María? You mention this to me because she complained about it to you. Is this happiness?' Salka fell silent. She wiped away tears. 'Don't you see that this is going to finish us as a family?'

'You talk as if you don't go to work. You're not always here for her.'

'Don't be unfair, Eysteinn. I do everything around the house. I'm the one who goes to the parents' evenings. I go to the school performances, and I drive her to training. I'm sorting out her confirmation on my own. Don't be unfair.'

'So why don't you quit that fucking job? You're paid peanuts and you're always complaining that you can't resolve this or that case. You complain about endless pressure. Why don't you quit and try … just try to enjoy life, Salka? There's nothing to stop you. Think of yourself.'

'I know you've been seeing someone,' she said, immediately regretting it. She hadn't meant to bring it up at this point.

'Salka,' he said, looking hard at her.

'I saw the emails.'

'Salka, this isn't…'

'No,' she said firmly. 'Don't say anything. The less I know, the less it hurts,' she said and felt the rage swell inside her. Instead of going for him, as she longed to do, she marched towards the door.

She sat in the car parked in front of the garage, jammed it into reverse, and put her foot down.

In the mirror, she caught a glimpse of María on her bicycle.

She heard the smash, the crunch.

She was there, and then she wasn't.

She saw María disappear from the mirror.

Salka dropped to her knees before the gravestone. She placed the white rose in front of it. The tears flooded down her cheeks, she buried her face in her hands and rocked back and forth.

She reached out and passed a hand over the lettering.

María Eysteinsdóttir
28th March 1998 – 14th December 2012
The memory of you is the light our lives

Salka took out her phone, scrolled through to María's number. She called and listened.

Hi, this is María. I'm soooo busy right now. Don't call back, I'll call you… If I remember.

A peal of laughter followed.

Salka went to the directory and deleted the number from her phone. She stood up, and made a sign of the cross over the grave.
'Goodbye, my love,' she said, and walked away.